"*Get your clothes off,*" he ordered.

"No, I—please," Sheena said. "Don't do this."

Billy jerked open her loose-fitting shirt and stared. "Wouldn't the men on the docks be surprised to see what ole *Sean* is hiding under 'his' shirt, now?" he asked, twisting the name so that it became a mockery. He removed the woolen cap that Sheena wore pulled low over her forehead, and cascades of red hair tumbled across her shoulders. Before she could stop him, he was unlacing her trousers.

"Now, Sheena, let's get a look at all of you," Billy said.

"Please stop," Sheena said, her pleading coming in a whisper of anguish.

BUT IT WAS TOO LATE. SHEENA O'SHEEL WAS ABOUT TO CAST OFF TO FATE, TO KISS THE PAST GOODBYE, AND SET SAIL ON HER ADVENTUROUS DESTINY!

THE
LOVE PIRATE

PAULA MOORE

A DELL/BRYANS BOOK

Published by
Dell Publishing Co., Inc.
1 Dag Hammarskjold Plaza
New York, New York 10017

ISBN: 0-440-14950-9

Printed in the United States of America
First printing—April 1980

BOOK ONE

1

From the dizzying heights of the uppermost yardarm Sheena O'Sheel had a view of the whole of Dublin. She could see the barges working their way up and down the Liffey, and the two cathedrals that dominated the city: Christ Church and, less than a quarter mile away, St. Patrick's, where her father's good friend Jonathan Swift was dean. Sheena could also see the buildings of Trinity College, where her father studied medicine, and, though a diaphanous haze of turf smoke covered the outlying parts of the city, she could even see the building where her father practiced his profession, and where he, Sheena, and her brother, Liam, lived.

Sheena was standing on the top bar of the mainmast, leaning loosely, confidently, against the upper spar, with little concern for the fact that the deck of the *Sea Mist* was some sixty-five feet below. The *Sea Mist* was one of more than two dozen vessels which lolled at anchor in Dublin Bay. Sheena had sneaked aboard, dressed as a boy, coming out with the lighter that was tied alongside to load and unload goods. This was her favorite diversion, one which she kept hidden from her father. She often boarded the ships in the harbors, exploring the mysterious holds and compartments, listening to the marvelous sounds of foreign languages, and dreaming the unlikely dream of some day actually going to sea herself.

"Hey, you, lad! What are you about up there?" a gruff voice called from the deck. "Get down from there, before you break your fool neck!"

The seaman started up the rigging after her. Sheena felt her heart beat faster with fear, not from the realization that she was so high but because she knew that if caught, her father would be informed and she would be banished from the docks.

Sheena began easing away from the mast, working her way out on the yard.

"Here, boy, don't go be doin' that now," the seaman called. "The farther out you get, the greater the danger. You just stay where you are, 'n I'll be to you in no time."

That was just what Sheena was afraid of. Over the seaman's protests, she inched farther out toward the end, until she reached one of the furling lines. She grabbed the line, then swung away from the yard and slid down it. She landed lightly on the deck, leaving her would-be rescuer high in the rigging.

"Somebody grab that boy!" the sailor yelled down, now angered that he'd been made a fool of.

Sheena looked around anxiously. Two of the deckhands seemed intent on catching her, so she turned and darted toward the open hatch which led to the ship's hold. She found a rope which hung down into the darkened interior, and slid down it.

The hold smelled of foul air and polluted seawater. She blinked a few times, trying to accustom her eyes to the darkness. Then, too late, she saw someone coming toward her down a shadowed passageway.

"And who might you be, lad?" the gruff-looking sailor asked.

"My name is Sean," Sheena said, giving the name she often assumed.

"Sean it is, ye say. You're a pretty boy, Sean," the sailor said, putting his hand on Sheena's cheek. Sheena could smell his foul breath and his touch felt repulsive to her. She began looking around, trying to find a way out. "How old would ye be, lad?"

"I'm sixteen," Sheena said. In this, at least, she wasn't lying.

"Sixteen it is then," the sailor said. All the while the sailor was talking he was gradually moving, circling around Sheena, until, with a start, she realized that he was moving to block her only exit! "Sixteen is jes' the right age ye know," the sailor said. His breath was coming in audible gasps now, and his tongue flicked out to lick his cracked lips. "I was broke in at the age of sixteen myself, ye know."

The sailor started unfastening his pants, and before Sheena's startled eyes, he exposed himself to her.

"A young, sixteen-year-old boy . . . most especial one as pretty as ye be, lad, is the best wife a seafarin' man could have. You know what they say, lad. Gash is fine, but one eye for mine."

"No!" Sheena shouted, jumping to one side, trying to avoid the repulsive sailor's advances.

"Here, now, don't be runnin' from ole Grunt. Grunt's gonna' treat ye right, he is."

Sheena tried to duck under and around Grunt, but he grabbed her in a move that was surprisingly quick. In an instant, he undid the hitch on Sheena's trousers and jerked them to her knees. As she was trying to escape him, she had presented only her backside, so Grunt was still unaware of her true gender.

"There ye go, lad. Bend over the canvas there 'n we'll be done in no time."

Despite Sheena's struggles, Grunt was able to push her over the pile of spare sail. Then, her stomach contracting in fear and revulsion, she felt him come up behind her, trying to gain entry into her nether parts.

"Step back from the lad, you buggering bastard, or I'll run you through with this blade!" a loud, authoritative voice called down the hold.

"Cap'n Miles, sir, I meant nothin' by it," Grunt shouted, his voice laced with terror. "Sure'n I was just funnin' with 'im."

"Pull your pants up, boy, and thank your lucky stars I saw you drop down into this hold. Grunt's the worst bugger on the seven seas."

"Thank you, Captain," Sheena said. She pulled her pants up, still facing away from the two men, so that in the dark hold her secret was still safe.

"What were you doin' on board my ship, anyway?" the captain asked as he and Sheena climbed the ladderway to regain the deck. "There's little enough to steal."

"It wasn't for stealing I came aboard, Captain," Sheena said easily.

"Then what was it?"

" 'Twas merely my interest in ships. I'll sail the seas some day, same as you."

The captain laughed. "Aye, 'n when I was a lad I had the same fire burnin' in me gut. But take a word of advice, son. Wait a mite longer. You've some changin' to do afore it's safe enough for you. Grunt's not the only bugger on a crew, and 'tis young, pretty boys like yourself that makes fair game for the pickin'."

"Captain, such things confuse me. Do the sailors not like women then?"

Captain Miles laughed again. "Aye, lad, they like 'em well enough. But they're long at sea and always without funds, and too often only the ugliest of the doxies to choose from. 'Tis but a small step from an ugly crone to a pretty young boy, and many's the sailor that's took it. Most take the step back when they can, but some, like Grunt, gets to where they like the boys better. Do you live in Dublin, lad?"

"Aye. My father's a doctor."

"A doctor, is he? That's a noble enough profession for any man. 'Tis a wonder you've no wish to follow him into the practice."

"Father has no wish for me to become a doctor," Sheena said.

"Here, now, and what sort of a father would not want his son to follow him? 'Tis only natural."

Ah, Sheena thought, *therein is the rub, for it is not a son, but a daughter who would be following him into the trade; and a lady doctor would be as unseemly as a lady sailor.*

"I see the lighter's going ashore now," the captain said. "Step lively, lad, and climb aboard. Come and see me in a couple of years, and if you've still a wish to go to sea, then perhaps I will be able to do something for you."

"Thank you, Captain," Sheena said, sliding down the rope to the lighter as effortlessly as a monkey.

The lighter was but a bay scow, wide of beam and shallow of draft. It was in no way an oceangoing vessel, but even in this—the roll of the waves, the spray of the sea, the taste of the salt, and the tangy, fishy aroma of the deep—Sheena took great delight.

Sheena thought of what had nearly taken place in the hold of the *Sea Mist* with the sailor called Grunt. Grunt thought she was a boy, and still would have had her, had the captain not intervened. And in that, Sheena added a new dimension to the sex education she was getting. Some men would have other men as surely as they would have women. She wondered, *Could one woman have another? But no,* she reasoned, *for there would be nothing on a woman that could be used as a man's tool.*

Sheena knew about men's tools and how they were used. She had discovered the secrets the doxies shared with the sailors, when, giving way to curiosity, she trailed one couple up to a room above a tavern, there to hide herself in a closet to watch what they did.

Sheena was learning about her own body too, for she would sometimes lock herself in her room to study her reflection in the mirror. Her hips, once as straight and slender as a board, had suddenly become round, and the nipples which had always nestled flat against her chest had turned into rosebuds, perched quite saucily on the pillows of flesh which were her breasts. And now a growth of hair, as fiery a red as that which grew on her head, sprouted at the junction of her legs. All this she had examined with eyes as green as the Emerald Isle itself, and she knew from what she had learned that there was many a sailor who would love to gaze upon this same sight. Gaze, and more, she knew.

Sheena's sexual education stopped there, for thus far she was innocent. But, though still a virgin, Sheena somehow sensed that she might be a person possessed of a passionate nature. Sometimes, during those moments of reflection, erotic thoughts played their temptations in her mind and, secretly, she wondered what it would be like to trade places with a doxy who was engaged with one of the more handsome sailors.

Sheena knew that it was doxies only who could take pleasure from such activity—decent women didn't think such impure thoughts—and she had to fight hard to keep such lustful musings in check.

The lighter touched ashore and Sheena stepped off. The dockboards were still slick from an earlier rain and with the spray tossed up by the rolling sea. A small bit of bread, wet and sodden, lay along the edge of the dank boards. A rat, his beady eyes studying Sheena's sudden intrusion into his domain, darted out to the prize, grabbed it, then bounded back to the comparative safety of one of the numerous warehouses along the docks.

Sheena hurried through the back alleys, taking a shortcut home. Her father was having Dean Swift over for tea this afternoon, and Sheena knew that she and Liam were expected to be there. It wouldn't do for her to be dressed as a boy. Her father would start asking embarrassing questions and soon discover Sheena's passion for the docks.

Sheena reached the back of the building which served as their home and her father's office, and climbed the trellis to sneak in through her bedroom window to change for tea.

Sheena gasped, for as she was climbing through the window she saw her brother sitting arrogantly in her room, waiting for her.

"So, Sister, you've been up to no good, I see," Liam challenged.

"Liam, what are you doing here?" she said.

"Father sent me up to remind you that Dean Swift is coming to tea. He feared that you would forget."

"I haven't forgotten," Sheena said.

Liam, at eighteen, was already beginning the study of medicine. He was working as an apprentice to his father, but he planned to attend the University in the near future. He could have been considered handsome, though his demeanor was somewhat arrogant and his personality selfish, so that it showed in his features. He was also a hedonist. He spent much of his time seeking sensual gratification, though this fact he had thus far hidden from his father.

"Where have you been?" Liam asked.

"I was out for a walk," Sheena said.

Liam shook his head and clucked his tongue, his eyes reflecting pleasure over Sheena's discomfort. "You took a walk dressed in such a fashion? What will Father say when he learns of this?"

"Liam, you won't tell him?" Sheena asked.

"I must tell him," Liam said. "I am your older brother, remember? It is my duty to see that you do nothing to disgrace this family."

"Liam, I beg of you," Sheena pleaded. "Don't tell Father of this."

"Very well, I won't speak of it," Liam said. "So, now, Sister, we each have a secret to share. I will not speak of your wandering about dressed in such a way, and you will not speak of seeing me visit the finer whorehouses of Dublin."

"Why should I speak of that?" Sheena asked. "For I know nothing of it."

"You say you know nothing of it, yet you followed me a fortnight ago," Liam said. "You are lucky that you weren't killed, for I feared a rogue had taken up the trail and I waited with a concealed dirk. Imagine my surprise when I saw that it wasn't a man following me, but my own sister, disguised as a boy."

"Then you *did* see me?"

"Yes."

"But, Liam, I was only curious as to where you went. Believe me, I had no intention of speaking about it to Father."

"Perhaps so, Sister, but it doesn't hurt to have a little protection, hey? And now that I have this little secret of yours, I feel my secret will be safe."

"I will say nothing. I promise," Sheena said.

Liam smiled, and started out of the room. "I know," he said. He pulled the door to, the smile of triumph still on his face.

No sooner had the door closed than Sheena began stripping out of her clothes to prepare to meet her father's famous guest.

2

An amazing transformation had taken place by the time Sheena had descended the stairs from her bedroom and walked into the drawing room where her father would be receiving. While the trousers, shirt, and hat had allowed her to pass as a boy, there was no mistaking the lovely young creature who stood there now. The dress she was wearing had a bodice which accented her womanly bosom, and it flared out over her hips, to hang in a full skirt in a shade of green which accented her eyes.

Sheena set the service in place for the tea. She had just finished when her father entered the room with Jonathan Swift.

"Sheena, dear, how lovely you look," her father said. "Tell me, Jonathan, have I not a daughter to warm the heart of any Irishman?"

"I think more than Irishmen would be aware of Sheena's charms," Swift replied graciously. "She is a beautiful girl, Kevin."

Sheena looked at the two men. Kevin, her father, was tall, strong-looking, and handsome. He was a well-respected doctor and he cultivated friends who were of high status, in order, he once explained to

Sheena, to be certain to find a husband worthy of her.

Sheena hoped that her father wasn't considering Jonathan Swift as a possibility. He was single, true enough. And as Dean of St. Patrick's Cathedral, a former figure in the English government, and a writer of some note, he would certainly meet her father's standard of worthiness. But he was forty-nine years old, eight years older than her father, and not at all handsome. Besides, he was a minister in the Church of England. Though he was a man of conscience, and outspoken for the rights of Catholic Ireland, he was still Protestant, and Sheena hoped that that would discourage her father from getting too serious with such thoughts. Nonetheless, she did get the feeling that her father sometimes seemed to push them together.

"Liam," her father said when Liam entered a moment later. "See how beautiful your sister is?"

"Dresses become her," Liam said. "It makes one wonder why she would want to wear anything else."

"Liam!" Sheena gasped. "You promised."

"Promised? Promised what?" Kevin asked.

"Nothing, Father, nothing at all," Sheena said.

"I would question her more closely, Father," Liam said. "After all, blood will tell, and we can't be too careful of her, now, can we?"

There it was again, Sheena thought. This mysterious reference to her "bad blood." What did it mean? What were they talking about? Why did it always come up whenever she did something wrong? And how did one get bad blood in the first place?

"That's enough of that, Liam," Kevin said sharply. "We have a guest, and we'll not be discussing such things now. Jonathan, please forgive us."

"Think nothing of it, Kevin," Jonathan said. "It is in the nature of a family to have disagreements. I remember my own childhood and often wonder how

16

things would have been if Stella . . ." His voice trailed off and Sheena knew he was speaking of Esther Johnson, the woman he almost married in England.

"Please try one of the biscuits, won't you? Sheena baked them," Kevin invited.

The tea seemed to drag on and on, the more so, because Sheena knew that her father would have words with her afterward. Oh, how she hated Liam for this. They had had a bargain, and Liam had broken it. Well, then she'd just break her end of the bargain as well. Perhaps her father would be just as interested in how Liam spent his time gambling and lying with the doxies.

Jonathan Swift took his leave after a while, and Sheena and Liam waited in the drawing room for their father, who had accompanied Swift to the door, to return.

"It will be interesting to see what Father has to say," Liam said, smiling in obvious enjoyment as he anticipated the upcoming scene.

"You promised you would say nothing," Sheena hissed.

"I reconsidered my promise, Sister, dear. After all, it was for your own good."

"I hate you, Liam," Sheena said.

"Here, I'll have none of that," Kevin said, returning at that moment. "He is your brother, girl. You can't be hating your own brother now."

"I'm sorry, Father," Sheena said. She stood up and started gathering the cups and saucers from the tea. "I'll just clear this mess away."

"No, you can get it later," Dr. O'Sheel said. "We have something to discuss."

"Here it comes," Liam said triumphantly, though just loud enough for Sheena to hear.

"Liam, it was not right to bring up a family problem before a guest," the doctor said. "Though I appreciate your calling my attention to any such matter as may need it. And now I ask you to explain what you were talking about."

"I was merely remarking, Father, how beautiful Sheena is when she is properly dressed. And I commented on it, as she is in the habit of going out wearing only men's clothes."

"Going out? Going out where?" Kevin asked, turning to Sheena. "And why would you be dressed in men's clothes?"

"I choose men's clothes as a disguise, Father," Sheena said contritely. "For it is only in such a disguise that I am able to do what I like to do."

"And what is that?"

Sheena looked downward at her hands, now folded in her lap. She was quiet for a moment before she spoke. "I like to visit the ships, Father."

"You what? You go on board those vessels?"

"Yes, Father."

"But why, girl?"

"Can't you guess, Father?" Liam asked. "She does have her mother's blood, after all."

"Liam, that is quite enough," Kevin said.

"Father, I am just trying to get you to be honest with yourself. We are both men of medicine. We know the scientific truth of bad blood."

"What is this bad blood you are always talking about?" Sheena asked. "You are a doctor. If I have bad blood, why don't you take it out of me?"

Liam laughed. "We couldn't take that much out," he said. "Half the blood in your veins flows from your mother. And she was a—"

"Liam!" Kevin shouted. "That is quite enough."

"She has to know about her mother sometime, Father," Liam said.

"No!"

"What are you talking about?" Sheena asked. "What

about my mother? She's dead. She died when I was a baby."

"I do not wish to speak again of your mother," her father said, putting his fist to his forehead. "Now, as for this other thing. You are forbidden to wear any clothes which are not proper for a young lady of your age. And you are never again to set foot aboard a ship. Do you understand?"

"But, Father, I love the ships. I want to—"

"I forbid it!" Kevin said, pounding his fist into his hand. "Do you understand me?"

"Yes, Father." Sheena looked at Liam, then thought of the bargain they had had, now no longer binding. "And Liam?" she said. "I suppose you will ask Liam to show more prudence in his behavior as well?"

"Liam's behavior has been above reproach. It is you who have brought me grief."

"And yet Liam visits the brothels to lie with the whores," Sheena said.

"Brothels? Whores?" Kevin said. "Where did you learn of such words? From the ships?"

"It doesn't matter how I learned of them," Sheena said. "But I do know of them, and I know that Liam visits them often."

"She lies, Father," Liam said easily. "You know yourself that I've no time for anything but my studies. Besides, it is but her way of trying to get even with me for doing my brotherly duty."

Kevin sighed. "I fear you are right, Liam. Sheena, telling lies about your brother will not help your situation."

"But I am not lying, Father," Sheena said.

Sheena's father kissed her on the forehead. "You must remember that when Liam or I correct you, it is because we love you. Now go to your room and recite the Lord's Prayer one hundred times, then pray for His forgiveness."

"Yes, Father," Sheena said contritely.

Sheena left the room with tears stinging her eyes. She climbed the stairs quickly, rather than give her brother the privilege of seeing her cry.

Sheena lay on the bed with her hands behind her head, staring at the ceiling. She cursed the twist of fate that caused her to be born a girl. If she was a boy, she would leave right now; just crawl through that window and go down to the docks, then sign on with the next ship leaving port. Why, she'd stow away if need be.

Sheena heard a sound just outside her door, and she quickly started on the Lord's Prayer, as if she had been saying it all along.

". . . hallowed be Thy Name, Thy Kingdom come, Thy will be done . . ."

"You don't have to fool me, Sister," Liam said, stepping into the room.

Sheena leaped from her bed and swung at Liam, catching him off guard and raking his face with her fingernails. He shoved her back and held his cheek. "What did you do that for?" he asked, as if genuinely surprised.

"Because you lied to me. You promised you would say nothing, then you told Father. Why did you do that?"

"Because I was afraid that you might get angry with me and tell Father what I was doing. This way he won't believe you."

"But I wouldn't have told," Sheena said. "And now you have ruined it for me. I can never go to the ships again."

"Then I have done you a favor, Sister. For that was the way of your mother."

"Why do you speak so often of one who is dead?"

Liam laughed. "Your mother is not dead, girl."

"What?" Sheena asked, gasping for breath. "What

are you telling me? Of course she is dead. She died when I was born."

"If she is dead, she is dead drunk," Liam said. "Your mother is a whore, Sheena. A doxie of the docks, a visitor of the ships. That is why you have tainted blood."

"But no, that surely can't be," Sheena said. "Father would have told me."

"Father has told no one. He is ashamed of it. That is why he brought you home to raise. You are his penitence." Liam laughed. "You are his one hundred Lord's Prayers."

"You are lying!"

"No, dear sister, I'm not lying," Liam said. "I've heard whispers of it, and I checked it out myself. It is true. Check for yourself, if you don't believe me."

"Check it out for myself? How?"

"Why, you could go see the old crone, I imagine," Liam said. "I think she goes by the name Hazel, though heaven knows what her real name is."

"I will check it out," Sheena said. "I will. And when I find that you have lied to me, I'll, I'll . . ."

"You'll what?"

"I'll carve your heart out!"

Liam laughed. "Sister, if I'm lying to you, I'll supply you with the knife."

3

Despite her father's express command that Sheena no more affect the dress and disguise of a boy, she felt compelled to do so one more time. She violated her father's wish because Liam had told her that she could find the woman he said was her mother at a tavern known as Billy's Blood.

Billy's Blood was one of the taverns right on the dock, and in the row of the worst of them. When Sheena stepped through the door she saw such a collection of riffraff as she had never seen before. Whores and slatterns of all ages and every degree of filth and ugliness, some with obvious signs of the pox and others with bastard brats nearby, occupied the tables and stood near the bars. There were seamen of every nationality there, some with hands stuck into the blouses of the nearest tarts, tweaking teats with as little shame as if they had been milking a cow.

Sheena walked up to the bar and ordered a tankard of ale. This was not unusual for her. She had entered taverns before to broaden her horizons and quaff the ale that she drank even at home, in her father's presence. But never before had she been in a tavern of such disrepute. A doxy from the end of the bar sidled down to stand beside her. She smiled, and Sheena saw that two of her teeth were missing.

"Well, now, lad," the doxy said. "Out looking for a good time, eh?"

"I'm looking for someone," Sheena said. "I was told she would be in here."

"Oh, you've a favorite already, is that it?" the doxy teased. She called out to the others in the bar. "Girls, 'ave any of you caught this young lad's fancy now? He won't lie with just anyone. He has a favorite."

"Sure now, 'n it was me, boy, for don't you remember telling me what a good time I gave you?" one old crone called. Those at the table with her laughed uproariously at the joke.

"I want to talk to Hazel," Sheena said, her cheeks flaming in embarrassment but her determination driving her on.

"Oh, Hazel is it?" the slattern at the bar said. "It would be Hazel, for she's still the queen of Billy's Blood. But she's come many a step down to here, I'll tell you."

"Then Hazel is here?"

"Hazel, it's you the lad wants to lie with. Have you a taste for young meat tonight?" the woman called.

At a table near the back of the room, a woman sat with a bearded man. She was badly dissipated, though the dim light was generous to her. And in comparison with the other women of the place, she was a prize indeed.

"I'm Hazel," the woman said easily. "Do I know you, boy? I don't remember you."

Sheena started for Hazel's table. So this was the woman Liam said was her mother. Could it be true? She felt a nervousness in her stomach and a quickening of her pulse.

"Stand away, lad, if you've no wish to run afoul of me," the bearded sailor said. "As ye can see, I'm conductin' business with the lady now."

"What business?" Hazel asked. "I've yet to see a coin. You, boy, do you have a copper?"

"Aye," Sheena said, producing the coin.

Hazel smiled. "Then you have my attention. And you," she said to the bearded sailor, "find yourself another table upon which to lean your drunken elbows."

The sailor was outraged by Hazel's rebuke and affronted by the boldness of the youth who had taken his place. He jumped up quickly, letting out a bellow of rage, and swung at Sheena with a knife in his clenched fist, making a long, lazy arc toward her.

Sheena saw the move and easily sidestepped the clumsy attack. The sailor, who Sheena now realized was besotted with drink, recovered and tried again. This time Sheena backed way from him, baiting him toward her, until he lunged again; then she stepped away just in time for the sailor to crash into the stone fireplace. He fell to the floor, unconscious, from his own devices.

"Good show, lad," the bartender said. "You two, a free tankard of ale if you'll deposit this drunken oaf outside."

Two sailors, as rough-looking and nearly as drunk as the bearded one who lay on the floor, jumped to do the bartender's bidding.

"Here, sit with me," Hazel said. "You're a brave young boy. Many's the man who would have quailed before such a brute."

"Thank you," Sheena said.

Hazel smiled. "So, you want to lie with me, do you? Have we lain before? I don't remember you."

"No, we never have. Someone gave me your name."

Hazel's smile grew broader. "Oh, I understand now. You've never lain before, have you? And you was given my name as someone who'd break you in, gentle and proper. Is that it?"

"No," Sheena said. "I don't want to lie with you."

The smile left Hazel's face and a hard light snapped on in her eyes. "Oh. I'm not good enough for you, is that it? Well, you'll find none better in these parts."

"That's not it," Sheena said. "It's something else. Something I want to ask you."

"Give me the money," Hazel said.

"What?"

"I said, give me the money. My time costs just as much whether I'm lyin' or talkin'."

Sheena handed the coin to the woman, who dropped it down the space between her breasts.

"Now, don't ye go chasin' the coin now," Hazel teased.

"No, I won't," Sheena replied, not understanding the joke.

"Okay, lad, what's on your mind?"

Sheena took a deep breath, then, finally, blurted it out. "Are you my mother?"

"Am I your what?" Hazel said. "How dare you ask a lady such a question? I've mothered no sons, and certainly none as old as you."

"I'm not a boy," Sheena said.

"What do you mean you aren't a boy?"

"I—I've no wish to disclose the fact in such a place," Sheena said. "I've come in disguise."

Hazel put her hand on Sheena's chest and squeezed one of the small but firm breasts. "What the—Why, blow me down if you aren't tellin' the truth, girl."

"Please," Sheena said. "Don't betray my confidence."

"All right, girl, I'll keep your secret. But tell me, why would you be thinkin' I'm your mother?"

"It was told me by my brother."

"Well, there you go then. I've already told you that I bore no sons."

"My brother and I have the same father," Sheena said. "We do not have the same mother."

Hazel looked at Sheena with a strange look on her face. "Tell me, girl, would you be . . . but no, surely not."

"What is it? Do you know of something?" Sheena asked anxiously.

"Your father," Hazel said. "Would he be a doctor now?"

"Yes," Sheena said. "Yes, he is a doctor!"

"Would his name be Kevin O'Sheel?"

"Yes, yes, that is my father!" Sheena said excitedly.

"Faith, and you are my own sweet daughter," Hazel said. She stuck her hand out and touched Sheena on the cheek.

"Then it's true?" Sheena asked. "What Liam said is true?"

"It is true, Sheena," her father's voice said. It cut through the smoke and banter of the tavern as sharply as a sword.

"Father! What are you doing here?"

"No, Sheena. The question is, what are *you* doing here?"

"The girl came to see her own mother. Now, where's the harm in that?" Hazel said. "After all, I've not seen her since she was a baby. We've a right to see each other."

"You have no rights at all," Kevin said. "You lost those rights when you abandoned the baby on my doorstep."

"Sure, an 'twas for the good of the child I done so," Hazel said.

"And for the good of the girl you should leave her be now," Kevin said.

" 'Twasn't me who looked her up," Hazel said. "The girl came callin' on me, as would be natural. Now that she's seen me, we've a right to visit now and again."

26

"No!" Kevin's voice thundered. "I forbid you ever to see her again. She bears the cross of your blood now. You'll not add to her troubles by teaching her your sinful ways. What could she learn from you except the art of whoring?"

"She wasn't born to a whore and you know that," Hazel said. "Time was when—"

"You are going too far, woman!" Kevin interrupted. He reached out and grabbed Sheena, pulling her away from Hazel. "We've struck a bargain and I've kept it. And by all that's holy, I'll see to it that you keep yours."

" 'Tis an unfair bargain," the woman said.

"Nonetheless it was agreed to," Kevin said. "Come, girl, we must quit this—this place of the devil."

"No," Sheena said. "Father, I have too many questions. I can't go just yet."

"Do not defy me, girl!" Kevin shouted angrily. "I have spoken and you will obey!"

"Please, Father, just a moment more, I want to—"

The barroom had grown quiet during the exchange as everyone, even the most grizzled of the seamen, had turned to watch and listen. Now the quiet was interrupted by the popping sound of a slap, as Kevin drew the palm of his hand sharply across his daughter's face.

"Father!" Sheena shouted in pain and shame. She put her hand to her face.

"Girl, oh, girl, see what you've made me do?" Kevin said contritely, pulling her to him in an embrace. While holding Sheena close to him, he looked over her shoulder at Hazel. "If you ever see this girl again," he said, "it will be in peril of your life."

Kevin, with his arm wrapped protectively about his daughter's shoulders, led her from the tavern. Even before they reached the door the noise returned to its original level, as the patrons realized that the show was over.

4

For the next two weeks Sheena was on her best behavior. She dressed every day as if she were going to a
party, and she did or said nothing to upset her father.

She even held her tongue when her brother found
some unkind remark to make.

After all, Sheena thought, Liam had been right.
Her mother was a whore, and that meant that she did
have bad blood. Perhaps it was the bad blood that
drove her to do the things she ought not to do; she
didn't know. But, bad blood or no, she intended to
show her father, and especially Liam, that she could
be as good as anyone.

Although it was difficult to take abuse from her
brother without responding in kind, the hardest thing
for Sheena to do was give up the ships. Sometimes in
first light of morning, she would look through her
window and down toward the bay. There she could
see the masts of the tall ships, bold black exclamation
points stabbing at the sky. It was at those times she
found her new life most difficult.

Nevertheless, Sheena had the willpower to adjust to
almost any situation, and she was prepared to settle
into the quiet, orderly life that her father wanted for

her. But during the third week something happened that would change the course of Sheena's life forever.

The stage was set by a very routine occurrence. Dr. O'Sheel, as was his Wednesday custom, left early in the morning to make the rounds of his patients who lived in the countryside near Dublin. As usual he charged Liam with the responsibility of the office, but in a departure from the usual, he also asked Liam to "keep a close, brotherly eye" on Sheena. "She is doing very well," he said. "But I fear that the blood may yet win, should we relax our vigil for but an instant."

"Don't worry, Father, I shall be alert for any misdoing," Liam assured him.

Dr. O'Sheel put his hand on Liam's shoulder and squeezed it affectionately. "You're a good boy, Liam O'Sheel," he said. "Would that your sister had your sense of duty and family loyalty."

"'Tis born in me, Father," Liam said. Liam followed his father out to the carriage, receiving last-minute instructions on the conduct of the office. As both men were engaged in conversation, neither of them saw the lone figure slip in through the side door and go quickly up the stairs.

Sheena had already cleaned her father's bedroom and that of her brother. She was working on her own room when she heard the knock on the door.

"So, Liam, you have learned the courtesy of a knock, have you?" she said. "Pray, come in."

"'Tis not Liam, girl, but your own mother who seeks a word with you," Hazel said, slipping in through the door at Sheena's invitation.

"You!" Sheena said, putting her hand to her mouth to stifle an involuntary shout. "What are you doing here? You know what Father said."

"Your father's said a lot of things," the old woman said. "Most of what he's said is God's honest truth, girl, for 'tis a slattern I truly am, yourself bein' a witness to the fact. But some of the story's not been told, and I feel you should know it."

"Please," Sheena said. "Please, I beg of you to leave at once. I fear for both of us should we be discovered."

"Don't send me away, girl," Hazel begged. "Not until I've had a chance at my say."

Sheena thought she heard a noise and she held her hand up to signal for quiet. She stepped to the door and listened for a moment, then closed it and returned to the old woman who stood by her bed, looking at her with a silent but eloquent plea.

"Very well," Sheena said. "But please be quick."

The old woman grinned, and here, in the cold, cruel light of day, her features were more harsh. Whereas she had managed to appear almost passable in the tavern, it had been due to a trick of lighting and the concealment of face paint. As if reading Sheena's mind, the grin left the old woman's face and she looked down quickly. "I was not always the ugly old crone you see before you," she said.

"I'm sorry," Sheena said quickly. "I've no wish to be unkind."

" 'Tis a sweet child you are," Hazel said. "It would warm any mother's heart to have a daughter the likes of you."

"I'm not sweet," Sheena said. "I've distressed Father many times. He says it's because I have—" Sheena suddenly stopped, realizing that what she was about to say would hurt Hazel.

"Let me finish for you, girl. He says you have bad blood, am I right?"

"Aye," Sheena said. " 'Tis your blood he's speaking of, I fear."

" 'Twas for this I wanted to see you, girl, and to set your mind at ease."

"How can you set my mind at ease now, for I have seen with my own eyes the truth of things?"

"You see, but you do not know," the old woman said. "For I have not always been what I am. True enough, girl, my blood is now bad. But it went bad after your birth, and not before. The blood you have is that of a servant girl, poor enough, but honest of heart and tender of spirit. A girl who fell in love and then was, by that love, deceived."

"You mean my father?"

"Aye," Hazel said. "Listen good, girl, and I'll tell you the story of how you came to be."

"Yes, I want to hear the story," Sheena said, forgetting all about her fear in the prospect of learning of her past.

" 'Twas a night when the surging sea, slashing rain, and howling winds beat against my poor cabin with all the fury of the torrents of hell," Hazel started. "Such a noise made the rain that I could barely hear the pounding at my door. I lived alone, in a small thatched hut behind the great house of O'Sheel."

"My grandfather's house," Sheena said. "I know it. And the little hut, I know it too. But it is for the servants."

"Aye, lass, and 'twas a servant girl I was, for your grandfather too. I came to the fine old gentleman with letters of credentials from my own parents' master, and from the village priest as well."

"Did you answer the knock at the door?" Sheena asked.

"Aye. And when I did, I saw none other than Doctor Kevin O'Sheel, the son of the gentleman in whose house I served. He was wet to the bone, fit to be drowned. His hair was plastered to his head by the rain, and his clothes were soaked through. But his eyes, girl, were still as blue as the summer sky, and when he smiled at me, sure'n I thought my heart would break again, as it did when he married your brother, Liam's, mother almost two years before."

"Then you knew him before?"

"Knew him, yes, and loved him too."

"What happened when you opened the door?" Sheena wanted to know.

" 'Dr. Kevin,' I asked. 'What is it? What is wrong?'

" 'Well, now, will you be letting me in, girl?' he says. 'Or shall I be forced to stand in this storm, no better treated than a mere beast?'

" 'Come in, of course, come in,' I says, stepping back to let him in. He took off his hat and poured the water from the brim, as though it were a pitcher on a stand, and he looked at me with that own sweet smile never leavin' his face.

" 'Is something wrong with your father?' I asked, for I feared for the old man.

" 'There is nothing wrong with anyone,' your father said.

" 'Then why would you be comin' to my poor house in the middle of the night, in the middle of such a storm?' I asked, now puzzled by it all.

"But your father just looked at me, girl, and his eyes grew deep and I could see the red fires of hell in the bottom of them. I grew frightened then, for 'twas obvious what was on your father's mind. And my condition was not one to discourage it, for standin' in the rain as I had done had made my nightgown so as one could see right through it. And then I was a fine, handsome girl, same as yourself.

" 'You shouldn't be in here like this,' I says. ' 'Tis in no way decent.'

" 'It isn't decent you say?' your father asked, stripping out of his soaked shirt and exposing the bare skin of his chest to me. 'Is this the same girl who let me make love to her in my own father's bed four years ago?' And, lass, I'm 'shamed to say that on that count he was right," Hazel explained.

" 'But that was different, mi'lord,' I said. 'You weren't married then.'

" 'Why was that different?' he asked, now slipping

out of his trousers. Oh, he was a handsome man, girl, and in the soft light of the candle I lit, I could see that the young boy I had dallied with in the secret chambers of your grandfather's house had grown angular, flatter, and promised even more for a girl. I felt a catch in my stomach, and a wantin' that was craven, but I tried to fight it off.

" 'It was different,' says I, 'because as long as you wasn't married there was always the chance that you—'

" 'Would marry you?' he asks, laughing.

" 'Yes, sir, I suppose that,' I says.

"Your father laughed again. 'Then tell yourself that now, girl, for 'tis as likely as it ever was.'

" 'No,' I says. 'For 'tis not the same for all your sayin' it.'

"The smile left your father's face, and he reached for my nightgown, tearing it impatiently, exposing my bare skin to his eyes. 'I'm in no mood for games, girl,' he said. 'My wife's turned me away from her bed, so I'll be takin' my pleasures where I can find them.'

"I begged him not to, but he laughed at my pleas and forced me back on my bed. He came down over me then, laying his flesh against mine, taking what he knew I couldn't deny him. He was the master's son and I the servant maid; he the husband of another and I the unmarried girl. But for the moment we shared something. Outside the storm continued to rage, but all its fury couldn't bother us, for we tasted such sweetness that we paid little note to it."

Hazel finished the story and Sheena noticed, with surprise, that she was crying.

"That was the night you came into being, girl," she said, dabbing at her eyes with a handkerchief. "So, you see, I was not a doxy then. I was an honest girl, betrayed by her own love. And you were of that love born."

"What happened after that?" Sheena asked.

"From there the story is no longer pretty," Hazel said.

"But tell me anyway, please?"

"Your father and his wife and their son, who is your brother, Liam, returned to Dublin. But there was a carriage accident on the way, and your father's wife was killed. And, oh, I know my sorrow now is God's own punishment for my wicked thoughts then, but when I heard of the accident, I felt happiness. Oh, pity for the woman's suffering to be sure, but happiness, for 'twas certain I was that your father would be for marryin' me now. But your father had no such ideas as marryin' a serving maid. Then, when my belly swelled with you, your grandfather turned on me for not disclosin' the identity of the father, and he made me leave. I had saved enough o' me wages to live until you was born, and then I placed you in a basket and left you on the doctor's doorstep. The doctor looked me up as I knew he would, and demanded to know the reason I had left you there. I told him I was hopin' that he would want to be marryin' me now, but he said he still had no intention of doing so. I cried and begged him to, but he refused. Then he offered to strike a bargain, and 'twas for your own good I agreed."

"What was the bargain?" Sheena asked. "For I heard him mention it to you before."

"The bargain was that he would raise you as his own child and guarantee you your birthright. But I was never to see you again as long as I lived."

"So that is why I thought you dead."

"Aye. 'Twas to seal my end of the bargain, so to give you what was rightly yours."

"It was a . . . a noble sacrifice, Mother, and I love you for it," Sheena said, reaching to put her arms around the woman's neck.

"No," Hazel said, backing away from her. "I'm not deserving of your love, or to be called 'Mother.' You

34

see now what I've become. And in that, your father is right. I should never see you again, and you should never see me. But I wanted you to know how the beginnin' was, so that you would not fear the bad blood your father speaks of."

"I do not fear it, Mother," Sheena said. This time when she put her arms around the woman, the woman allowed it, and they stood locked together in a tearful embrace.

Finally they parted, and Hazel, wiping away the tears, smiled at Sheena. "I want to get a good look at you, girl, for this is truly the last time I will ever see you."

"No," Sheena said. "It mustn't be. We'll find ways to meet again. Now that I have found you, I don't want to go the rest of my life without seeing you."

"But you must not see me again, girl. There is nothing I can do for you save bring you misery. Your father can offer you the world. You are better off doing as he wishes."

"But that isn't fair," Sheena protested.

"Life isn't fair," the older woman said. "But I've learned to live with it. And you will too, I'll wager. Now, I must be going."

"Wait," Sheena said. "At least let me make certain the way is clear for you."

Sheena stepped over to the door, opened it, and stuck her head out into the hall. She looked and listened, but heard nothing. "Come," she said. "No one is about."

Hazel pulled the shawl over her head, then stepped out into the hallway. She stopped, took Sheena's hand in hers, gave it one last squeeze, then moved quickly down the stairs.

5

Liam ducked behind the door when he overheard Sheena offer to see if the way was clear. Then, after Sheena's mother left, he slipped by Sheena's door and started after Hazel. He would show her that his father meant business when he ordered her to stay away from Sheena. And he would show his father that he could be depended on to carry out his instructions.

And there was another reason he followed her. A reason that he wouldn't admit, even to himself.

The woman moved quickly down the narrow alley-way and onto one of the wider streets, then turned to head for the docks. No doubt there she intended to find a willing sailor who would lie with her for the price of a tankard of ale, Liam thought. Inexplicably, Liam felt the beginnings of an erection, and he rubbed himself unthinkingly.

Liam thought of the story the old woman had told Sheena. From the time he was old enough to realize that he and Sheena had different mothers, he had wondered about it. He had often overheard things from the servants at his grandfather's estate: whispered conversations which hung in the air when an O'Sheel approached; veiled suggestions which didn't quite register; and knowing looks. Finally, from a stableman he bribed, Liam heard a story much like the one the woman had told Sheena. And from the same stableman he learned the identity of Sheena's mother, and discovered also that she was a doxy. He looked her up one day, not really knowing why he wanted to see her, but feeling a great sense of superiority in locating her and observing her from the bar without the woman ever knowing he was there.

The woman turned up the alleyway which led to the back entrance of Billy's Blood. Liam followed her.

"Hey, you, wench!" he called out. "Wait a minute. I want to see you."

The woman stopped and stood there for just a moment as if gathering her wits about her, then, with an almost imperceptible shrug of the shoulders, turned. She pasted the practiced smile of her profession on her face as she greeted the man who had hailed her.

"Oh, it's a young one, you are," she said. "Would you be lookin' for a good time?"

"And what makes you think an old cow like you can give me a good time?" Liam asked cruelly.

The smile left the woman's face.

"If you've no wish for my services, why did you hail me?" she asked.

"You don't know, do you? You really don't know who I am?"

Shutters were pushed open from a window on the upper floor and a woman emptied a chamber pot, the offal landing so close that Liam and Hazel had to step out of the way to avoid being splashed.

"Should I know you?"

"Look at me closely, whore, for I am your daughter's brother," Liam said coldly.

"You would be Liam then," the woman said.

"Not Liam, whore. To you I am Doctor O'Sheel."

"Your father is the doctor," the woman said.

"And I his apprentice."

"What do you want with me?" Hazel asked. "It bodes evil for me to be seen with you or your sister. That is against your father's wishes."

"Then why did you visit my sister today?"

"Faith, 'n you saw me visit the girl," Hazel said, covering her mouth with her hand. "And what'll you be doin' about it?"

"I intend to tell my father, as a dutiful son should."

"No, please, I beg of you not to do that."

"Are you frightened of my father, old crone?"

"Yes. But not for myself. 'Tis for the girl I'm frightened."

"You should have thought of her before you went to see her. Now it's too late," Liam said.

"Please, don't speak of this. I'll do anything you say. I'll give you anything you want."

Liam laughed cruelly. "And what could you have that I would want? I daresay you've not the price of a drink among your worldly holdings."

"Then I appeal to your mercy," Hazel said.

"I have no mercy," Liam replied.

"But surely there is something I can do for you, or you would not have bothered to call me down. Name what it may be, and I shall do it."

"Anything?" Liam asked, hating himself even as he asked.

Hazel had spent many years in the business of selling her body to men. She had known all sorts of men; rich and poor, old and young, handsome and ugly, black and white. If there was anything she was expert in, it was in reading the nuances of want, and anticipating the shadings of desire. And, much to her surprise, she recognized the unmistakable signs of lust in Liam's face.

Her smile returned, this time with as much seduction as she could muster. "Well, now," she said throatily. "Perhaps we'll be able to strike a bargain at that, eh? Come with me."

Liam felt his pulse quicken and his breath shorten. What was it about this woman that had him aroused? She was old and ugly and he was young enough and had money enough to be able to satisfy his cravings with any of a dozen young, beautiful girls. But even as he asked himself the question, he knew the answer.

This woman was Sheena's mother. From her womb had come the beautiful girl who was Liam's sister. Liam had been watching his sister for three years now, and during that time he had developed a lust for her which was all-consuming. It had been born from the moment he noticed her changing from girl-hood into young womanhood. There was a small hole in the wall that separated Liam's room from his sister's, and he spent hours there, spying on her as she bathed, or changed clothes, or simply examined her own budding body in pubescent curiosity.

Driven though Liam was, he knew he could never give in to the incestuous lust that burned inside him without being destroyed by it. It was to satisfy this forbidden lust that Liam became a sensualist, seeking relief in the fleshpots of Dublin. And now, here in this whore before him, who was the very mother of the object of his lust, he hoped to satisfy his hunger once and for all, and thus live, forevermore, free of its terrible cravings.

Liam followed her through a door which opened off the alley. The door itself was so small that he had to bend double to step through it, and the stairway was so narrow that he had to twist his body sideways to ascend. The stairway was dank and dark, and smelled foul from the scattering of hundreds of chamber pots and the frequent emptying of bladders.

"This is my room," the old woman said, opening a door and stepping inside. "I'll open the window and give us a little light."

"And air," Liam added, flaring his nostrils in distaste. "How can you stand this filth?"

"I have become used to it. I take little notice of it," Hazel replied.

Hazel began stripping out of her clothes, calling upon all the tricks of her professional experience to entice the young man who would be her lover. She used a shadow here, a soft light there, a movement to hold her body just so. As if by magic the person who had been a hard-looking woman in the cruel light of day was transformed into a sensual creature.

"Now, this is what you want, isn't it?" she asked in a husky, sexy voice, beckoning him to her nakedness.

"Yes, Sheena, this is what I want," Liam answered thickly. He loosened his belt and dropped his trousers, starting for the woman.

A flicker of confusion, then a look of understanding came across the woman's face. She chuckled softly to herself, then took the boy into her. "That's it, my big strong brother," she cooed into his ear. "Make your sister feel so good."

"Whoresister," Liam said, taking out the lust and anger he felt for his sister on this woman who was now her surrogate. His lust was born of animal desire. His anger was born of the lust. "Whoresister, whoresister, WHORESISTER!!!" he screamed as he vented himself of the final surges of passion.

But it didn't work. Afterward as he was dressing, he looked at the haggard old crone with whom he had just lain, and he was filled with disgust. He hid his disgust behind a weak smile, then reached slowly for the heavy candlestick on the bedside table.

6

Liam waited anxiously for his father to return that evening. When he came in, Liam begged his ear for a "grave discussion."

"Very well, Liam," Dr. O'Sheel said, closing the doors to the library to ensure their privacy. He returned to take a chair in front of the fireplace, across from his son. "Now we are alone. What do you wish to discuss?"

"It is about Sheena's mother," Liam said.

Dr. O'Sheel sighed and pressed his fist against his forehead for a moment before looking up. "Did Sheena disobey my express orders not to go see her?" he asked.

"No, Father," Liam said. "And in all fairness, in this instance, I feel Sheena was innocent. The old crone came here."

"What? Why did you let her in?" Dr. O'Sheel asked. "You knew my instructions."

"Aye, Father, I knew them well. But somehow the hag gained entry without my knowledge. I only discovered her as she was leaving."

"Then I shall call on her," Dr. O'Sheel said resolutely. "And I will fill her with such fear as to ensure that she never sees Sheena again."

"That won't be necessary, Father," Liam said nervously.

"It won't? And why not?"

"There is still more to tell you. I want to tell you, yet I fear it mightily."

"Fear it? Fear what? Liam, you have been a loyal and true son, worthy of my love and admiration. I should think you could tell me anything without fear."

"But this is most grave, Father."

Dr. O'Sheel put his hand on Liam's shoulder and squeezed it affectionately. "All the more reason you should feel secure in speaking with your own father," he said.

Liam looked at his hands for a moment before he began to speak. Finally he started, hesitantly, quietly, as if testing each word before he spoke it.

"I was busy with morning patients," he said. "I chanced to look around and saw Sheena's mother leaving by the back door. I called out to her so that I could again give her your instructions, but she pretended as if she didn't hear and hurried on about her business. Well, I knew that she should be spoken to on your behalf, so I excused myself from the patients and hurried after her."

"Oh, and that is why you are worried, because you excused yourself from the patients?" Dr. O'Sheel asked with a smile. "Do not worry, for you did the right thing. I did want my wishes expressed to the woman."

"No, Father, there is more," Liam said.

"Then, pray, continue," Dr. O'Sheel invited. He began filling his pipe, then took a burning ember from the fireplace to light it as Liam went on with his story.

"I trailed her back to the tavern where you saw her with Sheena. She went through a door in the back and up a foul set of stairs, and I followed right behind. I finally reached a door which I surmised led to her room. I knocked on it and she invited me in."

"Go on," Dr. O'Sheel said. "What happened next?"

Liam took a drink from the tankard of ale that was on the table beside the chair, then, wiping the foam from his lips, continued.

"I began to talk to her. I said, ' 'Tis Father's desire that you not see my sister. And as I am her older and loving brother, as well as my father's obedient son, I wish to inform you that I intend to tell him of your presence in our house during his absence.' "

"Well spoken," Dr. O'Sheel said. "What did she say to that?"

"She said she had a right to see her. I told her that it was for Sheena's own good that your instructions be followed and advised her that if she had a true mother's love for the girl, she would obey those instructions. She said that she had no mother's love for Sheena, but sought her out for the advantage she might derive from such meetings."

"Advantage?" Dr. O'Sheel asked, his eyebrows raised. "Of what advantage does she speak?"

"I wondered as well, Father, and so I asked her that selfsame question. And to it she replied: 'Perhaps her loving father will see fit to pay me a few bob to stay away from the girl.' "

"The greedy old hag!" Dr. O'Sheel said. "And so the true measure of her love is known! What did you do then?"

"I tried to plead with her, to tell her that Sheena was my own sweet sister and I wanted no harm to come to her, as would be likely if the old woman continued her evil ways."

"And how did she receive such an honest plea from a loving brother?" Dr. O'Sheel questioned.

"By mocking me, Father."

"She mocked you? How?"

"She removed her clothes and invited me to her bed," Liam said. "As if I would have interest in the old crone that she has become! Then, when I declined, she grew angry."

"A woman spurned often grows angry," Dr. O'Sheel said knowingly. "What did she do then?"

"She picked up a heavy candleholder from the table by the bed and attempted to use it to bash my brains out."

"Good lord, son, were you hurt?"

"No, Father, I parried the blow. But . . ."

"But?"

"In parrying the blow, the candleholder was somehow brought down over her own head."

"Ha!" Dr. O'Sheel said, laughing. "A fine bump on the head may be just the lesson she needs."

"'Tis more than a bump on the head, Father," Liam said. "For the old woman is dead."

"Dead?"

"Aye, Father, she is dead. She is dead, and I killed her."

"Well—well, perhaps so," Dr. O'Sheel sputtered. "But if so, it was an accident! You were acting in defense of your own life, did you not just say so?"

"Father, there were people who saw me go into that room," Liam said. "They may have recognized me."

"'Tis no matter. When the police make their inquiry, we shall merely relate the story you have just told me."

"But suppose they discover that the old hag was the mother of Sheena? Would you want that, Father? Can you see what Sheena's chances would be for marrying Dean Swift, should it be known that her mother was a whore?"

"Yes," Dr. O'Sheel said, his face now filled with worry. "Yes, I see your point. 'Twould not only be Jonathan Swift who would shy from her, but all others of quality as well. Faith, son, and what are we to do now?"

"There is only one thing to do, Father. We must quit Ireland."

"Quit Ireland? Leave this place of our birth? But our home is here; my medical practice, soon to be yours."

" 'Tis a sad thing we must do, true enough," Liam said. "But we must also think of Sheena. To stay in Ireland means to condemn the poor girl to a life of spinsterhood."

"You are right," Dr. O'Sheel said. He smiled at his son. "And you are willing to make this sacrifice for your sister?"

"Aye, Father, I am willing," Liam said.

Dr. O'Sheel stared at Liam for a long while, then put his fist to his forehead and pressed it tightly. His eyes misted, and a tear formed and rolled down his cheek. Finally he got up from his chair and walked over to embrace his son.

"I am truly an honored man," he said. "I have pleased God to have a son such as yourself."

" 'Tis not my doing, Father," Liam said. "For goodness is born in me of both sides. My poor sister is not so blessed, and thus we must make extra allowances for her."

"That is true, that is true," Dr. O'Sheel said. He sat back down and wiped his eyes with the back of his hand. "Now, if we are to quit Ireland, where shall we go?"

"We shall go to London, Father."

"Aye, perhaps we could. London is a huge city with room for many enterprises. I am certain that a doctor would have little difficulty in establishing a new practice."

"We would have no difficulty if you had your friend Jonathan Swift supply us with letters of introduction to the correct people."

"No," Dr. O'Sheel said. "I will not do that."

"But why not, Father? Surely it would make our adjustment in London much easier."

"I've no doubt but that it would," Dr. O'Sheel agreed. "But I'll not presume upon the friendship of Dean Swift."

"Then I fear we shall be in for a difficult time of it," Liam suggested.

Dr. O'Sheel smiled and put his hand on his son's shoulder. "It can't get too difficult for us, now, can it, Liam? We've the stuff it takes, right enough on that."

"Aye, Father," Liam said, hiding his disappointment. Liam had counted on a quick entry into London society and London clubs, by way of introductory letters from someone as respected as the Reverend Doctor Swift.

7

Sheena wasn't told why they had to leave Dublin, or even that they were leaving. She was just awakened before dawn one morning and hurried down to the docks, where she, her father, and her brother boarded a ship bound for England. She wanted to leave some word with her mother, to let her know what was happening to her, but of course her father had anticipated that very thing. It was for this reason the departure was made in haste and in the dark of night. He thought it best that Sheena never learn what happened to her mother.

Sheena enjoyed the voyage across St. George's Channel, short as it was, but England, and especially London, found little favor with her. In fact, Sheena hated London, and with good reason, for there the family no longer enjoyed the luxury of a house and were confined, instead, to two small rooms in an attic hovel.

The living quarters wouldn't have been so bad if Sheena could have gotten out and around, but London wasn't like her beloved Dublin. London was filthy, and not just in the seamier parts of town. The stench of rotting garbage and of human and animal excrement was everywhere. It was no wonder that on the few occasions when Sheena did go for a walk, she noticed that the fine ladies of London rode about in their carriages clutching bouquets of roses or perfumed handkerchiefs to their noses.

Sheena encountered another situation entirely new to her. She was immediately recognized as Irish by her brogue, and it was the nature of Englishmen to treat the Irish as second-class subjects of the Crown. Sheena, who had never encountered prejudice before, often found herself the butt of cruel remarks.

"Please, Father," she begged after two months of misery in the city. "Let us return to Dublin."

"I'm sorry, girl, but that we can never do," her father replied. "We must stay here."

"But you've not even a practice here," Sheena said. It was true. Kevin had discovered that Irish doctors could find few patients in London, and couldn't even find employment as medical apprentices.

"I'll soon find something," Kevin promised.

"You've not told me why we left," Sheena said. "Nor will you tell me why we can't go back. Why must we continue our suffering?"

"Girl, there are things of which you are totally unaware," Kevin said. "Things which affect our family, and especially you. You should be grateful that we are here, and especially grateful to your brother, who has made a great sacrifice on your behalf. After all, 'tis for your own good that we have come."

"Why is everything that is for my own good an unhappy thing?" Sheena asked.

" 'Tis more than I can explain for the moment," Kevin said. Kevin reached for his hat. "I'll be going to the pub now, girl, the better to avoid your nagging questions."

Kevin left his daughter and walked along the cobblestoned streets to the Red Bull Inn, a pub he had been frequenting since arriving in London. It was only in the pub, with his hands wrapped securely around a tankard of ale, that Kevin could find any happiness now, for Sheena was right: London was a poor place for the O'Sheels. In Dublin he had been Dr. O'Sheel, a man of substance, the son of Himself who owned the great House of O'Sheel. But in London he was Kevin O'Sheel the Irishman, no better off than the poor souls who dug for potatoes on his father's land.

There was another reason Kevin was ready to leave London. He was worried about his son. Liam, who had been so bright with promise while in Dublin, was now being infected by the vices and sins of London. Why, 'twas only the other day that Kevin had espied his son on the arm of a doxy. Poor Liam, he had made such a gallant sacrifice to save his sister from a life of misery, but in so doing had subjected himself to the degradations of London. Now, Kevin knew, he must leave London for the sake of his son.

But how? He had asked himself this question many times. As yet he had no answer. It had taken all his money to quit Dublin and bring his worldly possessions to London. Since reaching London, he had found no source of employment sound enough to keep body and soul together and still have enough money for the expense of another move.

If Kevin had not decided how he was going to move, he had decided where he would move to. He would take his family to America, to the Carolina colonies. He had heard much about the Carolinas since arriving in England. He recalled a conversation he had had with Timothy Braugh just a fortnight ago.

Timothy Braugh was a coarse man, given to crude language, and Kevin could not but note that the two of them would have never become acquainted were they still in Ireland. Braugh was of a station far below O'Sheel. However, such were the depths to which the O'Sheels had descended since coming to accursed London: that any Irishmen they met, of whatever birth, would have been their mates. Timothy was speaking again of America, as he often did during the time Kevin had known him.

"'Tis a wealthy man my American brother is, 'n that's a fact," Timothy said. "He's offered me passage to the new world, but it's married to an English woman I am 'n she's no taste for the Colonies."

"Your brother was wealthy when he went to America then?" Kevin asked.

"Wealthy?" Timothy asked, laughing. "I'll tell you how wealthy he was. 'Twas to escape debtor's prison that he fled this country."

"Then how was it he could make his fortune?"

"There's land in the Carolinas," Timothy said. "Land for the grabbin', and it's fine land too for the growin' of tobacco and the like."

"Aye, I've heard of the farms there," another said. "They're called plantations, and they're built on the blood and sweat of human misery."

"Why say you such a thing?" Timothy challenged.

"It's God's own truth I speak," the third party said. "For the plantations are worked by slaves; Africans who are bought and sold like livestock."

"Aye, that's true," Timothy said. "For my brother himself owns many such creatures. But 'tis the way of things there."

"It's the devil's way," the speaker said.

"Perhaps not," Kevin said.

"Doctor O'Sheel! You, an educated man, could see the right in slavery?" the speaker asked, his voice showing surprise over Kevin's statement.

"Aye. I see it as no different from the poor Irish tenant farmer."

"I can vouch for that," Timothy said. "'Twas from just such a family that myself came."

"Or the way all of Ireland is being held in bondage to England," Kevin added.

"Here, here," the other two men said, and the three of them touched glasses and drank.

"And in this institution of slavery, I can see a greater good," Kevin continued. " 'Tis truly the work of the slaves that is opening up the Carolinas and building a new world. And at the same time, the heathens are being brought to the word of God. 'Tis no more noble thing a man can do than bring heathens the word of God. Africans who are thus enslaved are thus enriched."

" 'Tis right enough you are on that point, Kevin," Timothy said. "You know, you should go there. 'Twas not only my brother, but many an Irishman who's gone to America 'n made his fortune. And most was lowborn too, sir, not like yourself, a noble gentleman and an educated man. Why you, sir, would be a rich man in no time if you went."

Kevin was still thinking about that conversation and pondering the best way to reach America when he arrived at the Red Bull Inn. He pushed through the doors and, seeing that Timothy was already at the table they regularly shared, started toward it. The inn was cloudy with tobacco smoke and noisy with the coarse conversation of seamen ashore, for it was a place frequented by sailors.

"Welcome, Doctor," Timothy greeted. "Sure 'n it was so certain I was that you'd be here that I've already ordered a tankard of ale. Ah, here comes the fair lass with it now."

As Timothy spoke a buxom wench approached, carrying Kevin's ale. She served it with a smile.

"She's a pretty thing, true enough," Timothy said after the girl left. "It's been said that she'll bed, if the man is a gentleman and his purse is accommodating."

"No," Kevin said. "I was once guilty of such a sin, and I've paid for it these many years in the sorrow of bringing into the world a child of corruptible nature. I've learned my lesson and shall not repeat the error."

"Press-gang!" a sailor yelled, sticking his head through the door. "Beware, mates, or you'll find yourselves conscripted!"

There was a flurry of activity and a sudden babble of voices, as dozens of men got up and hurriedly attempted to leave. Suddenly a group of club-wielding ruffians came in through both the front and rear doors, and those who were trying to leave were forced back inside.

"What is this? What's going on?" Kevin asked.

"A press-gang," Timothy said. "You mean you've nay seen a press-gang before?"

"Never," Kevin admitted.

"A press-gang's them what takes the sailors for their ships. Conscription they calls it. 'Tis more like kidnappin', for they have the king's authority to take what men they need, whether the men want to go or no!"

"You mean take them by force?" Kevin asked.

"Aye. But have no fear, you'll be in no danger. They mostly takes a few what's passed out drunk, and then only them with the look o' the sea about them. You'd not pass for a sailor, Doctor O'Sheel."

The press-gang was led by a big bushy-haired, bushy-bearded man. He brought four men with him. He stood over at the bar, smiling evilly and tapping his hand lightly with the short length of club he carried. He watched his men as they methodically dragged a few drunks to the bar and deposited them at his feet.

"A motley crew, this," he said.

"You want us to fetch some more, Dog?" one of the club-wielding sailors asked.

The door opened and a young man, about twenty-four years old, stepped inside. Strongly built, he had thick black hair and a complexion which, naturally dark, had been further turned by the hours he spent on deck in the sun. He had a strong chin and a well-formed mouth, topped by a neatly trimmed mustache. When he smiled he showed a row of even, white teeth, and his cheeks displayed dimples. His eyes were brown, with splinters of green. As he looked around the tavern all eyes looked toward him.

"Well, well," the man said. "This looks like an impressment party to me. And you," he said to the big bushy-haired one. "You are uglier than the hounds of hell. As Captain Collier described you to me, you must be the one they call Dog."

The sailors, those who had not yet been conscripted and who were standing fearfully to one side, now laughed nervously.

"I'm called that," Dog answered. "And who might you be?"

"The name is William Drumm, though it shall be Mister Drumm to you, Dog. I am the new first mate of the *Cassandra,* just signed on." Drumm looked at the three men who had thus far been impressed. "Return those men to their tables," he ordered. "I do not ship with impressed men."

"The cap'n won't like that," Dog said sullenly.

"The captain will be happier with a crew of volunteers," Drumm said. "And I intend to provide him with just such a crew. Lads, hear me. I need volunteers for the ship *Cassandra,* sailing tomorrow for the Carolinas."

At the mention of the ship's destination, Kevin's interest perked up.

"I'll come," one of the tavern whores said. She smiled broadly, showing her toothless gums. The men, now relieved of the fear of impressment, laughed uproariously.

"Aye, you probably would come at that," Drumm said, joining in the laughter. "But I'll be needin' men. Able-bodied seamen, cooks, carpenters, sailmakers—

any and all types anxious to serve a good ship with a willing crew."

"Say, I've sailed with Mister Drumm," one seaman said. He was a big man, bald-headed with a gold ring in his ear. "Come along, Ed," he said to his friend. "Mister Drumm's a good mate to sail for."

"Thanks, Carter," Drumm said, recognizing the sailor. "It'll be good to have an old shipmate aboard."

"Damn me, if 'e's as good as all that, I'd sooner sail with 'im than to wait 'ere and be impressed by some other gang for a ship that God knows nothin' about. I'll sail with 'im," another sailor said, and he started after the first two.

" 'E's the proper gentleman, 'e is," the old whore said. "And pretty too. Are you sure I can't come along, sweetie?"

Again the men laughed, and a few more moved over, until Drumm was satisfied that he had enough and indicated to Dog that he should take the new crew to the ship.

After Dog left, Drumm bought an ale for himself. The other customers, relieved that the press-gang was gone, returned to their own animated conversations and drinking.

"Mister Drumm, 'twould be an honor if you would be joining us, sir," Kevin invited.

Drumm brought his ale with him and sat at the table in the chair offered him. "Thank you," he said. "Drink is much better with company."

Kevin introduced Timothy and himself to the young officer. "You did say the *Cassandra* is bound for the Carolinas?"

"Aye," Drumm said. "We sail tomorrow, Why the interest, sir? You don't have the look of a sailing man."

"I'm a doctor," Kevin said. "Could you use a ship's surgeon?"

"Aye, we could that," Drumm said. "For I would

have to serve in that capacity, otherwise, and I've no skill for it, nor love of it."

"I've a reason for wanting to go to the Carolinas," Kevin said. "I'd take it kindly if you'd accept my services."

"Kevin O'Sheel. You're Irish then?"

"Aye. You've no love for the Irish?"

"No love for them, no hate for them. I'm American."

"You mean you're an Englishman living in the Colonies?"

"I consider myself American, as do the others who live there," Drumm said. "So, Doctor O'Sheel, if you wish, I'll sign you on with the crew."

"I've two persons with me," Kevin said.

"Who?"

"My son and daughter."

Drumm rubbed his mustache. "I don't know, Doctor, this changes things. The *Cassandra* is not properly fitted as a passenger ship."

" 'Tis only the passage we seek," Kevin said. "We'll not complain of the quarters."

"How old are they?"

"My son is eighteen," Kevin said.

"Eighteen, is he? Then he can help work his passage?"

"Aye. The girl's but sixteen, a mere child. But I'll be responsible for her," Kevin promised. "Please, Mister Drumm. I must get to the Carolinas."

Drumm ran his hand through his hair, then broke into an easy smile. "Doctor, I fear the wrath of my captain when he learns of this bargain I have struck, but 'tis done. Be at the *Cassandra* at first light of the morning."

"Thank you, Mister Drumm. You shan't regret this," Kevin said, shaking Drumm's hand happily.

8

In London, in 1718, there was scarcely enough time in one day for the poor people to earn their bread, so long before the sun rose they were out working, trying to stretch the hours to meet their needs.

Fishmongers, their wagons loaded with yesterday's catch, pushed their carts through the narrow, twisting back alleys. They moved through the garbage and sewage, hawking their wares, protected from the stench by the peculiar odors of their profession.

With the fishmongers went the vegetable-peddlers, the bread-sellers, the milk-dealers, all filling the morning air with their calls, given in the singsong voices that identified them to their personal customers.

Joining the early morning procession was the O'Sheel family: Kevin, anxious that he was doing the right thing; Liam, resentful at having to go but unwilling to remain behind; and Sheena, who was ecstatic with joy. Sheena's excitement was boundless, not only because they were leaving London but because they would be embarking on an ocean adventure. Just the thought of the cruise set her blood to racing.

"We must move quickly," Kevin said. "For I was told they would leave with first light."

"Tell me about the ship, Father," Sheena said. "What kind is it?"

"What kind? Well, I really don't know," Kevin replied. "Though I'm certain it will be adequate for the voyage."

"I truly hope so," Liam said in a disgusted tone of voice. "I hope we aren't embarking on some scow."

"It could scarcely be worse than what we must put up with now," Sheena reminded him.

"In this I feel your sister is right, Liam," Kevin said. "There, ahead, I see the ships. I hope we are on time."

As they walked down the cobblestoned street Sheena looked toward their destination. At the end of the street, only a short distance away, she could see the masts of several ships stabbing toward the sky. The masts, though free of sail, were stretched so tall as to almost grab the low-skirting clouds, and thus making the predawn darkness even blacker. Sheena was so excited that she wanted to break into a run but, realizing how unseemly that would be, she checked her impulse so that she arrived at dockside with her father and brother.

There were two seamen standing on the dock. They stared at Sheena with unabashed interest, surprised to see such a lovely creature in their midst.

"Excuse me, gentlemen," Kevin said. "Could you point out the *Cassandra* to me?"

The seamen, still staring with unchecked interest at Sheena, pointed to a ship just three slips down. There was a great deal of commotion on the dock alongside the ship, and it was obvious that the vessel was preparing for departure.

"Oh," Sheena said. "Isn't it beautiful?"

The *Cassandra* was a little over one hundred feet

long, copper-sheathed and square-rigged. It was officially listed as an "armed transport of His Majesty's Navy," and, as they drew closer, Sheena could see that there were cannons on board.

A gangplank was stretched from the dock to the ship, and Sheena and the others walked up it, then stepped onto the deck.

"So, surgeon, you've come in time, I see," a voice called. "And this would be the daughter? But surely there is some mistake? I expected a mere child. I see a beautiful young woman."

Sheena turned to look into the face of a tall, handsome sailor. He was strongly built, with thick black hair. She took in her breath sharply. She couldn't help herself, for he was certainly the most handsome man she had ever seen. Quite inexplicably, it seemed as if she could actually feel her blood moving through her veins. What was it about him? No man had ever made her feel like this before.

"Mister Drumm, if you could spare yourself, sir, would you see to the ship's stores?" the captain called from the quarter-deck.

Sheena looked up to see a short, disagreeable figure of a man. His face was round, without a saving characteristic; in its natural state the lower lip seemed to protrude slightly, giving him the appearance of being contemptuous of everything.

"Aye, Cap'n Collier," Drumm answered easily. He smiled at Sheena as he left to attend to his task.

"Surgeon, a word with you, please," the captain said. "And bring your daughter."

Kevin and Sheena walked over to answer the summons.

"I have decided to take you," Captain Collier said. "But it is against my better judgment."

"But why, sir? I am a qualified surgeon."

"It has nothing to do with your qualifications, sir, but with your daughter."

"My daughter?"

"We will be long at sea," Captain Collier explained. "My crew is composed of ruffians in the main, and I must exercise the strictest discipline over them to keep them in line. I feel the presence of a woman will make my task more difficult."

"But she is but a girl, Captain," Kevin protested.

"Have you not eyes to see with, man? She is a woman, full grown, and with charms enough to heat the blood of any man."

"Captain, I will try by all in my power to avoid any situation which might cause you unpleasantness," Kevin promised, though secretly deriving much pleasure from the captain's comments. He wondered if the first mate shared the captain's opinion.

"And you, girl, will you cooperate?"

"Aye, Captain," the girl said. "I've no wish to be a burden."

"Then perhaps there will be little trouble on the voyage. You, Dog," the captain yelled, and Kevin saw the bushy-bearded man who had led the press-gang the night before. "Show the lady to your cabin. She shall have it. You will quarter yourself with the crew."

"Aye, sir," Dog said.

"I'm sorry if I've put you out of your room," Sheena said as she followed Dog down a small ladderway and into the bowels of the ship. The odors below, though they would be considered unpleasant by most, were exciting to Sheena, and held the promise of adventure.

Dog laughed. "It's naught to be upset over," he said. "There's little enough to it."

It was dark between decks, the hold being lit by a few dim lanterns which burned orangely in their gimbal mountings. Very little of the light diffused through the hold, but what illumination there was allowed Sheena to observe her surroundings. There were coils of rope and kegs and boxes of goods scattered about. There were a few sailors working with something on the other side of the great, dark cavern, but she was unable to make out what they were doing.

"Here you'll stay, miss," Dog said, pointing to a small door. He opened the door and held his hand out grandly. "It's all shipshape for you. I'll just take my things, and you can have your own stowed here."

"Oh, it's grand," Sheena said, her eyes reflecting the gold of the lanterns. The excitement she felt over the impending voyage was obvious in her voice.

"Best you stay belowdecks, miss, leastwise till we get underway," Dog advised. "The cap'n, he don't like passengers on the deck."

"And the first mate?" Sheena asked. She wanted to bite her tongue for asking the question, for she had no wish for it to get back to the first mate that she had expressed an interest in him.

"The first mate I know nothin' about, ma'am. He's just signed on for this voyage. I've never sailed with him."

" 'Tis of no matter," Sheena said. "I will remain out of the way."

Sheena walked over to lie on the bunk after Dog left. She was still a little tired from the very early awakening, and the gentle rocking of the ship, the comforting breeze through the air scupper, and the muffled sounds combined to provide a soothing effect. Within a few moments she was asleep.

9

Sheena was awakened by the whistle of the boatswain's pipe.

"All hands," she heard Drumm's voice say. "Turn out."

There were more shouts and a great bustle on deck. Sheena went topside to watch the proceedings.

"Here, Miss O'Sheel," Drumm called out as he saw her standing at the hatch. "You can watch if you please, but stand to the rail, out of harm's way."

As Sheena watched sailors were climbing aloft and crawling out on the arms.

"Loose the topsails," Captain Collier said quietly, and Drumm repeated his order in a loud voice.

The topsails filled, and the *Cassandra* began to move.

"Loose the forecourse and the mainsail!"

The canvas billowed and boomed like thunder, and the ship felt as if it were leaping forward under the sails.

"We've a good following wind, Captain," Drumm said. "With it and the current, I calculate we'll pass through the mouth of the river and into the open sea in time to catch the tide. We're underway, sir."

"Very well, Mister Drumm, set the watch, please."

"Aye, aye, Captain."

"Mister Drumm," a sailor called.

"Aye."

"The mizzen skysail halyard is fouled, sir."

"Can you shake it loose?" Drumm asked, looking toward the very top of the aftermast at the dangling errant rope.

"We cannot, sir."

"Very well, send a man aloft."

" 'Tis on the outer tip of the yardarm itself, sir. It would take someone of less than one hundred and twelve pounds to reach it. We've no one that small."

"Dog, see to the deck," Drumm ordered, then started up the mizzenmast himself.

"You'll not be able to reach it, sir," the sailor who had called attention to the problem said.

"Well, better to try now than after we're in the open sea," Drumm called back.

Drumm knew that his own weight, one hundred and sixty pounds, was far too great to reach the line directly, but he hoped to be able to figure some way to reach it with another line. When he got to the top of the mast, though, he realized that his plan would be useless. The halyard was not badly fouled. It would be simple to free it if he could just reach it. But there was no place to support a bo'sun's chair that would allow its occupant to be swung out to the knot. He cursed his luck and climbed back down the mast.

"What's the problem, Mister Drumm?" the captain asked when Drumm reached the deck.

"It's not a severe one, Captain," Drumm said. "It could easily be loosed if it could be reached. But, as yet, I've no idea as to how to reach it."

"Best you find an idea, Mister Drumm," the captain said. "I'll not put to sea with a crippled ship, and I'll not put about for so small a problem."

"Aye, Captain," Drumm said. "Carter," Drumm

called to the sailor who had first noticed the problem.

"I'm here, sir," Carter said, approaching the first mate.

"We've got to rig some way of swinging a man out to the knot," Drumm said.

"That's no good, sir," Carter said. "I thought of it, but you would have to attach the block up there at the —Lord help me, sir, 'tis the girl!" Carter interrupted.

"The girl? What girl?"

"There, sir, going up the mizzenmast," Carter pointed.

"Mister Drumm, will you order that girl down at once, sir!" the captain suddenly shouted. He'd seen Sheena at about the same time as Carter had, climbing quickly up the mast.

"Miss O'Sheel, come back down," Drumm said, starting for the mast on the run.

All the sailors on board had stopped in the midst of their tasks. They watched as Sheena, still dressed in the finery she wore aboard, climbed to the very top of the mizzenmast, then started working her way out the yard toward the fouled rope.

Sheena had overheard the problem and knew at once that she could solve it. She weighed just under one hundred pounds, and she had been climbing about on ships for over three years. Of course this was the first time she had ever climbed the rigging in a dress, and it was causing her more problems than she had anticipated, for the skirt itself was acting like a sail and was near to blowing her off her perch.

"Miss O'Sheel," Drumm said, now even with her in height, though unable to come out on the yard. "What do you think you are doing?"

"I'm freeing the line for you," Sheena said. She reached the knot and in a few seconds had the rope freed. A cheer floated up from the seamen on the deck and the captain bellowed in a loud voice, "Belay that, you swabs! Bend your backs, or I'll have you to the whipping tee. Mister Drumm, order the girl down at once!"

"I don't understand," Sheena said. "I thought you and the captain would appreciate my help."

"We could have done it without placing you in danger," Drumm said angrily. "Now, would you please come down?"

Sheena grabbed the line she had just freed and slid down it to the yard below. Then she moved to the mast and climbed down the rigging, reaching the deck before Drumm did.

"Daughter, you have disgraced me!" her father said. "Go to your cabin at once."

"If it had been Liam and not I who untangled the knot, would you feel disgrace, or pride?" Sheena asked.

"It was not Liam," Kevin said. "The supposition is of little merit. The fact is, I am in disfavor with the captain and disgraced by you. Return to your cabin at once."

"Yes, Father," Sheena said, starting toward the hatch with downcast eyes. She was truly hurt by the reaction of everyone. She had thought that by proving herself, she could be accepted. But it only served to make the situation worse.

As Sheena started toward her cabin she heard the captain berating Drumm, and she caught Drumm's angry glance just before she descended the ladder. Though the captain's fury and her father's displeasure had upset her, it was the look of anger in Drumm's eyes that disturbed her most. For in the dream she had had during the short nap she had taken earlier, Drumm had been the sailor in the bed when she traded places with one of the doxies. It had been a vivid dream, and she had awakened from it with a tingling sensation which she knew wasn't entirely due to the excitement of the voyage.

* * *

Sheena stayed in her cabin for the rest of the day, listening to the constant roar of the wind in the sails, the singing of the ropes, the creaking of the masts, and the rushing of the water. She ate no breakfast and passed up lunch, but as the dinner hour approached she grew hungry and went up on deck, hoping to find her father and find out what the eating arrangements were.

When Sheena reached the deck she saw that they were now far at sea, and she inhaled deeply, enjoying the clean, fresh smell of the salt air, far away from the fetid odors of shore. Liam was standing near the rail, looking ashen.

"Liam, what is it?" Sheena asked.

"I suffer from seasickness," Liam said. His face was bathed in perspiration. "Do you not feel it—the accursed rolling of this ship?"

"Oh, yes, but I think it is exciting," Sheena said. "Maybe you are just hungry. I know I am."

"Do not speak to me of food!" Liam said sharply.

"I'm sorry," Sheena apologized.

"Ah, there you are, Miss O'Sheel," Dog said, approaching Sheena and her brother. "The cap'n's compliments, ma'am, and 'e asks that you do him the honor of dining with the ship's officers tonight. We've got good salt pork. The worms have na' 'ad a chance to start up yet," he added in a cruel jest toward Liam, whom he knew to be sick.

"Excuse me," Liam mumbled. He moved down the rail and began to throw up.

"It wasn't necessary to torment him, sir," Sheena said with a flash of anger.

Dog laughed, then looked at Sheena. "Perhaps I'd best tell the cap'n that the O'Sheels aren't up to dinin' tonight."

"Not at all," Sheena said easily. "I would be delighted to join the officers for dinner."

"I'll pass the word on, ma'am," Dog said.

10

William Drumm thought of the three O'Sheels who had signed on board. Dr. O'Sheel had yet to prove himself, for there had been no occasion for his services. The doctor's son, Liam, would be carried on the roster as a surgeon's apprentice. It was an unheard-of luxury for a vessel this small, but Drumm knew there was little else the boy would be able to do. They'd only been at sea for half a day and Liam had done little save stand at the rail and "feed the fishes," as the sailors say when speaking of someone who throws up from seasickness.

The beauty and charm of the girl, Sheena, had not gone unnoticed among the men, and Drumm had taken notice of her as well. The girl was a delight to the eyes: supple of form, hair the color of burnished copper, eyes as green as the waters of the Caribbean sea, and a face so lovely that it made men turn to jelly. And yet there was something about her, a defiance of authority, a rebellious attitude, that set her apart from any girl Drumm had ever met. The business of her climbing the mizzenmast to free the rope, for example, was itself an example of that defiance. Could any man tame that defiance, Drumm wondered?

Captain Collier had ordered his first officer to muster all hands aft, and Drumm had just done so. Along with all hands, the three O'Sheels were on deck. The doctor, who as a surgeon was a ship's officer, was standing with Drumm and Dog, the other two officers. Liam was technically a midshipman, so he stood with Eric Russel, the officer candidate of the voyage. Sheena, as the sole passenger, stood over near the rail, observing the proceedings. She was, it seemed to Drumm, watching him closely.

Captain Collier stepped through the door that led out of his cabin and climbed the three steps to the quarter-deck. They were short steps, physically, but the gulf that separated the seamen from the quarter-deck was as wide as the ocean itself. The quarter-deck was the officer's territory, and any seaman who trod there without an express invitation did so in peril of a thorough lashing, or worse.

"Mister Drumm, have you mustered all hands?" Collier asked.

"Aye, aye, sir."

"No young girls in the rigging, I trust?"

Sheena giggled at the inference, but she saw immediately that it was no laughing matter either to Drumm or her father, so she swallowed the laugh.

"No, sir," Drumm replied.

"Very well, we shall get on with it."

Collier cleared his throat, then looked out over the assembled crew. It was standard procedure for the captain to muster all hands soon after getting underway. It was his chance to let the sailors know what he expected of them during the voyage, and it was the sailors' chance to size up their captain.

Captain Collier paced back and forth on the quarter-deck, looking at the men. He puffed on a pipe and remained silent for several moments. There were, during this time, only the sounds of the sails and the creaking of the ship's fixtures as she answered the wind.

"Well, me lads," Collier said finally. "So you've shipped on board the *Cassandra,* and you'll be wantin' to know what kind of ship she be, eh? Let me tell you this." He took the pipe from his mouth and pointed with the stem. "All ships are the same. It's the men who make a good ship. Aye, the men. If we get along well together, we'll have a comfortable trip. If we don't, you'll feel that you've signed on for a tour in hell and me, the devil's mate. All you've got to do is obey your orders and do your duty like sailors, and you'll fare well enough. You'll find that we shall make an easy passage of it, and you'll think me a clever enough fellow. But if you've a mind to be a lazy slaggard, you'll find that I can be as harsh as any captain in the king's fleet. Now, I have nothing else to say. Mister Drumm, set the watch, sir."

Captain Collier returned immediately to his cabin, and Drumm set the watch as directed. Those who weren't on watch returned belowdecks. The girl, Sheena, he noticed, stayed above, and leaned over the rail, looking out to sea.

Drumm, as officer of the watch, had the quarterdeck, and he paced back and forth, seeing to the mechanics of the ship, but mostly just enjoying the moment. It was this part of sailing that Drumm liked best. It was the quiet time, when one could appreciate the perfect silence of the sea, and be alone with one's thoughts. Drumm's thoughts, he noticed, were, disturbingly, of the girl.

The ship's prow was pointed toward the west, and the bowsprit stretched out toward the setting sun, which was a great orange disc, just balanced on the horizon. Before the sun, and stretching all the way to the *Cassandra,* was a wide band of red, laid out like a carpet on the sea. The few clouds which dotted the western sky had purpled, and even the great white sails of the ship were rimmed with gold.

So beautiful was the sunset that Drumm simply

watched it, letting thoughts of the girl drift from his mind. Then, after the colors had faded, he turned to look at Sheena, only to see that she had left the deck. He was sorry she had, for it had been truly a magnificent sight, and sharing it with her, even from separate stations, would have drawn them closer.

Drumm left the quarter-deck and took a turn about the ship. He checked the set of each sail, looked at each sailor's work, then returned to the quarter-deck. As he returned, he happened to look down toward the air scupper which led into the second mate's cabin, the one now occupied by Sheena O'Sheel. And when he did, he saw something which made him stop short.

There, in the second mate's cabin, was Sheena O'Sheel. She was dressing for dinner, and she had two dresses lying on the bunk, trying to make her choice. And, at that precise moment, Sheena was completely nude.

Drumm rarely "slept cold" when ashore, as the sailors put it. But he was hard-pressed to remember anything that charged his blood as intensely as this chance glimpse of Sheena O'Sheel in the nude. In that moment, Drumm knew that he would have her, before this voyage was completed.

"Mister Drumm," the helmsman called. "The wind's getting ahead, sir."

Drumm was startled by the helmsman's call. He had been so busy with his own private thoughts and with the beauty of the sunset—to say nothing of the beauty of Sheena—that he had neglected his duty. True, as the helmsman had said, the wind was coming around and the clouds were beginning to gather together. Likely, they'd be in for bad weather shortly.

"Mister Drumm," Captain Collier called, appearing in his doorway at that moment. "Don't you think you'd best give the order to trim the yards?"

"Aye, Captain, I was about to," Drumm said, his cheeks flaming in the embarrassment of having the captain publicly correct him for the second time during this short voyage.

"Trim the yards," Drumm ordered, and the sailors of his watch, many of whom had been lost in their own thoughts, moved into action.

Drumm moved a coil of rope with his foot, blocking the air scupper into Sheena's cabin, in order to reserve for himself the view he had just seen.

Potter, the captain's steward, had set up a table in the open area of the bay just forward of the captain's cabin. The table was set with white linen and ship's crockery. Occupying the position of honor on the table were a large hoop of cheese, a bottle of wine, and a bowl of apples. Seated around the table were the captain, Dr. O'Sheel, Sheena, and Dog. There were two empty places, one for Liam, who wouldn't be joining them, and one for Mr. Drumm, who was making arrangements for Midshipman Russel to relieve him on watch.

"My son sends his regrets, Captain," Kevin apologized. "He is feeling ill from the sea."

"He'll be gettin' his sea legs soon, I reckon," the captain said. He carved off a large piece of cheese and handed it to Sheena. "You seem to have adjusted to the sea quite well, Miss O'Sheel. You've sailed before?"

"Only the short distance from Ireland to England," Sheena said. "But I love it."

"My daughter has always had a fascination for ships and for the sea, which I find perplexing," Kevin explained.

Mr. Drumm joined them at that moment, excusing his tardiness.

"We started without you," the captain said matter-of-factly.

"I apologize, sir," Drumm said. "There was some difficulty with a luff tackle. It's repaired now."

"Then, please join us," the captain invited, shoving a piece of cheese into his mouth as he spoke.

"Miss O'Sheel," Drumm said, as he sat across from her. "You look lovely tonight. And I do think the green is more becoming than the blue. You made a wise choice."

Sheena felt her face burning. How could he know she had been trying to decide between a blue dress and this green one? Then she remembered hearing his voice from right over her cabin at that precise moment, and being startled by it. Good heavens, she thought. Surely he had not seen her? She was naked then. She looked at him with questioning eyes.

"The blue you wore when you came aboard was quite attractive though, and I daresay it would have been just as impressive now," Drumm went on.

So, Sheena thought with a sigh of relief, he was talking about what I had on this morning, and not about the decision I was trying to make in my cabin. But, as she looked at him, she saw a twinkle in his eyes which seemed to suggest that there was more to it than that. Again she wondered if he had seen her. But how? The air scupper perhaps. Could one see through the air scupper?

Sheena left the question unasked, and their conversation continued in generalities, though the idea that he may have seen her naked stayed with her, dominating her thoughts. Sheena enjoyed a forbidden delight over that possibility. It suffused her with a warm glow that was very pleasant.

Even as they were talking, Sheena noticed that the ship was rolling more. It had been gradually increasing in intensity until finally even Sheena was able to discern the difference between the vigorous chop of the ship now, and the quite gentle rolling of it earlier.

Captain Collier got up from the table and walked through his cabin to the stern windows. "The sea has risen, Mister Drumm. Could you find it in yourself to excuse yourself from the charming Miss O'Sheel's company to relieve Midshipman Russel, please?"

"Aye, sir," Drumm said, aware that once again the captain had deemed it necessary to remind him of his duty.

When Drumm returned to the deck it was quite different from the serenity of the sunset an hour earlier. Then, the *Cassandra* had been floating as serenely as a painted ship on a painted ocean. Now she was plunging through heavy seas, and the waves were beating against her bows and flying over the deck. Midshipman Russel, a young man of seventeen, was holding tightly to the security line. He was soaked through by the water.

"Mister Russel, did you not think my presence on deck would be desirable?" Drumm asked.

"Aye, sir," the midshipman said. "But I had no wish to disturb you at your meal."

"A foundering ship would be quite a disturbance, don't you agree?"

"Aye, sir," the midshipman said, hanging his head in shame over his error.

"Well, come along, lad. We must take action. Get all hands topside. We must take in sail. Turn to! Turn to!" he shouted.

The men came running.

"Reef the topsails," Drumm ordered. "And see that there is a proper furl, lads."

The topsails were furled, one by one, but the wind continued to build, until, with a great, tearing sound, the mainsail on the mainmast ripped open from top to bottom.

A handful of sailors climbed the mainmast and began working on the torn sail, managing to secure it just in time to take care of another torn sail, working in the rain and fighting the windblown sea, until at last the ship was secure again.

Drumm kept all hands at their stations until he

heard four bells of the midnight watch. By then, 2:00 A.M., the wind had abated and the sea had calmed. A brisk quartering breeze was all that remained of the storm, and it was the kind of breeze that would blow them along in good fashion. Drumm put on sail, then dismissed everyone except those who would normally have the watch.

"You there," Drumm said a moment later, watching one of the sailors start belowdecks. "Come here."

The sailor started toward him. Just as the sailor reached him, Drumm grabbed the sockcap from the sailor's head, allowing cascades of red hair to fall down.

"I *thought* so!" Drumm said angrily. "Miss O'Sheel, just what do you think you are doing?"

"I was helping," Sheena said. "I can climb the rigging as well as any man."

"You little fool. You've meant nothing but trouble for me since you set foot on this vessel," Drumm said. "Get to your cabin at once!"

"You can't order me around like one of the sailors!" Sheena replied hotly.

"If you're going to act like a sailor, I can order you about like one," Drumm said.

"Mister Drumm, what is the commotion, sir?" Captain Collier asked, sticking his head out the door of his cabin. He saw Sheena. "Good Lord, not again. Go to your cabin, girl. Mister Drumm, you report to me."

"Aye, sir," Drumm said.

Sheena returned to her cabin as the captain ordered, unable to understand why Drumm was so upset with her. After all, she had worked as hard as any man during the storm, and, to her delight, none of the sailors were the wiser. It wasn't until Drumm recognized her that she was compromised, though how he recognized her, she had no idea.

Once in her cabin Sheena stripped out of her wet clothes. She was just reaching for her nightgown when the door burst open, and she saw Drumm standing there.

"You!" she said, so angered by his sudden intrusion that she momentarily forgot the fact that she was nude. "What are you doing here?"

"You've shamed me before the captain again, Miss O'Sheel," Drumm growled angrily. "And I'll have no more of it."

Suddenly Sheena remembered that she was naked. She held the nightgown in front of her body, trying to preserve some modesty. "Get out of here," she ordered.

"No, Miss O'Sheel, I have no intention of leaving," Drumm said. He reached out and grabbed the night-gown in Sheena's hand, then jerked it from her grasp and tossed it to one side. "Not until I've been compensated for the grief you've caused me."

The movement was so unexpected that Sheena was momentarily stunned, and Drumm took advantage of that situation to grab her and pull her to him, mashing his lips down on hers.

Sheena's head began to spin. What was happening to her? She should be angry with him for breaking into her room like this, and yet under the spreading pleasure invoked by his kiss, she found it impossible to hold an edge to her anger.

"And now, Miss O'Sheel," Drumm said, pushing her toward her bed. "As you seem to have difficulty in deciding whether you wish to be a man or a woman, I shall take it upon myself to show you which it shall be."

Drumm pushed Sheena down on her bed, then began unbuckling his belt, sliding his wet trousers down his long, muscular legs.

"No," Sheena said, sitting up. "I'm not some whore to be taken by any sailor who comes along!"

Drumm pushed her back down. "You'll be taken by me, Sheena O'Sheel, and you'll like it." Drumm held her down with the weight of his knee as he tore at the rest of his clothes. Within a moment he was as naked as she, looming over her, staring down at her with lust-inflamed eyes, which, even in the dimmest of light, revealed his intent.

"I'll not let you do this, you bastard," Sheena said, fighting against him, and now against herself too. For her own passions were rising, and she blamed the betrayal of her body on the bad blood that flowed in her veins.

"You can't stop me, Miss O'Sheel," Drumm said. "Why try to fight?" He spread her legs then, and forced himself into her.

Sheena felt a searing pain as he entered. She fought against him, raking her nails down his back, producing lines of blood with her scratches, but the struggles only increased Drumm's resolve and he thrust deeper, until the pain subsided, and Sheena felt herself surrendering to the pleasure of it. No, not surrendering to, *embracing* the pleasures of the moment. The time she had spent before her mirror, examining the wonders of young womanhood and thinking of the things she had seen between the doxies and the sailors, now came back to betray her. This was what it was all about. *This,* the sudden burst of pleasure that started small, in the core of her being, then moved out to engulf her, finally overtaking her in a shattering climax, which left her gasping for breath and clinging to the naked shoulders of the man who was over her.

"Mister Drumm, report to the brig at once, sir. You are relieved of all duties on board this ship," Captain Collier's ice-cold voice said. "And you, miss, cover your nakedness at once!"

The captain stood in the door of the cabin, surveying the scene. His eyes were flashing like the eyes of the avenging angel.

"Captain Collier, I—" Drumm started to say.

"Say nothing to me, sir, lest I decide to forget, as you seem to have forgotten, that you are an officer, and have you flogged and hanged from the yardarm. As it stands now, sir, you will at least be given a formal court-martial ashore, before you hang for rape."

"Rape? But this wasn't rape, Captain, surely you could see. . . . Sheena, tell him . . ."

"Please, just leave me alone," Sheena interrupted him, covering herself in shame and looking away.

"Sheena, are you listening to what he is saying? For God's sake, girl, tell him you *enjoyed* it."

"Will you go peacefully, sir, or must I summon a detail of men?" Captain Collier asked.

"I'll go," Drumm said, exhaling a sigh. He looked toward Sheena. "It would appear, miss, that you have won this brief war which has developed between us."

Sheena wasn't listening. She closed her ears to it as tightly as she shut her eyes. But she knew that Drumm was right. She had enjoyed it, even more than she had thought possible during the wildest flights of fantasy. And in her mind that could only mean one thing: Her mother had lied to her when she told Sheena that her sins wouldn't be visited on her daughter. The blood that coursed through Sheena's veins was as wanton as the blood which coursed through the veins of any doxy.

Liam and her father were right. Sheena had bad blood.

11

No one was told why Drumm was confined to the brig.
There was much speculation, for none of the sailors
had ever heard of a first officer being confined like a
common sailor. Some of the crew, Carter and his
friends among them, even muttered darkly of a mutiny.
Such talk was carried on only in the utmost secrecy
though, for talk of a mutiny was as serious as the
offense itself.

The captain had guarded the reason of Drumm's
confinement so well that not even Sheena's father and
brother knew that Sheena had been raped, and Sheena
was thankful for that. But though she was thankful,
she was also ashamed. She was ashamed that she had
enjoyed it, but equally ashamed that she had lacked
the courage to admit it, and thus spare Drumm im-
prisonment. But, she told herself, once the voyage was
completed, she would say whatever was necessary to
prevent Mr. Drumm from actually being hanged for
his crime.

Dog became the new first officer, succeeding William
Drumm. Sheena was certain that Dog didn't know
what had happened, but his behavior around her always bordered on the insolent and so she was most

uncomfortable near him. She avoided him when she could and kept always aware of where he was, so that she could move before he approached her, without seeming to do so. Chances are, had Captain Collier not been injured, Sheena would never have spoken to Dog.

They were eight days out when the captain received his wound. It seemed harmless enough at first. A particularly heavy swell hit the ship just as the captain was starting down the ladder from the quarter-deck. The swell threw him into the sharp edge of a piece of lumber which had been left there by the ship's carpenter, and the point of the wood tore a large, jagged cut in the captain's leg.

The captain bandaged his own wound, which seemed little more than an annoyance, and continued about his business without a second thought. Within a few days, however, the leg began to swell, and the wound became infected, though the term used for it was putrefaction.

In less than a week the captain found that movement became increasingly painful. Then one morning he awoke in such agony that even to touch the leg caused excruciating pain.

He called for Dr. O'Sheel.

"I've seen legs like that before," Dog said as Dr. O'Sheel examined the wound. "It's going to have to come off, ain't it?"

"I'm afraid so," O'Sheel said. "Captain, why didn't you come to me before? You've let it go on too long."

" 'Twas but a small wound of little consequence," the captain said. "I did not think it worth the bother."

"But you can see how the putrefaction has spread through the whole of your leg," Dr. O'Sheel said, pointing to the black-and-blue skin. "If it gets to your body, it will poison you. Dog is right. The leg will have to come off."

"No!" Captain Collier said. "I'll not be a peg-legged captain! You'll not take that leg off, Surgeon."

"But I've no choice, sir," Kevin replied. "It's either lose the leg, or lose your life."

"I'd rather take a chance with me life," the captain said. "Treat the leg, Doctor. Don't take it off."

Kevin cupped his chin in his hand and stared at the leg for a moment. He started poking around the edges of the wound, noting the captain's wince each time he did so. He clucked to himself.

"What does that mean?" the captain asked.

"There's only one thing we can try," Kevin said. "Your leg seems to have a good amount of laudable pus. Perhaps if we drain that it will carry the poison away from your leg. But it will be a painful process."

"How much more painful could it be than cutting off the leg?" the captain asked through clenched teeth.

"Very well, we shall try," Kevin said. He looked at Dog. "Where is my son?"

"He's at the rail, feeding the fishes again," Dog said derisively.

"Then find my daughter," Kevin said. "Ask her to come to the captain's cabin. Then bring me a charge of gunpowder, and some bread from the cook."

"Gunpowder? Bread? What sort of medicines are these?" the captain asked.

"Never you mind that, Captain," Kevin said. "My advice to you, sir, is to get drunk. Have you any rum?"

"Aye, a goodly amount I reckon," the captain said. "'Tis in my sea chest there."

"I'll get it," Kevin said, starting for the sea chest. "I want you well besotted when I start."

Dog laughed inwardly as he started for the girl. He knew that she would see him coming and move out of his way, but this time he would have an excuse to follow her until he caught her. She was well forward when he emerged from the captain's cabin, and, as Dog knew she would, she crossed to the opposite side of the deck when he approached the bow.

"Girl, why do you move away from me every time I come near?" Dog asked.

"I—I wasn't aware that I did," she replied.

"You do, girl, I can tell that easy enough," Dog said. He laughed. "After all, it ain't me you need to worry about. You don't see *me* in the brig, do you?"

"What?" Sheena asked in a shocked voice. "What do you mean by that?"

"Never mind. Your papa's in the captain's cabin, and they want to see you."

"He's in the *captain*'s cabin?" Sheena asked, her heart leaping to her throat. "Why? What does he want?" Fears that she was about to be confronted with the incident with Drumm nearly overtook her, and Sheena's knees grew weak.

"I'm not rightly sure what your papa wants with you, miss," Dog said. "Maybe he wants to talk to you about you'n Drumm." Dog chuckled to himself as he walked away, and Sheena realized that he knew about her shame.

Sheena crossed the deck to the captain's cabin. She drew herself up just before she went in. She would not grovel before her father.

"Sheena, good, I need your help," her father said as she stepped into the cabin. "Liam is incapacitated, and I must depend on you."

"You need my help?" Sheena asked, not understanding what was going on. She had been prepared for an ugly scene regarding Drumm, and it took her a moment to realize that it wasn't for that reason she was called.

"Yes, the captain's leg is in a bad way," Kevin said. "We are going to try and save it. Will you help?"

"Yes, Father," Sheena said, relieved to be off the hook. "Of course, I'll do anything I can."

"Good. I've sent Dog after a few things, and I want you to get a pan of hot water and some clean rags for bandages."

Sheena looked at the captain, who was pouring rum down his throat. Though the fog of intoxication was already beginning to set in, the captain seemed to perceive Sheena's worry about him telling her father. "Don't worry, girl," he said.

" 'Tis a brave man you are, Captain Collier," Kevin said. "Telling my own sweet daughter not to worry, when 'tis yourself who is in danger."

But Sheena knew that the captain meant she need not fear that he would speak to her father about Drumm, and she reached out and touched his arm gently. "I'll not be worrying," she said.

"The head that once was crowned with thorns
    Is crowned with glory now;
A royal diadem adorns
    The mighty victor's brow."

Captain Collier was singing drunkenly, and at the top of his voice.

"Doctor Kevin O'Sheel," he said. "You would be Catholic then?"

"Aye."

"Then I trust, sir, you've taken no offense from my Anglican hymn."

"No offense at all, sir," Kevin said. " 'Tis the same God, be we Catholic or Church of England."

"Aye, 'tis the same God," Captain Collier replied. " 'Tis only the accursed Pope who stands in the way of our being true brethren."

"And yet I called Jonathan Swift my brother, and he is the dean of Ireland's largest Anglican cathedral,"

Kevin said. "Now, Captain, would you be ready for me to begin?"

"Aye, I'm as ready as I'll ever be," Captain Collier replied. "I'm fortified with the devil's own brew and armed with Jesus's song. Begin your work, Doctor." Captain Collier took another drink, then started singing again;

"The highest place that Heaven affords
    Is His, is His by right,
The King of Kings, and Lord of Lords,
    And Heaven's . . . . Ooooooowwl!"

The piercing yell occurred as Kevin lanced the wound, cutting into the blue flesh with a sharp knife. The pus began draining away, and Kevin continued his operation, purging the wound of every vestige of the stuff. Finally it was nearly all removed.

"Now, girl," Kevin said to Sheena. "Take the gunpowder there and pour it all into the wound. Don't miss any of it."

Sheena poured the black powder from a powder horn, getting it well into the wound as her father directed.

"Now hand me the flintlock," Kevin directed.

"I . . . What are you going to do, Doctor?" the captain asked, biting his lip in pain.

But before the captain had time to worry, Kevin held the flintlock in position and snapped it, sending a spark into the gunpowder. It flared a brilliant orange, and fire and smoke leaped up from the captain's leg, bathing the room in a wash of bright light and sending its acrid smell through the cabin.

"Ye gods, man!" the captain yelled, but in an instant it was over.

"I've done it now, Captain," Kevin said soothingly.

"Surgeon, what were you about? You could've blown

my leg off with that damn-fool stuff," the captain complained, fear joining the look of pain on his face.

"No, sir. Powder explodes only when ignited within a confined space. This was necessary for the powder to burn away the remaining poisons."

"Then you mean my leg won't have to come off?" Captain Collier asked.

"We can hope and pray not, yes, sir," Kevin said. "Sheena, hand me the bread, please."

"'Twas naught but moldy bread," Dog said.

"That doesn't matter," Kevin said. "The bread will be used as a poultice to draw away any of the poisons that may be left behind. Sometimes the mold on the bread makes for an even better poultice, though I've no explanation for it. Sheena, place the bread on the wound and bind it in place with the bandages, please."

Sheena did as her father instructed, then looked up at the captain's face. "He is near to sleep now," she said. "The drink has done him in."

"That is good," Kevin replied, washing his hands in the basin of water Sheena had fetched. "For there is nothing can cure him now but time. You, girl, stay in here with him until he gets better."

"Yes, Father," Sheena said.

"Dog, I imagine the sailing of this vessel will be in your hands for a while."

"'Tis no matter," Dog said. "The course is laid in. We've but to follow it."

Captain Collier developed a fever during the night, and Sheena bathed his face in cool water. The fever was followed by chills, and both plagued him for two days. Sheena kept treating the fever with water, and combated the chills by piling extra comforters on the captain's bed. Finally, just before dawn of the third day, the fever and chills ceased and the captain began to sleep peacefully.

Sheena dozed in a chair, and as she dozed she had disturbing dreams of William Drumm. In her dream she saw him hanging from a gallows, turning in the wind. As he came around, his face suddenly became the face of her mother! She awoke with a start and sat for a moment to regain her composure. She saw the captain and listened to his soft, easy breathing. She crossed over to him and placed her hand on his forehead. It was cool.

The captain opened his eyes and looked at Sheena. "What are you doing here?" he asked.

"I've been attending to you," she said.

"Attending to me? Oh, yes, my leg. My leg! Did he?" Captain Collier raised up and felt for his leg. When he was assured that it was still there, he smiled and lay back down. "He didn't have to cut it off," he said.

"No," Sheena said, smiling. "He didn't have to cut it off."

"But the pain. It's gone," he said. "My God, girl, your father is a miracle healer!"

"I'm glad you are feeling better," Sheena said.

"Feeling better? My God, I feel great! I could dance the hornpipe! And you, girl. You've stayed with me? It must be what, the next day?"

" 'Tis near three days now," Sheena said. "You had a difficult time, though you're much the better for it now."

"I owe you for that, girl. And your father. I owe both of you a great deal."

" 'Twas merely my father's duty," Sheena said.

"No, for if he had merely done his duty he would have cut off my leg. He went beyond that, girl. And you as well, staying in here to tend to me. You've no duty beyond being a passenger. I will show my gratitude in some way."

"Do you mean that, sir?" Sheena asked.

"Aye, girl, I mean it. Why? Have you devised some way I can express my thanks?"

"Aye. 'Tis about Drumm."

"Have no fear, girl. He'll hang for what he did."

"No!" Sheena said.

"What?"

"I don't want him to hang."

"See here, girl. Are you trying to tell me that you invited him to your bed?"

"No. But"—Sheena couldn't put into words the statement that she had enjoyed it—"but I've no wish for him to hang."

Captain Collier sighed. "I see. You are still afraid that word of your shame will get out, aren't you? Not to worry, I understand such fears. Very well, I shall charge him with incompetence. Heaven knows, he has given me ample cause for such a complaint. He won't hang, but he'll be set ashore without papers. If he sails again, it'll be as a common seaman, where the chances are less likely that he'll ever again be in a position to molest a defenseless girl. And now, get your father for me, will you, lass?"

"My father?" Sheena asked apprehensively.

"Aye." Captain Collier smiled. "Fear not, little one. Have I not said your secret is safe with me? 'Tis only to give him his reward that I summon him."

Sheena smiled. "Forgive me, Captain. Of course I will get him."

A moment later Sheena brought her father into the captain's cabin. The captain was already out of bed, sitting at his desk, rummaging through papers.

"Captain, you shouldn't be about too early," Kevin warned.

"Nonsense, Surgeon, you've cured me," Captain Collier said. "I feel only a little soreness and some weakness, but the poison is gone, I know. Besides, if I don't get back, that damn fool Dog will run us aground somewhere."

"I'm glad you are feeling better," Kevin said.

"Ah," the captain said, pulling out a brown envelope. "Yes, I believe this is it." He opened the envelope and pulled out a paper and read it for a moment. "Yes," he said. "It is. Surgeon, I want to give this to you for saving my life." He handed the paper to Kevin.

"Captain, you don't owe me anything," Kevin said.

"You will allow me to reward you, sir," the captain replied. "I consider my life very valuable, and if you refuse my offer, it will cheapen it."

"Well, I've no wish to do that, sir," Kevin replied. "What is this document?"

"'Tis a deed," the captain said.

"A deed?"

"Aye, 'tis a grant from the king for ten thousand acres of land in South Carolina. It is very near Charles Town, I believe."

"Ten thousand acres? Captain, that is nearly a kingdom itself! Do you know what you are doing?"

"Aye," Captain Collier said. "Of what good is land to a sailing man?"

"Captain, with this much land, you'd have no need of the sea."

"No need of the sea?" the captain said. "Surgeon, I've saltwater for blood. How could I live without the sea? No, sir, the land means nothing to me, except as a way to reward you for your services."

"But how did you come by such a magnificent parcel?"

"I won it in a gaming house in London," Captain Collier said. "I thought someday to sell it for a fair price."

"But I've no money to pay for it. You'd be cheated of your fair price."

"What more fair price could I ask for than my life?" the captain said.

Kevin held the precious document in his hands and looked at the captain, with his eyes shining in excitement. "Captain, I don't know how to thank you. Because of you, my dream is going to come true for me, for my son, and for my daughter."

No, Sheena thought. *Not for your daughter. For the captain has just explained things to me. 'Tis not bad blood that flows in my veins. 'Tis saltwater. I'm not bad ... I'm just a creature of the sea.*

12

With a title free and clear, Kevin O'Sheel found, to his pleasant surprise, that the bank was more than willing to lend him the money to start his farming operation.

"Absolutely, Doctor O'Sheel," George Gordon, the banker, said. "You see, if you become successful, then it can only add new money to our economy."

"And if I am unsuccessful?" Kevin wanted to know.

Gordon smiled. "Well, then, Doctor O'Sheel, the bank will have a nice piece of property to sell. Either way, it's a good risk for our investors."

"I hope your bank does not have to get into the land business," Kevin said.

"To be sure, that is also my wish," Gordon said. He sat down to fill out the papers, then looked up at Kevin. "And what will you be calling your plantation?"

"Calling it?"

"Certainly, you must have a name for it."

"Oh. Oh, yes, indeed I do." Kevin thought of the green hills of his homeland, realizing, with a small catch of sadness, that he'd never see them again. "I'll call it Bonny Isle," he said.

Gordon filled out the papers, then loaned Dr. O'Sheel a substantial amount of money. " 'Tis none of my business how you spend the money," he said. "But if it were me, I'd be for buyin' my slaves first. Without someone to work your land, it is worthless to you."

"I agree," Kevin said. "Though I must confess my ignorance in such matters. How does one go about the purchase of slaves?"

Gordon laughed. "I suppose to someone new to Charles Town, such a thing would be unknown. But there's no problem, believe me. In fact . . ." Gordon began rummaging through some papers on his desk until he came up with a printed circular. "Yes, here it is, someone left this here this morning. You might use this." He handed the circular to Kevin, and Kevin read it:

NEGROES
100 NEGRO SLAVES 100
PRIME STOCK
Auction at Two O'Clock
Terms: Cash at Sale
SLAVE BLOCK
at Wharf Street in Charles Town

"I see," Kevin said. "Then anyone can go to this auction?"

"Anyone who has the money to make a bid," Gordon replied. He wrote out a little note and handed it to Kevin. "Show this to one of the officials. He will help you make a few good selections."

"Thank you," Kevin said, taking the note from Gordon. "I will return to the inn and pick up my son. As he will one day own Bonny Isle, I feel it important that he accompany me."

"Your son, eh?" Gordon said. He looked around, then got a strange glint in his eye. "If he's a sportin' lad, his blood'll run hot when they strip some of the wenches down, I'll wager."

"I've no desire to introduce the boy to such a sin,"

Kevin answered shortly, letting Gordon know that he heartily disapproved.

"Quite right you are too," Gordon said, recovering quickly. " 'Tis the curse of our institution, I fear, that such fornication does take place. But not to worry. The shield of righteousness is mightier than the sword of lust, and I have no fear but that your son, so armed, will be able to resist temptation."

"I am certain he will, sir," Kevin said. "After all, he is a loving and obedient son—the fulfillment of all a father's hopes."

"You are a lucky man to be so blessed. And is he your only child?"

Kevin got a worried look on his face. "No, I have another—a daughter. It is for her sake that I have come here to the Carolinas. She is in need of stern guidance."

"Which I'm certain you will be able to provide for her," Gordon said.

"I shall do my duty as a father," Kevin said. He put on his hat, thanked the banker for the loan of the money, then took his leave to return to the inn. He thought of Sheena as he walked down the street. After all, it was for her sake that they left Ireland. He hoped he had done the right thing by her. But, of late, she seemed dispirited, vague, and distracted. Her disquieting behavior seemed to begin at about the same time the first mate was jailed, and he couldn't help but wonder if there was some connection.

But no, he reasoned. What connection could there possibly be?

And then there was Liam. Kevin smiled. What a wonderful gift Liam had been. It was good to have a son to pass on his life's work and ambitions to. Loving of his father and concerned for his sister, Liam was the ideal son, and Kevin's chest swelled with pride when he thought of him.

In the inn, waiting for her father, Sheena stood at the window of an upper-floor room and gazed longingly back toward the harbor. She saw the masts of the ships, which sprouted from the waterfront like trees in a forest. How she wished she could simply walk out of the room, stroll down to the docks, and sign on one of the ships. How she envied Liam! He was a man, and so had it in his power to do so if he wished. Liam had finally adjusted to the pitch of the ship and was able to complete the voyage without the discomfort of seasickness, but he had no love for the sea, and thus no desire to do that which was within his power to do. To Sheena, that seemed grossly unfair.

As Sheena thought of the unfairness of the situation she blushed with shame, for she had been unfair to William Drumm. Because of her, William Drumm, a man who had her same love for the sea, was now confined to the shore. She tried to justify it by saying that he had, indeed, raped her. She hadn't invited him into her cabin. Though, in truth, she had responded so eagerly to his lovemaking that she felt she *must* have invited him in some subtle way. And the fact that she tried to deny that, seemed to her to be as unfair as the vagaries of life, which denied her access to the sea.

It was also a sin. For even now, as she thought of Drumm, Sheena felt a strange warmth suffusing her body, and she had to close her eyes to force the memory out of her mind, lest she go mad from the evil want of it.

Sheena's father returned then, and announced with pride and joy that he had been successful in borrowing the money.

"We'll build a place here that would have made my father himself proud to call his home," Kevin said. "Over here people name their plantations. Ours, I have named Bonny Isle."

" 'Tis a fine name, Father," Liam said. "It'll always remind us of home."

"And you, Sheena. Have you nothing to say of the name of your new home?"

Sheena wanted to say it would be better to be in Ireland than to have a piece of land that could only remind them of home. But she saw how much it meant to her father, and the words that formed in her mouth never found utterance. She smiled at him. "Aye, Father, Bonny Isle is a good name, I'm thinking."

"Good, good," Kevin said, rubbing his hands together eagerly. "Then we are all agreed. And now, Liam, there's men's work to do."

"Oh?"

"There is a slave auction being conducted this very day. Here, I have a bill on it," Kevin said, handing Liam the circular he had been given by Gordon, the banker. " 'Tis my intention that we should attend that auction and buy the Negroes we shall need for Bonny Isle."

"A slave auction?" Sheena asked. "Father, can I go too? I've never seen such a sight."

"No, and you shan't see one either," Kevin said quickly. "The idea that you would want to is appalling. 'Tis for men to see only."

Liam laughed at Sheena's disappointment. Sheena held her retort. She knew it would be a useless gesture to argue the matter any further, so she returned to the window to look at the ships and resume her musing. She had better enjoy the sight of them while she could, she decided, for Bonny Isle was nearly ten miles inland, and she would not be seeing the ships much longer.

"Mama, why are we in this place?" a pretty twelve-year-old girl asked. The girl's skin was smooth, and the golden color of honey. The woman to whom the question was addressed had very dark skin. She was tall and statuesque, and graced with the lines of beauty that adorn the blessed of all races. The place where they were, and that the girl had asked about, was a

holding cell for slaves, like a jail. The girl's mother
was standing at a window, holding onto the bars, looking at the gathering throng outside. She sighed. "We're
gonna be sold off in a slave auction, girl," the woman,
whose name was Elmyra, said. "We're gonna be sold."

"Are we both going to be sold to the same man,
Mama?"

Elmyra looked at her daughter. She had borne
Tricia to Charlie Holt, and he'd treated the both of
them well. Perhaps, in his way, he had even loved
them, though of course he had never said so. But he
had never provided Elmyra with the papers that would
mean her freedom, or the freedom of their daughter,
so when Charlie Holt died Elmyra and Tricia became
a part of his estate. And now, to settle claims against
his estate, Elmyra and Tricia were to be sold.

Elmyra looked back out the window and saw a group
of slaves newly arrived from Africa. She felt keenly
the sense of fear, rage, frustration, and shock they felt,
for she too had been brought to America from Africa.

It had been in her fifteenth summer, a happy summer, for she had been chosen to be the bride of Prince
Garth from the village of White Waters. She was, herself, an Ibo princess, and both villages were pleased
that there was to be a royal wedding. Not that royal
weddings were uncommon. But this one was said to
have been made in heaven because Princess Erta,
Elmyra's African name, and Prince Garth were in love.
Elmyra could scarcely wait until the feast of the moon,
at which time the palm leaves would be braided into
a rope, tying their spirits together for all time.

The day was approaching, and Elmyra was strolling
along the seashore near her village, looking for shells
with which to make her wedding jewelry, when she
saw the slave ship. She didn't know what it was. Never
before had her eyes beheld such a wondrous sight. It
was longer than twenty boats, with three large tree

trunks rising from it. Great white objects billowed from the tree trunks, as if the clouds of the sky had somehow been captured.

As Elmyra studied the boat she saw a smaller boat coming ashore, closing the distance rapidly. She considered running away, but her curiosity was too strong. The men in the small boat had come from the giant one, and she wanted to see what type of men could build such a craft.

When the boat landed a man with white skin approached her and, smiling, offered her a chance to get into the boat. She wanted to see more, to satisfy her unbridled curiosity, so she accepted the invitation without question.

The man spoke to her, but she couldn't understand what he was saying. He spoke to one of the other men, and the other man laughed, then ran his finger gently across the nipples of her bare breasts, she being dressed, at that time, only in a skirt. It was not an unpleasant sensation and Elmyra felt no danger from it, so she just returned the man's smile and was gratified that they all laughed.

When they reached the giant boat one of the men motioned to Elmyra to climb a rope ladder, and when she did, she saw that there were many more men with white skin. She was taken to one who was evidently the chief of them all, because although Elmyra couldn't understand English then, she could recognize the deference the others showed toward him.

The chief reached out and jerked her skirt off, so that Elmyra was naked. At first she thought he was merely curious about her, as she was about them, and as she could understand curiosity, she didn't resist. But within a short time she realized that he wanted something else, something she had thus far provided for Garth only, and she began to fight.

Two of the men who had brought her aboard grabbed her then and held her, while the third, the chief, used her. After he finished with her, she was led down into the bowels of the ship, where she was lashed against a bulkhead.

Elmyra stayed there for a long time. She refused what food was proffered her and turned her face when they spoke to her. After a very long while she heard noises up above, then a scattering of Kwaibo. Kwaibo was her language. Maybe now she could find out what was happening.

The doors were kicked open, flooding the compartment with light. It caused Elmyra's eyes to hurt at first, but the light also allowed her to look around the room. It was long and wide. There were several chains with cuffs attached, and they hung from the bulkheads, swaying slightly with the roll of the ship.

A solid line of blacks began to march in. They filed in slowly, with their heads hung in fear and subjugation.

"Who among you speaks Kwaibo?" Elmyra asked in her native tongue.

"I speak Kwaibo. What do you want?" a big black man asked. He was not in chains like the rest of them. He was well dressed and was carrying a weapon.

"What is this great boat? Why am I in chains? Who are all these people? Are you Ibo?"

"You ask a great number of questions, woman. Now I will ask you some before I answer. Who are you, and how did you get here?"

"I am Erta, daughter of the chief of the Village of the Sun, betrothed to Garth, prince of the Village of White Waters. Some men came in a boat and I went with them to view this great vessel."

"This is a slaver's ship, Erta, and it will take you to a far place called America, where you will be a slave."

"And you? Will you go as well?"

"No," the man answered. "I am Boraabamumu, of the Ijo people."

"I have heard of the Ijo people. Are you a slave hunter?"

"Yes," the man answered.

"Do you know Garth, of whom I speak?"

"I do not know him. I do know of the Ibo Village of White Waters, and I know of the Village of the Sun. I do not raid those villages for slaves."

"Go to the village. Tell them of my fate. I do not wish them to wonder where I have gone."

"I will send word, Erta. Good-bye to you," Boraabamumu said.

Elmyra couldn't keep an accurate track of the number of days and nights that passed after that. Occasionally, she thought it must be once a day, someone brought food down. It was unlike anything she had ever tasted, and at first she refused it. Soon, though, she realized that she had to eat to survive.

The conditions were horrible and many of the people suffered with seasickness, although they didn't know what it was. Gradually they began to die. As the food was brought in the dead bodies were carried out. Elmyra had no idea what happened to the bodies once they left the room, although she assumed that they were being eaten. She knew that some tribes ate the flesh of other humans, and she believed these white men belonged to one of those tribes.

During the long voyage Elmyra began to learn the language of the whites. Some of the blacks could speak it, as well as Kwaibo, and she worked hard to learn the new language in order to learn her fate.

One day as the man came in with the food someone was with him. It was the man who had first invited Elmyra into the boat on the beach.

"Well now, missy," the man said as he stood in front of Elmyra. "Boraabamumu tole me you was a princess."

"I am," Elmyra replied.

"What? You mean you've learned English while you been chained up down here?"

"Yes."

"Well, now, honey, s'posin' you just come along with me into a little space in the 'tween decks that I know about."

Elmyra couldn't understand all of what the man was saying, but she knew he wanted her to follow him. Perhaps now that she could speak with them she could persuade them to let her go.

"Come in here with me, my pretty little missy. I'm gonna make you feel real good," the man said. He opened a very small door and stepped into a passageway between decks. He turned and motioned for Elmyra to follow.

There wasn't enough room for Elmyra to stand erect. It was even darker than the area she'd just left. In this place she could hear water rolling and sloshing around.

"Now," the man said, turning around. He grabbed Elmyra and pulled her down to her knees, then pushed her over onto her back. The boards were damp and the edge of one of the beams cut into her legs. "Let's find out just how much of a princess you really are," he said. He began removing his clothes, and then, for the first time, Elmyra knew what he was going to do.

She smiled sweetly at him and held out her arms.

"There, now that's the sensible thing to do," the man said. "You just lean back and enjoy it. I've been pleasurin' black wenches ever since I got into this business, and I know what you like."

Elmyra could feel the heavings of him and smell the rancid odor of bad diet and no bath. He was grinning at her with a mouthful of crooked, yellow teeth. She let him get almost to her, then slipped the knife out of his belt and buried it in his gut up to the hilt. The man died without a sound, his smile changing to a look of surprise as he sank to the floor.

Elmyra left the cramped passageway and found her way back to the lower deck. She was never questioned about the man, nor was she bothered by anyone else for the remainder of the passage. Several days later she heard for the first time the name of the place that would be her new home for the rest of her life.

Carolina.

The conditions were greatly improved once they left the ship. They were locked in a pen that was larger and had light. They were no longer chained and they could sit about, gingerly rubbing wrists which had long since grown scar tissue. They were also given clothes to wear for the first time since leaving Africa.

They were taken to a big warehouse, where all the women were put on benches on one side of the room, and the men on the other side. One of the whites came around parceling out children, although in most cases the children and the women to whom they were given didn't belong to each other. It was just a matter of pairing off what was left alive of the children and the women.

When Elmyra stepped onto the block many of the men whistled and looked at each other with winks and smiles. She heard the white man who was standing on the block with her begin to shout to the crowd. Although she was beginning to understand some of the language, he talked so quickly that she could catch only a few phrases here and there. Things like: "princess"; "young"; "beautiful"; and the word the white men used when they talked about those with black skins, "nigger."

Elmyra was glad for the clothes she had been given. She had been stared at by all the men on the ship and now she could protect herself from the burning eyes of these men.

"Shuck that shift off there, girl," the man on the block was saying to her.

Elmyra realized that she was being spoken to but she couldn't understand what he wanted.

"I said shuck that thing off. These gentlemen want to see what they are buying."

Elmyra still didn't understand, so the man turned to two young blacks. "Here, you two nigger boys down there, come up here 'n shuck the dress off this here wench who ain' nothin' but a ignernt savage 'n cain't even talk English good yet."

The two complied and once more Elmyra stood nude before the burning eyes of the white men.

"Now, I tell you, this girl is so pretty that your wife might even get jealous!" the auctioneer said, and his comment was greeted with laughter.

The bidding was spirited until she was finally bought by a man named Abner Howell, who claimed her with a lustful glint in his eye and an exchange of ribald jokes with his friends.

Elmyra was given another dress to wear. She followed Abner Howell out of the market and into a place where men were drinking and playing cards. One of the card players was Charlie Holt, and Howell joined Holt's game.

"You, sit on the floor," Howell ordered Elmyra, and she obeyed, then studied the man called Charlie Holt. He had laughing eyes and a friendly face. She couldn't help but wish it had been someone like Holt who had bought her, instead of the man who had.

The men played cards for approximately two hours, with Abner losing steadily. Then Charlie Holt raised a bet against Abner Howell.

"Will you take my marker, sir?" Abner asked. "I'm a man of means, but I have no more money with me."

"I'd rather not take a marker, sir, if it's all the same to you," Holt answered pleasantly.

"Well, it ain't all the same to me. You're cheating me out of a winning hand if I can't call your raise."

"Are you calling me a cheater, sir?" Charlie Holt asked coldly.

"I'm just saying that I have the winning hand here and I can't call you if you won't take my marker," Abner whined, backing away from the glint of steel in Holt's voice.

"That's the way the game is played, mister," Holt said.

Abner looked over at Elmyra, then got an idea. "Wait," he said. "That nigger wench. She'd more'n cover the bet. Here's the paper on her." He shoved a piece of paper to the center of the table.

Charlie Holt turned to look at the girl, who was sitting quietly on the floor. He looked at her for a full minute. The room was very quiet, except for the labored breathing of Abner Howell.

"Very well," Charlie said. "I'll take the bet."

Abner smiled triumphantly, then turned up three tens and two nines. Charlie turned up four sixes and took the money.

"No one has luck like that!" Abner bellowed. He leaped up from the chair and pulled a pistol out of his coat pocket.

Charlie pulled a knife from his trousers and let it fly with a quick, underhanded throw. It buried itself in Abner's chest just as he pulled the trigger on the pistol. There was a flash, followed by an ear-shattering report, and a cloud of smoke. The pistol ball whizzed past Charlie's ear and crashed into the wall behind him.

Abner fell to the floor, gurgling as his life's breath escaped him.

Charlie calmly gathered his money, then put the paper of ownership of the girl in his pocket.

"What is your name?" he asked.

"Erta," she answered. In the African dialect it had a strange, harsh sound which Charlie couldn't understand. He waved the name away impatiently.

"I'll call you Elmyra."

And Elmyra it was, for the thirteen years she lived with him, riding the ups and downs with him as he won and lost fortunes at the card games.

And then one day Charlie met a man who was quicker with a gun than Charlie was with a knife.

Elmyra walked away from the window, sat beside her daughter, and put her arm around her. If there was any way it could be done, she would keep them together. "I hope we are sold together," she said, answering her daughter's question.

"You in there," someone shouted harshly. "You're next."

"I want my daughter to go on the block with me," Elmyra said.

"She can go on the block, but if you're sold separately, that's just too bad," the man said. "Now, get out there."

Elmyra blinked her eyes against the sun, bright now after the darkness of the cells. She was walking along the path toward the trading block when she happened to see a man getting his pocket picked.

"Sir," she shouted quickly. "That man is stealing your purse!"

The victim, heeding her warning, spun around in time to frighten the would-be pickpocket into dropping the purse. The thief shouted a curse and ran away, melting into the crowd. But the man's purse was saved, thanks to Elmyra's warning.

"I shall buy her," the man said.

"And my daughter, sir," Elmyra said. "Please, buy my daughter too."

"You don't want her, Doctor O'Sheel," one of the officials said. "She's never done a day's work in her life. She was some gambling man's mistress."

"Nevertheless, I shall buy the both of them," Kevin O'Sheel said. "She has proved to me that she is an honest woman, and her honesty should be rewarded."

"I agree, Father," Liam said. "We should buy her."

Liam had already considered the possibility of having such a handsome woman around, obedient to his will.

13

Elmyra felt a debt of gratitude toward Kevin O'Sheel for buying both herself and her daughter. He was thus able to buy several other slaves cheaply, who couldn't speak English, because Elmyra informed him that she would act as an interpreter.

In truth, Elmyra had as much difficulty understanding those who didn't speak her dialect as Kevin did, but Kevin never realized that. To him all the dialects sounded alike. Elmyra used his ignorance to her advantage, securing her position by making it seem as if only she could speak to the others.

Thus it was that by sheer will Elmyra became one of the most important fixtures on the plantation. It was a natural process of selection, because the task of running Bonny Isle was just too much for Kevin O'Sheel. His son, Liam, also found his abilities unequal to the task, but whereas Kevin O'Sheel never quit trying to learn, Liam gave it up entirely. He spent all his time gambling and drinking with the other swains of the county.

The only O'Sheel who had the capacity to manage Bonny Isle was Sheena. But her interest in the sea had never abated, and, though she more than held up her end of the work load, she never allowed herself to develop a true affection for the land.

When Elmyra saw that Sheena was capable of doing everything that she, Elmyra, was doing, she was at first frightened. For if Sheena perceived that she was not indispensable, then the careful little world Elmyra had built for herself might collapse. But Elmyra soon saw that Sheena was no real threat to her, for Sheena's heart was never in Bonny Isle.

And Elmyra saw something else as well. Elmyra saw the sensual nature that was inherent in Sheena's makeup. It puzzled Elmyra that Sheena should be masking this part of herself, even from herself. Elmyra was always honest with herself about her own feelings. Passions which were a part of Elmyra's personality were accepted by her without question.

Elmyra also knew, without being told, that Sheena had experienced passion with a man. She didn't know who, or under what circumstances, but she knew, and she knew that the memory of it was a constant companion to the young girl.

And, as no secrets were safe from Elmyra's keen perception, she was also aware of Liam's lust for his sister. In fact, it was so clear to Elmyra that she was amazed no one else seemed to notice it.

There, at least, Elmyra was wrong. Someone else had noticed it, and that someone was Sheena herself.

Sheena wasn't sure when she actually realized that Liam wanted her. At first, it was just a nagging sensation, a prickling of the skin, as if someone was watching her, though she was never able to find out who. Then, little things began to give Liam away. A glint in his eye, a shortness of breath when she came close to him, beads of perspiration across his lip . . . and sometimes even the unmistakable sign of an erection.

At first, Sheena was frightened. Then, she was repelled. Then, in sudden awareness, she realized that she could use this situation to her advantage. It was the perfect way to torment her brother, to pay him back for all his years of mistreatment of her, under the guise of "brotherly love." Now Sheena looked for opportunities. When she felt the skin-prickling indication that she was being watched at her bath, or in her bedroom, she would further inflame Liam's lust by putting on a show for him. She would strip nude, even when it wasn't necessary to remove all her clothes, and she would stay nude for a long time, fondling her breasts or other parts of her body in a way that was seemingly innocent but designed to push her brother to the limit of his endurance.

After such a show, Liam would be forced to walk down the hill behind the big house, alongside an open drainage ditch which ran year-round with muddy water from the rains and drained fields. The drainage ditch wound through a row of weather-beaten, unpainted shacks. These shacks were the slaves' quarters. Within a year, they housed more than one hundred human beings who were in perpetual bondage to Dr. Kevin O'Sheel.

Dr. O'Sheel meant what he said about bringing the heathen to God. He built for his slaves a small church, in which he observed every religious holiday with them, sometimes even managing to bring in a Catholic priest to celebrate mass.

For their part the blacks welcomed such observances. It was much easier to kneel at the altar than it was to kneel in the tobacco fields.

Dr. O'Sheel may have been concerned for their eternal souls, but his son, Liam, cared only for their temporal bodies. Kevin never visited any of the slaves, not even Elmyra, who tried on more than one occasion to entice him into her bed. But Liam, the slaves whispered among themselves, was like a bull in the pasture. He had a constant hunger for sex, and there were very few of the women over the age of sixteen who hadn't been called upon to warm his bed. It was a task for them, like any other task, and some could tolerate it more than others.

Elmyra was a particular favorite of Liam's, and he visited her at least three times a week. Elmyra, in that stoical way that had assured her survival thus far, tolerated Liam's visits and even managed to convince him that she enjoyed them. She knew that Liam would control the plantation one day and she reacted accordingly.

Bonny Isle prospered in spite of, rather than because of, Dr. O'Sheel's management. The land was too rich, the crops too plentiful, and the demand too great for it to be any other way. By the end of the first year of operation, Kevin O'Sheel had paid off the loan. By the end of the second, he was a very wealthy man.

With wealth came importance, and Kevin O'Sheel became a respected pillar of the county. Liam used the position to gain entry into the more jaded salons and parlors, though still without his father's knowledge. Sheena settled into the routine of Bonny Isle. Though the dream of going to sea never died, the futility of such a dream soon took dominance in her thoughts. Sheena knew with certainty that she would spend the rest of her days tied to the shore.

There were certain standards of decorum expected from the gentry, and Kevin O'Sheel saw to it that his progeny received the proper training to allow them to adhere to those standards. Sheena was given lessons in the gentle arts of flower arranging and needlepoint. The lessons were a beastly bore to her, but she saw no recourse but to abide them, for to rebel against them would have brought about her father's displeasure.

Liam, on the other hand, received instruction in horseback riding and in fencing. Liam was as averse to his lessons as Sheena was to hers. But Sheena would have given anything to trade places with Liam. Especially for the fencing lessons. She managed to arrange her classes so that she could always observe Liam's fencing lesson. Afterward, she would go out behind the barn, and when no one was watching her, practice what Liam had been taught that day.

And so it was that one bright afternoon Sheena was in the studio that had been built for just such purposes, watching Professor Fenelon instructing Liam in the art of fencing. As she was a regular observer now, neither Liam nor the professor thought anything about her being there. Frequently they forgot all about her. That was the way Sheena wanted it, for had she been noticeable, she would probably have been asked to leave.

"Non, non, non, monsieur!" Professor Fenelon said in exasperation after Liam had executed one maneuver very clumsily. He reached out to reposition Liam's hand for the third time. "You must always remember that the technique of good swordsmanship is based upon precision, speed, timing, and distance." Fenelon took the foil from Liam's hands and continued with his instruction, demonstrating the technique as he described it. "Observe, monsieur. The fencing attack is a coordinated hand and foot movement, with no wasted motion."

Fenelon moved with the grace of a ballet dancer. The foil danced in his hands, then thrust forward as quickly as the strike of a snake. "Do you see?" he asked, handing the instrument back to Liam.

"Yes, I see," Liam said. "But if you ask me, this is all rather foolish."

"But no, monsieur, it is not foolish," Fenelon said. "Your father has been in Carolina for only two years, but in that short time he has become one of the state's wealthiest gentlemen. And you, as his son, must know all the gentlemanly arts. Suppose a ruffian impugned your honor, sir, or the honor of your family?"

"I'd kill him," Liam said.

"To be sure, sir, that would be the only acceptable recourse. But how would you kill him?"

"What difference does it make? It should matter only that he be killed."

"It makes a great difference, monsieur. A gentleman must kill a ruffian in a gentlemanly manner, and that necessitates a duel."

"Then we shall use pistols."

Professor Fenelon slapped his hand to his forehead. "Pistols? Next you will suggest that knives be used, or rifles, such as those used by the uncouth mountain men. Heaven forbid, you may even suggest tomahawks and go completely savage!"

"It's just that I have no taste for such a weapon," Liam said. "I have my own ways of settling disputes."

"I know your ways, brother," Sheena said, walking over to take a foil from a rack on the wall. "You prefer stealth and concealment. The dirk you have concealed up your sleeve, or the tiny pistol in your boot top."

"Such things are necessary for a man in my position," Liam said. "Who are you to challenge me?"

Sheena tested the flexibility of the foil, then looked at Liam and smiled. "Oh, I don't question it, brother, I merely point it out. If I were a man, I would have no use for such tricks."

"Oh? And why not?" Liam asked derisively.

Sheena whipped the foil around in an exact duplication of the move made by Professor Fenelon. "I would be adept in the use of the foil," she said.

Liam laughed. "That is easy enough for you to say, Sister. But you have had no lessons. You do not realize how difficult mastery of that particular weapon is."

"I've had no lessons, true enough. But I have observed your lessons and I have learned from them."

"You've learned, have you? And I suppose you consider yourself proficient?"

"No," Sheena said. "But I am skilled enough to best you."

"Oh, ho! So you would challenge me to a duel?"

"No, not a duel, for I've no wish to kill my own brother. Merely a fencing match. I shall touch you in a vital spot with the tip of the blade. I will not bring blood. This would be a test of skill, would it not, Professor?"

"Yes, mademoiselle, it would be a good test," Fenelon said.

"Well, then, Liam, I put it to you. Shall we have a match? It will be a fine sport."

"A sport without a wager is no sport," Liam said.

"Then we shall have a wager," Sheena said.

"What shall we wager?"

"If I win, you will give me the balanced blade father bought you. I fancy such a weapon for myself."

"And what shall be your forfeit to me if you lose? A vase for arranging flowers?"

Sheena looked at her brother with narrowed, knowing eyes. "I shall willingly forfeit something you have long coveted," she said.

"And what would that be, dear sister?"

"That forfeit we shall keep in the family," Sheena said. "And as it would be a family affair, it is one of those things best kept secret."

Suddenly Liam realized that Sheena was offering to forfeit herself! His eyes grew deep, and he felt a burning sensation in the pit of his stomach as he thought of it. But, how did she know? He had never made the slightest move toward her, nor compromised his secret lusts, and yet, somehow, she knew!

"You are prepared to go through with this, with no reservations if I win?" Liam asked.

"Yes," Sheena said. "And you?"

"Yes, yes, of course I am," Liam said anxiously.

Sheena smiled, a mocking smile, at him. "No, Brother, I mean if you lose. Will you keep your end of the bargain?"

"Yes," Liam said. He took the foil from Professor Fenelon's hands, bent it, then released it. "Though what use you would have for it, I don't know."

"Wait," Fenelon said. "I protest this match."

"Why?" Liam asked.

"The young lady has had no lessons," he said. "It will not be a fair contest."

"She feels her skills are enough to best me. Let the match be," Liam said. He stepped back and assumed the position. "On guard!"

Liam, anxious to claim his forfeit and hoping to use his size and strength to his advantage, lunged forward with an immediate thrust. But Sheena, who was naturally athletic and as graceful as any dancer, was able to parry the thrust easily. Then she executed a riposte, or counterattack, catching Liam by total surprise and scoring at once.

"Touché!" Professor Fenelon said, clapping his hands enthusiastically. "Bravo, young lady. That was beautifully presented."

"Then you would consider me skilled enough to handle Liam's blade?"

"Skilled enough? But of course. You have the grace and movement of a champion fencer. Though it is for your brother to grant the forfeit."

Liam threw his blade all the way across the studio room and swore angrily. "Take your forfeit and be damned!" he shouted. The foil skidded along the floor, then sprang back from the wall and spun around. Liam pointed a finger at Sheena. "But you'd best be careful in offering to engage in such a wager, for the time will come, Sister, when I will be the victor. And when that time comes I shall collect my spoils without the least consideration."

"I shall never offer such a wager if I feel the slightest

chance of losing," Sheena said. "The issue of this contest was never in doubt."

Sheena's laugh followed Liam from the studio and rang mockingly in his ears. Damn her, he thought. She had inflamed him in the full knowledge of what she was doing, tortured him with a desire which hadn't gone away. He knew that what he wanted was forbidden, and yet he could not control the terrible lust that burned inside him.

Liam walked up to the front door of Elmyra's cabin. There wasn't actually a door there; it had been taken down for the spring and summer, and a piece of canvas had been hung in the frame instead. It was still early spring though, and the rain, when it came, and the wind blew around the edges of the canvas, so that the air inside the cabin was always chill and damp.

The canvas curtain parted as Liam stepped onto the porch, and Elmyra peered out. Her face broke into a practiced grin.

"Good afternoon, Master Liam," she said. "Have you come to warm my bed?"

"Yes," Liam said. "May I come in?"

"Of course you can. After all, it is your father's house. I just live here."

"It's my house as well," Liam reminded her. "I want you always to remember that."

"Of course, sir," Elmyra said easily.

"Mama, I'm going over to Dulcey's," Tricia said. Tricia had just washed herself and was stepping out from behind a screen when she saw Liam. She turned her back to him quickly, to prevent his seeing her.

Liam was thunderstruck. Tricia was only fourteen years old, and he had never considered her as anything but a child. But, as if seeing her for the first time, he saw how truly beautiful she was. He saw the girl's shoulders, then the smooth expanse of skin on her back, and finally the delightfully formed buttocks which were exposed.

Tricia reached for the piece of canvas she and her mother used for a towel and covered herself modestly before turning to face Liam.

"I'm sorry, Master Liam," she said softly, her voice falling on his ears like the tinkling of wind chimes stirred by the breeze. "I didn't know you were here."

"That's all right, girl," Liam said. "Sure'n a more beautiful lass I've never seen before. You could do it for me, girl. I know you could."

"Do it?" Tricia asked.

"I've had a fire burning away at my insides for many years now, and nothing there was that would put it out. But you could, lass. I know you could."

"How?" Tricia asked innocently, for she was still a young girl and had no idea what Liam meant.

Elmyra saw at once.

"No," she said. "Master Liam, please, Tricia is too young. Besides, only your sister can put out that raging fire, and you know it. Not my Tricia. Leave her be."

"My—my sister?" Liam asked, shocked at Elmyra's statement. "What do you—"

"Mama, what's he gonna do?" Tricia asked, suddenly realizing that something was amiss.

"He's not going to do anything, girl. You're going to run!" Elmyra said. "Run, girl! Run for your life!"

Tricia dropped the towel and dodged around Liam, then darted through the front door, running down the muddy path, screaming for help.

"You bloody bitch. You know!" Liam shouted, slapping Elmyra sharply.

Elmyra slapped him back.

"I'll have the skin off your back for this, you bitch!" Liam shouted, slapping Elmyra again.

Sheena was taking a walk at that moment. She saw the strange sight of the nude girl running through the muddy street.

"Tricia, what is it?" Sheena called. "What are you running from?"

"Mama," Tricia called back, not turning around, not stopping in her flight.

Had Elmyra whipped Tricia? It would be like her to do it, Sheena thought, if doing so would somehow maintain her position of authority over the others. So far, Elmyra and Sheena had maintained an uneasy truce. They both knew that Sheena could burst Elmyra's bubble of indispensability anytime she wished, but they also both knew that Sheena didn't want the added responsibility. Yet there were limits to the truce between them, Sheena thought, and if Elmyra had whipped Tricia, then she had exceeded those limits.

"Elmyra, if you've whipped that girl, you'll answer to me," Sheena yelled toward Elmyra's cabin.

Several of the other blacks poked their heads through the hanging curtains of their doors, saw the nude young girl running up the path, and saw Sheena's anger. White people's anger, they had already learned, was best avoided, so they pulled their heads back in and hoped she wouldn't come to their cabins.

"Elmyra, what did you do to Tricia?" Sheena asked, pushing her way into Elmyra's cabin.

"I've been stabbed, Miss Sheena," Elmyra said, staggering toward Sheena, her hands clutching the blood-stained dagger that protruded from her stomach.

"Elmyra! What has happened?" Sheena asked, her anger instantly dissolved in her desire to help. She caught the black woman as she fell forward, then eased her down to the floor. Instinctively she pulled the knife from the wound, though doing so unplugged the wound and allowed Elmyra to bleed more profusely.

"You!" Liam suddenly shouted, appearing as if from nowhere. "You've stabbed her!"

"What? No," Sheena said. "No, Liam, I didn't do it. I just—"

"Don't lie, girl, you've the dagger in your hand!" Liam said.

"But, Liam, I didn't do it. I swear I didn't!" Sheena said, standing up to let the knife fall to the floor beside the prostrate form of Elmyra.

"Don't worry, Sheena. When I tell Father, I shall intercede on your behalf. For after all, 'tis in your blood to be evil, and there is little you can do to combat it."

Sheena felt a sickness come over her. She didn't stab Elmyra, but she knew now that no one would believe her. She shuddered to think of what her father would do.

Elmyra could hear them talking but the sounds were muffled and coming from far away. She could see them too, but, strangely, she seemed to be looking down from above them, and she could see not only them but her own body, lying on the floor between them. But no, she thought. That's not her body. That body is old, and defeated, and enslaved. That wasn't her at all. She was in her body now, and she was fifteen, and she was searching for seashells, and there, ahead, waving at her from the waterfall was her Garth!

14

" 'Tis no secret that you've thought ill of Elmyra from the beginning," Kevin O'Sheel was saying to his daughter. He paced back and forth in his study, puffing furiously on his pipe, making a cloud of blue tobacco smoke, which rose to the ceiling then spread over the room. Liam was sitting smugly in a chair near the large, rolltop desk, and Sheena was on the settee.

"I didn't do it, Father," Sheena said. "I told you. I heard Tricia scream and I went to the cabin to see what had happened."

"The blacks say you called out threats to Elmyra before you went into her cabin," Kevin said.

"I was angry," Sheena said. "I thought she had whipped her daughter."

"If she had, 'twould have been no affair of yours," Dr. O'Sheel said. "The woman was the girl's mother, and 'twould have been naught but parental discipline. You had no right to interfere."

"Father, you know that Elmyra was a headstrong woman, given to having her own way," Sheena said. "She thought she was queen of South Carolina."

"I know that you never liked her," Kevin said. "Not from the beginning."

"You are always talking about how I treated Elmyra. How about the way Liam treated her?"

"What are you talking about? Liam got along very well with her."

"If sleeping with her was getting along with her, then I suppose you can say that he did," Sheena said.

"Father, I see that Sheena has returned to her old pattern of trying to absolve her own guilt by accusing others," Liam said. "It is obviously untrue, as I'm sure you know. But I harbor no ill will toward her for telling such lies, for she cannot help the things she does."

"How typical of you, Son, to bear up under the false witness of your sister. As a student of medicine, you can understand that it is, after all, her bad blood which causes such sin." Kevin walked over and put his hand affectionately on Liam's shoulder. His other hand he pressed against his forehead as if trying to form the next words.

"Sheena," he finally said. "I had hoped that by leaving Ireland and England we would be able to expose you to a life which would allow you to overcome the taint of your birth and allow my good blood to assert itself. Unfortunately such has not been the case. And therefore, after much prayerful consideration, I have come to a conclusion as how best to handle the situation."

"What situation?" Sheena asked. "Father, I told you, I didn't kill Elmyra!"

"Please!" Kevin said, holding his hand out to silence her. "Please, do not compound your sin by further lies. I do not know what terrible blood lust drove you to commit murder. But I do know that the same Christ who spared the thief on the cross in a last-second show of mercy will have mercy on a person who spends a lifetime of repentance. Therefore, in order to spare your immortal soul, I have made arrangements for you to return to Ireland and to enter the Convent of the Sisters of Solitude."

"The Sisters of Solitude? Father, the sisters there take a vow of silence! Were I to go there, I would not be able to speak for the rest of my life!"

"Aye. 'Tis better that way. You'll have a lifetime of silence to reflect upon your sins and ask the Lord for forgiveness."

"But surely, Father, you would not send me away so? 'Twould be like a prison for one who hasn't been called by God for such service."

" 'Twould be your opportunity to bring honor to the family," Liam said. "And 'tis better than you deserve for such a crime."

"Aye, your brother is right. You should consider yourself fortunate, daughter," Kevin said. "If Elmyra had been a white woman, you might have been hanged at the gallows, or at the very least sentenced to a colonial prison. In the convent, at least, you'll have the joy of knowing that you are serving God."

"No, Father, I won't go," Sheena said defiantly.

"You've no choice, girl," Kevin replied angrily. "I have made my decision, and you will go. You'll be sailing within the week."

"Father, please, hear me!" Sheena begged, tears springing to her eyes for the first time. "I didn't stab Elmyra. The knife was protruding from her belly when I entered the cabin."

"And where did the dagger come from?" Kevin asked. " 'Twas not the kind of knife common among slave folk."

"I don't know where it was from," Sheena said. "I only know that—" Sheena suddenly stopped in mid-sentence, for she realized for the first time where the dagger had come from. It was the same concealed dirk she had once seen on Liam's person. The very nature of its secrecy meant that the chances of anyone else having seen the knife in his possession were remote. She was trapped, for to tell her father that it was

Liam's knife would bring on the accusation that she was trying to shift the blame again.

"You only know what, girl?" Kevin asked, tiring of the long pause in her conversation.

"I—I only know that I didn't do it," she answered weakly. She looked over at Liam in such a way as to inform him that she now knew it was his knife. Liam smiled at her, knowing that there was nothing she could do about it.

"There will be much to do to prepare you for the convent," Kevin said. "Go up to your room now and meditate over your sins, and pray for the Lord's acceptance of what you are going to do for atonement."

"Aye, Father," Sheena said, rising from the settee and starting for the stairs which led to the second floor and her room.

"Liam," she overheard Kevin saying as she left. " 'Tis worried I am about Elmyra's daughter, Tricia. She's nowhere on the plantation, I'm convinced of that."

"Perhaps we'd better hire some slave chasers to hunt her down, Father," Liam suggested.

"Aye, I've thought of that. But 'tis a cruel lot that makes up the slave-chasing profession. I've no wish for harm to come to the girl."

"Surely, Father, we can request that she be treated gently when found. After all such men would be in our pay."

" 'Tis right you are, son," Kevin said. "Very well, I shall hire slave chasers on the morrow. 'Tis best for the girl to be coming home anyway."

The words of her father and brother dimmed as Sheena climbed the stairs. By the time she was in her room, she was no longer able to hear them at all. She lay on her bed and folded her hands behind her head, staring at the ceiling. Tears welled in her eyes and ran down the side of her face as she thought of what her father had in store for her.

She could not go to a convent! She just couldn't! She had nothing but respect and admiration for those women who could live such a life, but she knew that she didn't have the dedication or the faith for it. And, such a life would end forever her dream of someday going to sea.

She laughed to herself as the thought of going to sea returned to her. She was eighteen now, a grown woman, and yet the dream was as real to her as it had been when she was but a girl of thirteen, first beginning to sneak out of the house to visit the ships.

Sneak out of the house?

Sheena suddenly sat up. She walked over to the window and looked through it. She saw that it would be a fairly easy climb out to the large and fragrant magnolia that grew beside her room, and from there an even easier drop down to the ground. That's what she would do! If Tricia could run away, so could she. If a young black girl could make it, how much easier would it be for a young white man? Sheena smiled broadly. For when she did leave, it would not be as Sheena, but as Sean.

The crickets and frogs competed for the right to carry the night melody. To their songs were added the haunting call of the whippoorwill, and the gentle rustle of the trees, moved by an evening breeze.

The sky was dusted with stars and lighted with the greatest silver orb of the moon, so that Sheena had little problem in finding her way out of the window, down the tree, and across the rolling lawn to the woods beyond. A short walk through the woods, and she found the Charles Town Pike, a wide dirt road which led into the nearby coastal city.

Sheena was wearing men's clothes. She carried two more changes of clothes, plus a couple of biscuits and a piece of salt meat, wrapped in a handkerchief and tied to the end of the fencing foil she had won from her brother. She also had five pounds in gold coin tied up in a corner of the kerchief. She had taken them from her father's desk after everyone was asleep. It was stealing, she knew, but she also knew that without a little money to get her started, she would have a most difficult time of it.

The dirt road stretched out before Sheena, shining silver in the moonlight, looking almost like a river. The powdery dirt felt soft and cool to her feet.

Little puffs of dust rose with each footfall and were carried off by the wind. She walked on, oblivious to anything except getting away from her father and escaping the sentence he would impose on her. She had not planned ahead and had no idea what she would do once she reached Charles Town.

"Well, now, Argus, lookee here what we've got standin' 'afore us," a man's voice suddenly called from the shadows alongside the road.

The unexpected sound of the man's voice startled Sheena. She stopped short, her stomach contracting in sudden fear.

"Who is it?" she called out.

"Be ye lass, or be ye lad?" the voice from the dark returned. " 'Tis hard to tell from your voice, and in the dark."

"I'm a man," Sheena replied, pitching her voice a bit lower. "Who are you?"

Two figures emerged from the shadows.

"Well, now, lad, my name be Troy. Me partner's name be Argus. He don't talk, but he's an all right fellow. Where ye be headed?"

"I'm going to Charles Town."

"Charles Town, be it? Well, now, lad, you'll be wantin' a little information about Charles Town, won't ye? Like as where to eat, 'n where to sleep, 'n where a young fella like you can get hisself on wages. Argus 'n me, we'd be glad to supply you with that news, in exchange for a little money."

"I don't have any money," Sheena said.

"All right, then I'll just take a little something from your kerchief there. Open it up here in the moonlight 'n let me have a look-see. Never can tell what a body might find, eh?"

"No," Sheena said, taking one step back as Troy stepped forward.

"Well, now, Argus, lookee here at the lad, will ye? He's not bein' very generous with them of us what's in a bit of need, is he now?"

"Uhhn, aworl, ihmph," the other figure grunted, the savage, animallike grunts making Sheena's hair stand on end.

Troy laughed. "Ole Argus, he says whyn't we jus' take that little ole' sack of your'n anyhow. Come on, lad, hand it over, and Argus 'n me'll be on our way 'n you can go on your'n."

Sheena slipped the kerchief off the end of the foil, then assumed the guard stance as she had learned it by observing the fencing lessons.

"Oh, ho!" Troy laughed. "He's the proper gentleman, he is. He's going to stick me with his gentleman's sword." The smile left Troy's face, and he pulled a knife from his belt. "Now, lad, leave me friend 'n me have the bundle, 'n you go on, 'n no one's gonna get hurt."

Troy took another step toward Sheena. She whipped the sword out and flicked the point against his hand, stabbing it in about half an inch. Then she pulled it out quickly and put the point against Troy's throat. Troy dropped the knife, grabbed his hand and let out a scream of pain.

"Tell your friend without a tongue to withdraw," Sheena said.

"Argus, get back, get back!" Troy said, his voice reflecting pain and fear. "Easy lad, easy. Stick my throat with that thing the way you did my hand, 'n I'll be a dead man."

"Exactly," Sheena said. "Tell him to get far enough away from me so that I can't even smell him, and his stench carries a long way on this night air."

"Argus, damn ye, you want me kilt?" Troy shouted.

Argus grunted once and started down the road. When he was about one hundred yards away Sheena pulled the point away from Troy's throat. "Now, you," she said. "Join your friend."

"I'm goin', lad, I'm goin'," Troy said, turning and running up the road, leaving puffs of dust behind him.

Sheena watched until both were a safe enough distance away, then retrieved her kerchief and hooked it back on the end of the foil. She laughed aloud and jumped once for joy. She had never known such exhilaration as she felt at that moment.

BOOK TWO

15

"And what kind of work would you be doin' now, tell me that, lad? You don't look as if you could heft more than two-stone weight." So the warehouse foreman responded to Sheena's request for a job.

"But surely you've a position which requires brains over muscle," Sheena said. "I'm good with numbers, and I read and write very well."

The foreman rubbed his hand against a bristly chin. "I don't know," he said, looking at Sheena. "Maybe there's something for you at that. I could let you work for Billy. Fact is, if you prove out, you might wind up taking Billy's job away from him."

"I've no wish to take another man's job, sir," Sheena said. "Everyone should be able to earn their daily bread."

The foreman laughed. "Billy don't care nothin' about his daily bread," he said. "He's more interested in his daily tot o' rum. And perhaps a willing female to share his bed. He has a taste for liquor and an eye for the ladies that sometimes gets in the way of his work. Add to that his temper, which is always gettin' him into fights, 'n you'll see that I wouldn't be unhappy to see the man go."

"Then I'll learn his job as quickly as I can," Sheena offered.

"Ha! You'll work out all right, lad. You've got ambition about you, I can see that."

"Aye, I have ambition," Sheena said. "But 'tis not to stay on the docks."

"Oh? And what would you do?"

"I've a hunger to go to sea," Sheena said. "I want a berth on a merchantman."

"Sure 'n you'd best talk to Billy about that, for he was once a ship's officer, set ashore without papers as a punishment."

"What did he do?" Sheena asked.

"They tell that he laid with the captain's wife," the foreman said, chuckling. " 'Course you can never find out from ole' Billy hisself, 'cause Billy won't say nothin' about it. Knowin' his taste for the ladies though, I'd say it's probably true."

"When can I start work?" Sheena asked.

"You can start today," the foreman said. He handed a sheaf of papers to Sheena. "Here's the load manifest. See that it's put on board the *North Star*."

Sheena took the manifest. "Where is the dock foreman? Shouldn't I report to him?"

"Like as not, he's laid up drunk somewhere," the foreman said. "That's why I hired you." The foreman laughed. "Besides, I want to see his face when he shows up and sees the work done without him."

"What men can I use?"

The foreman laughed again. "Lad, just go down there with the manifest. You'll have 'em comin' to you askin' for the work."

Sheena took the pages and started out toward the pier where the *North Star* was tied. True, as the foreman had said, she was deluged with work applicants by the time she got there. That was because the workers were paid per ship, and if there was no ship to be loaded, they weren't paid.

"Where's Billy?" one of the men asked.

"Billy's not here," Sheena answered. "I'll be in charge of this loading."

"You? You're but a tot," one of the other men said. "Why should I work for a boy?"

"Why should you indeed?" Sheena asked. "I daresay there are enough others who are willing to do the work. You can cool yourself in the shade if you wish."

The others laughed at the dockhand, then began moving forward, volunteering their services. Within a few moments she had the entire crew signed on, and they began loading the ship.

Sheena really had no idea of what to do, but she could read, and she did have a good head on her shoulders. It was easy enough from the manifest to determine what the load was supposed to consist of, and the men themselves, when told to bring "fifty barrels of pitch," seemed to know what to do. So Sheena just relaxed and learned the ropes as she went along.

It was much easier than she had thought it would be. In fact it was so easy that she couldn't understand why she had spent the last two weeks hiding out in the room she'd rented, afraid to go out and find a job. It was only when she'd perceived that the money was running out and realized that she would have to do something that she'd gathered up the courage to come to the docks to seek employment.

"One hundred bales of tobacco," Sheena said, making a mark on the paper. "And that finishes this ship." She clapped her hands together. "Well, perhaps I'd best locate another manifest so as to get another ship."

"You done that real good, lad," one of the huge, sweating dockhands said, wiping his forehead with a handkerchief. "Like as not, Billy hisself coulda' done no better."

"Hey, Pennace," one of the other men said to the dockhand who was talking. "Lookit them two birds poking around down there. They're back again."

Sheena looked in the direction indicated and saw two men. One was tall, with a lean face and a mean look to his eyes. The other was shorter and broader, with a full beard and a bald head. Both were better dressed than the men of the docks, though lacking the finery of true gentlemen.

"Who are they?" Sheena asked.

"They're bounty hunters," the one called Pennace said, spitting on the ground as he said the words.

"Bounty hunters? What is a bounty hunter?"

"You know, lad. They hunt down thems what's got a price on their head," Pennace said.

"And it don't make no never mind whether 'tis the king's own reward or the bounty paid for a runaway slave. They search 'em all out, just the same," the other said.

"They're a mean lot," Pennace said. "They don't pay much attention to how they treat the poor buggers when they catch 'em, be they white or black."

The two men who were the subject of the conversation started over, and Pennace and his friend drifted away, so that when the men arrived, they found Sheena standing alone.

"Can I help you?" Sheena asked.

"They tell us you be the foreman today. Where at's Billy?" the tall man asked.

"I don't know," Sheena said. "This is my first day on the job, and I've not seen him."

"Well, then I s'pose we can confide in you," the tall man said. He pulled a piece of paper from his jacket pocket. "We got us a warrant here to look for two girls. A white girl what run away from her pappy, and a nigger girl what run away from the same place."

"What—what do you want with them?" Sheena asked, feeling a quick twist of fear, hoping her disguise would hold up under their scrutiny.

"We want to take 'em back, lad, so as to collect

the reward. The white girl, likely, will jus' get a whippin'. That is, if she don't cause no trouble. The nigger girl . . . well, they say she's a comely wench. We may find somethin' else to do with her, eh, Turk?"

"Yeah," Turk said, grinning broadly and grabbing himself between the legs.

"There's a bob in it for you, lad, if you should see either one of 'em 'n tell us about it like a loyal subject o' the Crown should."

"I'll—I'll keep my eyes open," Sheena said.

"Yeah, you do that," the tall one replied. "Come along, Turk. The little nigger girl's been seen around here. We'll find her, never you mind."

"When we catch her, Fox, I'm first," Turk said, rubbing himself as they walked away. "You may mind you got to bust that little ole' injun girl last week."

"I remember," Fox said. "But Turk, you hurt 'em somethin' awful when you lays with 'em 'n they ain' no fun after that."

Sheena watched them until they were gone, then, breathing a sigh of relief that her disguise was not compromised, headed for the next ship to load.

The mysterious Billy did not show up for the entire day, a habit not uncommon to him, Sheena learned. When she questioned the wisdom of keeping someone on the job who was so undependable, the foreman explained that until Sheena came along, there had been no one else available who was qualified to handle the job.

When Sheena returned to her room that night, she was not only confident that she could carry out her disguise, she now knew that she could even excel in a job that was regarded as for men only. It was a heady feeling. It made her think that the idea of going to sea was not as impossible as it had seemed.

It was dark when Sheena reached her room so she took the candle from the small bedside table and carried it next door to the tavern, where she lit it from one of their candles, then returned to her own room. Many people in the neighborhood used the tavern candle to light their own, as matches were expensive and reserved for emergencies only.

A golden bubble of light diffused through the small room as Sheena placed the candle on the table. Checking to make certain that the shutters were closed, Sheena began to undress for bed.

"Miss Sheena?" a soft voice called.

Sheena, startled by the voice, looked around quickly. There, sitting in the corner, her large dark eyes shining in the light of the candle, was Tricia.

"Tricia! What are you doing here?" Sheena asked.

"I don't have any place else to go," Tricia said.

"How did you know where I was?"

"I saw you leave the same night I left," Tricia said. "I followed you." She laughed. "I even saw you roust those two men. You sure are good with that sword."

"It's been almost two weeks," Sheena said. "Where've you been staying?"

"Here," Tricia said.

"Here? How? I don't understand."

Tricia smiled and pointed to the ceiling. Then without a word of explanation she climbed on a chair, pushed a ceiling panel to one side, pulled herself up into the loft, then replaced the ceiling panel. From Sheena's viewpoint, it was as if the girl had totally disappeared. A second later the panel was moved to one side and Tricia dropped back down to the floor.

"There's just enough room for me to lie down up there," Tricia said. "I stayed up there when you were here and came down when you left."

Sheena laughed, then held her arms out and hugged the girl enthusiastically. "I'm glad you decided to make your presence known," she said. "It's so good to see you." The expression on Sheena's face suddenly changed. "Oh, Tricia, you have to leave. You are in great danger. There are bounty hunters after you."

"Bounty hunters?"

"Slave chasers," Sheena explained. "Oh, they are awful men. I hate to think of what they will do to you when they catch you."

"What should I do, Miss Sheena?"

"I don't know," Sheena said. "You could go back, I suppose. How bad could it be? My father treats you well."

"I'm never going back there," Tricia said, and there was such feeling in her words that Sheena knew the girl meant them. "Besides, Mama's dead now. I don't have anybody to go back to."

"Tricia, I want you to know that I didn't kill your mama. Your mama and I never got along, as you well know, but I didn't kill her."

"Lord, Miss Sheena, whoever said you did? It was your brother, Liam, who killed her."

"I thought as much," Sheena said. "And yet he convinced Father that I did it."

"Your brother is a very evil man, Miss Sheena. I'm afraid to go back there. I'm afraid he'll kill me, like he did Mama."

"Then you won't have to go back there," Sheena said. "But where will you go?"

"I'll find a place," Tricia said. "Have you had your supper?"

"No," Sheena said. "I'm afraid I'll have to go without food until I'm paid tomorrow."

Tricia smiled. "Do you like cheese?"

"Yes, very much."

Tricia climbed onto the chair, reached into the crawl space above the ceiling, then pulled out a package. She unwrapped a large hoop of cheese.

"Tricia, where did you get that?"

"I found it," Tricia said.

"How could you find something like that?"

"It's easy," Tricia said. "If you know where to look."

Tricia broke off a piece and gave it to Sheena. "Uhmm," Sheena said. "I don't care where you found it. All I can say is it is delicious."

"I won't be here when you come back tomorrow," Tricia said. "I'll be going on to somewhere else."

"I wish there was something I could do to help you," Sheena said.

"You have helped. You let me stay here for two weeks."

Sheena laughed. "Maybe so, but I didn't know you were here."

"That doesn't matter. Anyway, I've got an idea of where I want to go. The thing is, I don't know where it is, or how you get there."

"Where would that be?"

"Nassau," Tricia said. "Mama said that's where her man wanted to take us. She said folks are a mite easier on the black person in Nassau. You ever heard of that place?"

"No," Sheena said. She smiled at the younger girl. "But whatever it is, I hope you find it."

"I'll find it," Tricia said, breaking the cheese into two large pieces and wrapping one piece back up. "Never you mind about that."

"What are you doing with the cheese?"

"I'm leaving some for you," Tricia said.

"Tricia, no, that isn't right. It's your cheese, and you'll be needing it in your travels."

Tricia smiled broadly. "No offense meant, Miss Sheena. But black folks on the run know better how to find food than white folks. And you are on the run too, so I know you could use the cheese."

"Yes, of course I could," Sheena said. "I just hate to take it from you."

"You didn't take it from me, Miss Sheena," Tricia said resolutely. "I gave it to you. Nobody's ever going to take anything from me again."

16

"Billy came in this mornin'," the foreman told Sheena when she went to work the next day. "His head was still besotted with rum and he smelled of the woman he had laid with, but he come in here like as if all would be forgiven as it always is."

"Did you forgive him?" Sheena asked.

The foreman laughed. "I put him on notice. When he saw all the work that was done in his absence, he was that shocked you could have knocked him over with a feather. Now he's down on the pier, workin' the men double hard, tryin' to prove that he's needed around here."

"Should I join him?"

"No," the foreman said. He pulled out another sheaf of papers. "Here is a new ship what come in durin' the night 'n is layin' off waitin' to be unloaded. By rights it should wait for Billy, but it comes to my mind that you might be able to get a crew together 'n do it now. That way I could watch the two of you 'n make up my mind as to which one of you I should keep."

"Why not keep both of us and double your work?" Sheena asked.

" 'Cause that also doubles the pay, lad," the foreman answered. "It's best to double the work, but pay only one. And if there's only one job, I'll get double the work out of whoever has it. 'Course, you'd best be on the lookout for Billy. I don't figure he's gonna be any too pleased with what I've got in mind, and he's like as not gonna' try 'n make trouble for you. He's bigger and stronger than you are, lad, so if you've got wits about you, you'd best find a way to protect yourself."

Sheena took the bill of lading from the newly arrived ship and left the small office to gather a crew. The fact that she might be putting Billy out of work didn't bother her, for if Billy couldn't do the job, he didn't deserve it. But the warning about Billy did disturb her. She knew that she would be no match for a man in a fight which valued strength over agility and brawn over brain. She would, as the foreman suggested, have to use her wit to avoid trouble.

Sheena strolled out to the end of the pier as she had the day before, but on this day no one volunteered to work on her crew. She saw several who were not working, but when she approached them they turned away from her. Finally she inquired as to the matter.

"Billy said to wait right here," one of the men said. "He told us we'd get the next ship."

"Don't you hear what I'm saying?" Sheena asked. "I have the bill of lading for that ship in my hand here. We can get right on it. You don't have to wait." She held the sheaf of papers out to show the men.

"Billy said don't work for anybody else," the spokesman for the group said again.

"Oh, he did, did he? Then suppose you just tell me where this Billy is. I think I should have a word with him."

"He's easy enough to find," the spokesman said. "Billy's him what's bossin' the crew around down there."

Sheena saw the work crew at the end of the pier and started toward it. She had hoped to be able to avoid trouble. But she was finding it thrust upon her, and there was little she could do save meet it head-on. That meant this was no time for meekness, so she took a deep breath and prepared for whatever might come.

"Billy," she called as she approached the men. "Billy, you stinking rumpot, I would have a word with you!"

"You may have it," a tall, strongly built man said. He pushed his hand back through his thick black hair, and smiled at his challenger, confidently, impudently.

For a moment Sheena was shocked into silence. For there, before her eyes, was none other than William Drumm, the first officer of the *Cassandra*, the one who had robbed her of her virginity two years before.

"You!" Sheena said. "I might have known it was you!" Anger overtook her at that moment.

"I beg your pardon, lad?" Billy Drumm asked easily. His face twisted in confusion. "Do I know you?"

For an instant Sheena felt such outrage that she was ready to reveal herself to him in order to vent it. But at the last second she controlled herself.

"No," she said. "No . . . it's just that I've been informed that you won't let the men unload my ship."

"Your ship?" Billy Drumm asked easily. He smiled and pointed to the schooner in the harbor. "Would you be talking about the *Marcus B.*, which lies at anchor in the bay?"

"Aye, you know the ship. And you've so instructed the men that only you can oversee her unloading."

"Lad, what do you know of the *Marcus B*?" Billy asked.

Sheena looked at the ship, lying low and sleek in the water. Her masts were wand-thin and free of sail.

"I'd make her about thirty tons," Sheena said. She looked at the bill of lading. "And she's carrying wool. What more is there to know?"

"How about her captain? Do you know who he is?"

Sheena looked at the bill of lading again. "Captain J. Ledyard."

"J. Ledyard. That name means nothing to you? 'Mad Jack' Ledyard?"

"The freebooter?"

"One and the same," Billy said.

"But what is he doing here? How came he to Charles Town?"

Billy laughed. "Lad, are you so innocent that you don't know the Charles Town merchants make up the marketplace for the pirates?"

"But the governor of South Carolina has issued warrants for the pirates. I know this, for I've read of the warrants in the papers."

"Aye, lad. But 'tis only a show. In the meantime the pirates plunder the seas, then bring their booty to Charles Town, where the merchants gladly pay a lesser price for goods than they would pay were the goods legitimately transported."

Sheena looked toward the *Marcus B.* again. "I don't see the Jolly Roger," she said.

Billy laughed again. "Lad, sure'n if you weren't after my job I could like you for your innocence. It would be folly to fly the ensign in Charles Town harbor, now, wouldn't it?"

"Aye," Sheena said. "Of course, you are right."

"It's for your own good, lad, that I handle the work here. You aren't cut out for the docks anyway. Best you find yourself another occupation."

"You should know about changing occupations, Mister Drumm," Sheena said hotly.

"What?" Billy asked, gasping. "See here, how do you know my name?"

"I—I heard it from the foreman," Sheena said, realizing that she'd made a mistake.

"No," Billy said. "For I've given my true name to no one." He stared at Sheena more closely. "You couldn't have been one of the sailors who shipped with me. It's been two years since I was to sea, and you're too young. Who are you?"

"My name is Sean," Sheena said.

"Sean what?"

"As you've seen fit to conceal your last name, you can understand that I've no desire to reveal mine."

Billy rubbed his chin and stared at her, and Sheena noticed for the first time that the mustache he had sported so proudly when he was an officer of the king's fleet was now missing. Whether he had shaved it off in an attempt to disguise himself or had removed it in the shame of his demotion, she had no idea. She did know, however, that she could not long undergo his intense scrutiny without having her identity compromised. She spun about in anger and walked away from him.

It was a serious blow to her pride, but Sheena had to report back to the foreman and inform him that she was unable to get the men to unload the ship. To her surprise the foreman didn't seem too upset by it.

"There's many who won't board Ledyard's ship," he said. "Talk is, he sometimes forces 'em into the brethren, though I've never known a man who went as didn't want to."

"Then what Billy said is true? The *Marcus B.* is a pirate ship?"

"Aye. But 'Mad Jack' has a letter of marque from the king himself. His goods have been plundered from Spanish ships as an act of war. 'Tis not illegal to do business with the man, if that's what you're a thinkin'."

Sheena looked toward the ship again and saw two

of the crewmen moving about on the deck. For an instant she had the mad, impetuous desire to be with them, passing herself off as a man, sailing the high seas, searching for prizes to capture and booty to share.

"Here," the foreman said, handing Sheena some more papers. "You may take inventory of the warehouse. Be true with your figures, lad."

Sheena took the papers and started toward the warehouse. It would be a dull substitute for the life of a privateer, but it was employment, and she needed that now to keep body and soul together.

Such inventory as had been done before had been poorly executed, and Sheena found that it was necessary to devote the rest of the day to procuring accurate numbers. By the time she was finished and had taken the results to the office, night had fallen and she had to walk home through a dark, twisting lane.

Sheena wished for her rapier, for with it she would have felt more secure. As it was she was nearly defenseless, depending solely on her disguise to offer some protection against a would-be attacker. She could hear water gurgling through the open sewers, and the impatient squeak of the rats that lived under the board sidewalks. She hurried on, trying not to think of the time she'd almost been buggered in the hold of a ship in Dublin, when even passing as a boy did not protect her from a sexual attack.

Sheena was passing by an open alleyway, thankful to be just a few short blocks from her room, when a hand suddenly thrust out of the dark, grabbed her arm, and jerked her roughly off the boardwalk.

"Help!" Sheena started to yell, but a hand was cupped across her mouth to stifle the cry.

"Don't worry, little one. I'll remove my hand in a moment and you can yell all you want, for all the good it'll do you," a voice hissed in the night. The

138

hand was pulled away. Sheena, struggling unsuccessfully to escape, cursed him.

"Now, now, is that any language for Sheena O'Sheel to use? The daughter of one of South Carolina's most respected gentlemen?"

"You *know* me?" Sheena asked.

"Aye, I know you, girl. And you know me as well," the voice replied. At that moment, a door cracked open and a bar of golden light splashed out into the alley, falling on the face of her abductor. Sheena gasped when she saw him.

"It's you, William Drumm!"

"I'm called Billy now, as you know," Billy said. "William had a fine sound to it for an officer's name, but for a dockhand, Billy is good enough."

Sheena struggled against him again. "What is it?" she asked. "What do you want with me?"

"It's taken me some time to figure out who you are, but now that I have, we've a score to settle, lass."

"A score?"

"Aye. It was not enough for you to have me set ashore without officer's papers. Now you've come to take this job as well. Well, I won't allow it, Sheena."

"What do you mean you won't allow it? I've heard you are so often besotted that you are unable to work. 'Tis no fault of mine if you cannot hold your job, Billy Drumm."

"Maybe not, girl. But 'tis your fault that I've found myself in such a fix, for had you been honest with the captain, he would never have charged me with rape."

"But you weren't charged with rape," Sheena said. "Had you been, you would have been hanged."

"The captain explained to me that it was to protect your reputation that the charge was not lodged," Billy Drumm said. "Instead, I was charged with incompetence. William Drumm, the best officer in the fleet, charged with that which is beneath the dignity of a common seaman. And now I'm marooned here with the wharf rats."

"I'm sorry about that," Sheena said. "But I'm afraid there's nothing I can do about it."

"I think maybe there is," Billy said, pulling her down the alleyway with him.

"What? Where are you taking me? Let me go!" Sheena protested.

"Not for a while, Sheena," Billy said. He looked at her and laughed, a low, mocking laugh. "You see, I've paid long and dear for but a few moments pleasure. Now I intend to have what I've already paid for."

17

Billy's grip on her arm was too strong for Sheena to break, and she was afraid to scream. If it became known by anyone else that she was woman, she might be in even worse trouble. Her only hope seemed to lie in going with Billy to wherever it was he was leading her, and then to try, in some way, to reason with him.

They walked through the maze of alleyways, crossing cobblestoned streets and open, rushing streams of sewage. They passed drunken men who leaned against the brick buildings, and groups of whores who, mistaking the both of them for men, offered their bodies with obscene gestures and crude words. Finally they reached their destination, Billy stopping beside a door which opened off one of the alleys.

"In here," Billy said, opening the door and shoving her in. He stepped in behind her, then closed the door and bolted it.

"Why have you locked it?" Sheena mocked. "Are you afraid someone will get you?"

Billy didn't answer. Instead, he lit a lamp, then adjusted it so that the room was bathed in a bright yellow light.

Sheena examined her surroundings, trying to determine a means of escape. There was, however, only one door, and that was bolted and guarded by Billy Drumm. The only window was high and much too small for her to squeeze through. There was a bed, a chair, and two chests, with a pitcher of water and a bowl on one of the chests.

"Get your clothes off," Billy said, beginning to open his shirt.

"What? I have no intention of doing any such thing," Sheena said.

By now Billy had removed his shirt and had started with the lacings of his pants.

"I said take off your clothes."

"And if I refuse?"

"Then I shall remove them by force," Billy said easily. "The end result will be the same, Sheena. I am going to have you, whether you allow me to do so willingly, or whether you fight me. It makes little difference."

"Why are you doing this?" Sheena asked.

"I told you why. You let me face a charge of rape, and yet you clearly enjoyed our little tryst fully as much as I."

"I *did not* enjoy it," Sheena said, her cheeks flaming in anger and embarrassment.

"You did enjoy it, Sheena," Billy said. He was completely nude now. His hard, muscular body gleamed golden in the light. He looked like the bronze statues in the museum, the ones that Sheena used to sneak away to look at sometimes when she was much younger.

"I've had many women, and I know when they enjoy it and when they don't," Billy went on.

"But I didn't enjoy it," Sheena said. "I don't have bad blood. I don't, I don't."

Sheena sat on the edge of the bed and began to

cry. Her reaction so shocked Billy that he moved to her, not roughly but gently. He sat beside her and put his hand on her shoulder.

"Bad blood?" he asked. "What do you mean, bad blood?"

"Nothing," Sheena said, sniffing and looking for a handkerchief.

"Sheena, enjoying a man does not mean you have bad blood. It only means you are alive."

"You don't understand," Sheena said. "My mother is a—a—"

"A what?"

"A doxy," Sheena said, barely able to get the word out. "And my father and my brother say that I have the same evil blood she has. They say I do evil things because of it. I left home because of something very bad that happened."

"Something that you did?"

"No, I didn't do it. Liam did it. But they wouldn't believe me because I have bad blood."

"If you are innocent, that should prove there is nothing to what they say about your blood."

"But the other things that they say are true," Sheena said.

"What other things?"

"I—I have—sinful thoughts," Sheena said. "You are right, I did like what you did to me, and I've remembered it many times. Sometimes at night I remember it, and I almost ache with the wanting of it."

"Then girl, for God's sake, why did you say nothing in my defense?" Billy challenged.

"Oh, but I did," Sheena said. "The captain granted me a favor for nursing him back to health, and it was my request that you not be hanged."

Billy stood up and took a few steps to the middle of the small room, then looked back at Sheena, still sitting on the edge of the bed. He held his hand out to take in the room and sighed. "My God, girl, this is worse than hanging, for here I'm with the living dead."

"I'm sorry," Sheena said.

"Sorry doesn't get me a berth at sea," Billy said. He looked at her, and his anger over his predicament showed in his eyes, which grew narrow and piercing. "I said get your clothes off," he ordered again.

"No, I—please . . . don't do this," Sheena said. "I told you that I enjoyed it. Help me fight this wantonness."

Billy jerked open her loose-fitting shirt, then stared at the two small, though perfectly formed breasts, which were thus exposed. "Wouldn't the men on the docks be surprised to see what ole' Sean is hiding under *his* shirt, now?" he asked. He twisted the word "his" so that it became a mockery.

Despite her continued protests, Billy removed the woolen cap that Sheena wore pulled low over her forehead, and cascades of red hair tumbled across her shoulders.

"Now, Sheena, let's get a look at all of you," Billy said. He unlaced her trousers and slipped them down past her knees, over her ankles, and then clear, to be tossed in a heap on the floor beside the pile of clothing that was his own. She sat on the bed wearing only a shirt, and it hung open to expose the smooth-skinned, red-nippled breasts. Her hair, which fell across her shoulders, was matched in its brilliance by the spade of hot coals that crowned the junction of her legs.

Billy's need grew strong and evident, and Sheena, seeing this, felt her own breath quicken despite her efforts to combat what was happening. Billy sat beside her and put his hand behind her head, drawing her mouth toward his.

"Please, stop now," Sheena said, her pleading coming in a whisper of anguish. She was trying to fight him and her own racing passions as well.

Billy kissed her with burning lips and Sheena's resolve melted under the heat. She opened her mouth to his, tasting this experience hungrily. Then, when his hand went to her breast, she surrendered herself to him fully, no longer possessed of the strength to fight him and her own hungers, subservient to his will.

Billy gently removed the shirt so that Sheena was as naked as he, then stretched her out on the bed and lay beside her, moving his skilled hands across her body, kneading the flesh of her breasts until they were throbbing with pleasure, dipping adroitly into that area where all feeling seemed to be concentrated.

Billy positioned himself over her. Then, much more gently than he had on the ship, he thrust into her. Despite herself, she raised to meet him, pushing against him to share with him this thing which was now so much a part of both their bodies.

She gasped with the pleasure of it and cried with the joy of it, freeing herself from all thought save this building quest for fulfillment. Her body was like the restless sea, storm-tossed and wave-mounting, latent with the promise of more. At the peak, a crest of pleasure burst over her like the crashing of the largest breaker. It was a pleasure so intense as to be beyond her ability to measure it. It was far greater than the sensation she had felt up to that instant, and it surpassed by many times that which she had felt and remembered from two years before.

Sheena was unable to control her reactions to the orgasm. Though she tried to hold back her screams of joy, moans of pleasure escaped her lips, and she threw her arms around Billy and pulled him to her, trying to accept all of him into her womb, until the last shudders of ecstasy died away full moments later.

"Now, Sheena," Billy said sometime later. "Deny that you found that pleasurable."

"I cannot deny it," Sheena said. "I did indeed find it pleasurable. Oh, Billy, it was more thrilling than anything I've ever experienced in my life."

Billy smiled. "Aye, lass, I'm glad you can accept it now, for we shall have much more of it."

"No," Sheena said.

"Why do you say no?" Billy asked, clearly puzzled by her answer. "Did you not just admit that you found my bed pleasurable?"

"Aye," Sheena said. "And it only convinces me that Father was right. I have the mark of the harlot, and there's but one thing I can do to overcome the taint left on me by my mother. I must go to the convent as he says."

"The convent? What are you talking about?"

Sheena explained her father's intention to send her to Ireland to join the Sisters of Silence.

"It was fear of that which caused me to run away," she concluded.

"And right you were to leave, too," Billy said. "Such a life is not for the likes of you."

"No, Billy, 'tis the only thing for me now," Sheena said. "There I shall be free of all temptation, and I can spend the rest of my life in silence, praying to the Lord for forgiveness."

"You mustn't go," Billy said easily. "You won't go."

"But I must, and I am," Sheena replied.

"No," Billy answered calmly. "For I shall keep you prisoner here until you've come to your senses."

"Prisoner? How could you do that?"

"It would be easy," Billy said. "This very room was once used as a detention room for the Charles Town customhouse. The walls are heavily constructed; the door is made of oak and can be locked from outside. I'll simply lock you in by day and return to you by night."

"You wouldn't do that?" Sheena asked.

"Oh, but I would."

"Why?"

"Because you've bedeviled me these last two years, Sheena, and I've harbored a hunger for you, which I intend to satisfy."

"And to satisfy that evil lust, you would keep me prisoner? How could you torment me in such a way?"

"Why should it be such a torment?" Billy asked. "Did you not just say that you would willingly take a vow of silence and be a prisoner for the rest of your life?"

"But this is different!" Sheena said.

"I fail to see the difference, Sheena," Billy said. He laughed. "I shall keep you my prisoner for one month, and if at the end of that month you still wish to join the convent, I will set you free. How does that set with you?"

"It doesn't set with me at all, sir. You've no right to do such a thing," Sheena said hotly.

Billy laughed again. "I've the right to do it," he said. "Because I've the power to do it."

18

During the next three weeks Sheena was kept as Billy's prisoner. True, as Billy had stated, the room was so constructed that escape was impossible, though Sheena did try several times over the first couple of days. Finally, resigned to her fate, she began to occupy her days by keeping the room spotlessly clean and reading the many books on seamanship which Billy had kept from his days as a ship's officer.

After a short time Sheena found that the days weren't all that unpleasant. She had time to be alone with her thoughts and to try and understand the confusing turn of events that had brought her to this point. Also, she enjoyed Billy's books. She even enjoyed, she was surprised to discover, the idea of keeping Billy's room clean and neat for him. When he commented upon the improvement in the place on the fourth day, she beamed under the compliment.

She fought him during the first several nights he came to her, but it always ended in the same way. His strength prevailed and her own weakness betrayed her, so that the sessions of lovemaking ended with Sheena clinging to him in ecstasy, begging for more.

Only later, after Billy was asleep and she lay awake in the dark of the night listening to his soft, even breathing, did she have time to consider the sinfulness of her ways.

One night, shortly after Billy's lovemaking had lifted her to the stars, Sheena lay beside him, listening to the sounds from outside. She heard a drunken sailor's shout, a whore's raucous laugh, the hoofbeats of a postrider bound on some night mission, and she drew close to Billy, feeling warm and secure and glad to be there with him. That marked the last night she fought his advances.

At the beginning of Sheena's fourth week of confinement, she and Billy sat at the table, eating the stew she had prepared for them.

"I've been offered a berth," Billy said easily.

"As an officer?" Sheena asked.

"Yes."

"But how can that be? You have no papers."

Billy stood up and walked over to the fireplace to remove the teakettle and refill his cup. He rolled the cup back and forth in his hands, then took a swallow, before he answered.

"The owner who's offered the berth doesn't always respect such rules as may be established by maritime commissions," Billy said. "I've no need of papers to sail with him."

"Are you going to accept the offer?" Sheena asked.

"Yes."

"When will you sail?"

"I sail with the morning tide," Billy said.

Sheena felt a pang of disappointment. *No!* she wanted to cry. *Not so soon.* But she knew that such an expression of concern would be unseemly, so she hid it rather than show Billy how she felt.

"I suppose you will have the decency to set me free before you leave?" she asked sarcastically.

Billy laughed.

"What are you laughing about?" Sheena demanded, angered by his insolence. "I suppose you think I've *enjoyed* being kept here, locked in like an animal in a cage?"

"You must have enjoyed it," Billy said.

"You have taken cruel and unfair advantage of me, sir," Sheena said with downcast eyes. "I have admitted to you that it is my bad blood which causes a weakness of the flesh. I am unable to resist you at night, though I did try."

"I'm not talking about that, Sheena," Billy said. "I'm talking about the daytime, while I was gone. You've been perfectly content here."

"I've kept myself occupied," Sheena said. "But only because escape was impossible."

"And how do you know it was impossible?"

"Because I tried to escape," Sheena said.

Billy smiled at her. "I've left the door unlocked every day for two weeks now," he said. "You could have walked away anytime you wished."

"What?" Sheena asked. "But you didn't tell me."

"If you really wanted to escape, I wouldn't have had to tell you," Billy said. "For you would have tried the door every day. You didn't want to leave, did you?"

Sheena felt her cheeks flaming red. She stared at her hands for a long moment before she answered, softly, "No."

"Then I was right?" Billy asked, stepping over to her quickly. "Girl, could it be possible that you might return my love?" He dropped to one knee beside her and took her hands in his, looking into her face with an intense gaze.

"Yes," Sheena said. "I love you, Billy Drumm."

"Oh, Sheena, darling, but this is wonderful!" Billy said. He laughed. He pulled her up from the chair and squeezed her, then started dancing around the room with her.

"Wait a minute," Sheena said. " 'Tis true, then, Billy Drumm, that you love me as well?"

"Aye, lass," Billy said, stopping his dancing and looking into her eyes intently. "There were no truer words ever spoken."

"And yet you would leave me on the morrow?"

"But I've a berth, Sheena, and it has always been the way of seafaring men to leave their womenfolk behind."

"Billy, if you love me, don't leave me behind," Sheena said.

"Girl, are you asking me to give up my chance to go back to sea?"

"No," Sheena said. "I'm not asking you to stay ashore. I'm only asking you to take me with you."

"Take you with me? Are you daft?"

"No," Sheena said. "Billy, I've always wanted to go to sea. Now, what better way to do it than with the man I love?"

"No," Billy said. "That's impossible."

"Why?" Sheena asked. "I saw officer's wives on board some of the ships in England. I know it is sometimes done."

Billy sighed. " 'Tis not a gentleman's ship I'll be going aboard," he said. "I told you I would be sailing for a man who takes little notice of regulations and the such. 'Twas the only way I could get an officer's berth without papers."

"Then all the more reason he shouldn't care," Sheena said.

"Sheena, I'll be sailing with 'Mad Jack' Ledyard. I'm joining the brethren. I'll have to sign the articles, and one of them says that women are not allowed aboard the ships."

"Then I'll come aboard as a man," Sheena offered.

Billy laughed. "I could just see that."

"Billy Drumm, I've passed as a boy many times," Sheena said. "I'm slim, and bulky clothes can conceal my breasts easily. And I can climb, and run, jump, fence—do anything a boy can do. You saw me at the docks. Did any of the men there suspect that I was a woman?"

"Well, no," Billy agreed. "But . . ."

"But what?" Sheena asked. "I have done this often, Billy Drumm. Many's the time I've sneaked on board ships disguised as a boy, and no one was the wiser. Why, even on the *Cassandra* I worked in the rigging during the storm, right beside men who never knew who I was."

"Aye," Billy said. "Well I remember that."

"Then you'll take me with you?"

Billy laughed. "Don't you think people will begin to get a little suspicious if they see us sharing the same cabin?"

"Yes," Sheena said. "But they'll suspect the wrong thing. They'll think only that I'm some fair young boy who's caught your fancy. I've learned that such things are quite common on board ships denied women." She remembered her introduction to the idea on the day she was mistaken for a boy by the sailor called Grunt. "Sure'n I'll be your boyfriend," Sheena added, her eyes twinkling in amusement.

"Very well, Sheena, I'll take you with me," Billy said.

"You must call me Sean," Sheena warned. "You must get used to it."

Billy laughed. "Aye, Sean it is then." He rubbed his hand through her red hair. "Tell me, Sean, how did a lad such as yourself come by such beautiful hair?"

"Oh, shall I cut it off?" Sheena asked.

"No," Billy said. "There are many lads who have hair as long as that. Leave it, for it pleases me much."

"I'm glad it pleases you," Sheena said, moving closer to him and turning her lips up to be kissed. "For that's what I enjoy most, Billy Drumm. Pleasing you."

19

It was before dawn the next morning when two figures "borrowed" a skiff from the warehouse and pushed away from the shore. They shipped oars, wrapped them in cloth to dampen the sound, then rowed, silently, across the bay toward the dark, looming shadow of a ship.

To anyone who saw them, they were two men, though in fact only Billy Drumm was a man; his partner Sean was really Sheena.

"Are you sure you want to go through with this, Sheena?" Billy asked quietly.

"Hell's bells, Billy, if you don't start calling me Sean, the whole plan is going to fail."

"Aye. But I've a hard time remembering."

"Best you do remember," Sheena said. "Don't forget Article Ten."

"I can't forget it," Billy said. "In fact, it's about all I've been able to think about since I agreed to this crazy idea."

The Article Ten to which Sheena referred was in the Privateers' Code of Conduct, known most commonly as the Pirates' Article. Piracy, even sanctioned piracy such as that practiced by privateers operating with a letter of marque, was a part of sailing which operated outside any maritime controls. Therefore privateers had their own laws, laid down by a sort of pirates' constitution, which provided a set of guidelines for everyone to follow. The laws were in fact quite democratic, and the life of a common seaman on board a privateer was many, many times more bearable than the life of a common seaman on board a vessel of national registry. There was no absolute, dictatorial authority of the captain over the men, as on merchant ships, and even punishment issued by the captain was held to certain restraints, subject to the approval of a majority of the crew.

There were, however, certain guidelines which were so strictly enforced by the members of the brethren, as the privateers called themselves, that anyone who "went on account," or signed the articles and then violated them, was subject to the death penalty. Members of the brethren had a powerful superstition against women on board their ships. Article Ten addressed itself to just that.

"No women except those as may be taken prisoner shall be allowed on board the ship," Article Ten read. "Any man who brings a woman on board the ship will suffer death."

"Maybe we should go back," Billy suggested.

"No," Sheena said. "We can do it, Billy, I know we can."

A few moments later the boat bumped against the side of the *Marcus B.* and Billy and Sheena shipped oars. Billy grabbed a line and held the boat firm against the ship's hull.

"Ahoy the deck!" he called.

A bald head thrust over the rail and looked down at them. "Who be you, and what do ya want?" the head called.

"Billy Drumm, to come on account," Billy called.

"So, you've a wish to become one of the gentlemen

of the sea, eh?" the sailor replied. "I'll drop over a ladder."

A rope ladder zinged down and slapped against the side of the hull. Billy started to hold it out to make it easier for Sheena to climb, but she gave him a cautioning glance. He smiled, then started up the ladder before her.

There were two lanterns burning just abeam of the main mast, one mantled with green, the other with red. The ship's deck was wet with the morning dew, and the lights left green and red splashes on the deck.

"Who be this with you?" the sailor asked, as Billy and Sheena stepped onto the deck.

"My name is Sean," Sheena said. "I've come to go on account as well."

"Does he be your faggot?" the sailor asked.

"Aye," Billy said. "But he can hold his own with the work and the fighting."

"Is he an accommodating lad, or your boy only?" the sailor asked, looking at Sheena with an interest that she recognized as carnal. He had a gold earring in one ear, and a red silk scarf knotted around his neck.

"I'll not be sharing him with the crew," Billy said.

"'Tis a shame, lad," the sailor said, never taking his eyes off her. "A little spice is nice, if you get my meanin'."

"I get your meaning," Sheena said. "But it's Billy's bed I'll be warming."

"Then you'll have to marry him," the sailor said.

"Marry him?" Sheena asked in surprise. "What do you mean?"

"Mad Jack's run into this problem 'afore," the sailor explained. "Dog, he had himself a pretty young boy, 'n the boy commenced to flirtin' with the others in the crew. It near 'bout to caused as much trouble as a woman, so Mad Jack said that anyone as wants to stake claims has to get married, all legal and proper, same as if they was marryin' a woman."

"I don't know about that," Billy said.

"Why not?" Sheena asked. "Like the man said, it would be all legal and proper."

Billy smiled broadly. "Yeah," he said. "Yeah, I suppose it would at that. Very well, we'll take care of that. Now, where is Mad Jack?"

"Like as not he's in his cabin," the sailor said. "Just go on in. We ain't your formal king's navy around here." He laughed at his joke.

"Thanks," Billy said. "Oh, how are you called?"

"Hedge," the bald sailor answered.

Billy walked aft to the captain's cabin and stood just outside the door, which opened onto the middeck. Hedge had told him to walk right on in, but all his training dictated that he knock first and be invited to enter, so he hesitated for a moment. Sheena, seeing his hesitation and realizing what it was, pushed the door open for him, giving Billy a gentle nudge, and they walked inside.

The cabin was well-lighted by a lantern. A large man, maybe six feet four inches tall, stood behind a table, looking at a map. The man had a great black beard and long hair which hung in two braids. A scar, which climbed up from the tangled beard, passed through his left eye and ended as a puffy mass of scar tissue just above his eyebrow. His eyes were as black as his beard, and they shone brightly in the lantern light. The man looked up as they entered.

"Captain Ledyard?" Billy asked.

"Aye, some calls me that," the big man said. He laughed, and his laugh was as deep and resonant as the booming of a cannon. "Some calls me a lot worse."

"I'm Billy Drumm. I was told by Mister Penobscott that you needed a new first mate, so I signed on with him."

"Penobscott? That lily-livered landlubber? What the hell does he know about anything?" Ledyard said.

"I was under the impression he owned the ship."

"He owns it," Ledyard admitted. "But I'm the captain. I'll make the decision as to who I sign on as first mate. Though you're welcome as a hand if you wish."

"No," Billy said. "I'm a ship's officer, Captain Ledyard, set ashore without papers. I'll not sail again unless it is in my proper position."

"Ship's officer, eh? I've got one of those on this ship. Sailed for the king's navy he did, till he went on account. He's as worthless as teats on a cannon, Mr. Drumm. I've no need for another just as worthless."

"Who would he be?" Billy asked.

"Miller Simmons," Ledyard said. "Only nobody calls him that. He's called—"

"He's called Dog," Billy interrupted. "And he is worthless. I hope you'll not compare him to me."

Mad Jack Ledyard put his hand in his beard and pulled at it for a moment. "I see," he said. "So you know Mr. Dog, do you? Very well, Mister Drumm. I'll take you on board, but you'll be the one to tell Dog that you're taking his place."

"I'll do that, Captain," Billy said.

Ledyard directed his gaze toward Sheena, who had been studying him all this time. He was a repulsive character, yet Sheena could feel a tremendous strength in the man. It was a strength of will as well as a physical strength, and that she found fascinating almost to the point of an attraction, though that feeling she easily put aside.

"And what about you, mate? You want to be a midshipman on board a corsair?" he laughed.

"No," Sheena said. "I'll do whatever needs to be done."

"You're a bit smallish," Ledyard said.

"I'll hold my own," Sheena said.

Ledyard looked at Sheena a bit longer, then looked at Billy. "Would he be your faggot?"

"Aye," Billy said.

"I can't see what pleasure there is in that. I only like women myself. But there's them what like young boys, so I turn a blind eye to my own feelin's. But it can sometimes cause as much trouble as bringin' a woman on board, so when such is the case, I have a special way of dealin' with it. Have you heard my rules about marryin' faggots?" Ledyard asked. "That's how I keep down the trouble."

"I've heard," Billy said. "We want to be married."

Ledyard picked up a tankard of ale he had been drinking and took another swallow, then belched loudly. He stuck his fingers into the ale and then sprinkled a few drops onto Billy and Sheena. "I pronounce you married," he said. "I'll pass the word to the crew, 'n the lad becomes your responsibility. There's still one or two as may make a try for 'im, but you've the right to fight for 'im now, if need be."

"I don't need anyone else to fight for me," Sheena said. "I'll handle my own battles."

"Feisty little son of a bitch, ain't he?" Ledyard said. He picked up the ship's logbook and handed it over to Billy. "Sign your name to the Articles, mates, 'n you'll be part o' the brethren, right enough."

The door to the cabin opened just as they finished signing their names, and Dog came in. Sheena recognized him at once and felt her cheeks burning, for this would be the big test. If Dog didn't recognize her now, she felt that she would be safe.

"Haw," Dog said, looking over at Billy who stood behind the plotting table. "I heard that you was on board. Well, I hate to inform you, *Mister* Drumm," he said, screwing his mouth up at the word "mister," "this vessel already has a first officer, and that's me."

"Dog, you wouldn't make a good seaman on a garbage scow," Billy said. "You've been relieved."

"By whose orders?" Dog asked.

"By mine, as I'm the new first officer, and thus empowered to issue such commands," Billy said. "Now quit this ship, or go before the mast."

"Cap'n, does you aim to make him first officer over me?" Dog asked.

Ledyard laughed. "Don't you think he would be a good one, Dog? He's the training of a gentleman; you can tell that by his bearing."

"Get him to tell you why he was set ashore without papers."

"The reasons are on record at the maritime offices," Billy said. "I don't have to explain."

"Well, I'll tell you why then," Dog said. "He was set ashore 'cause he raped a young girl what was a passenger on the ship. I seen 'im do it. I was watchin' through the air scupper 'n I seen ever'thin. Then I went 'n tol' the cap'n."

Sheena's cheeks flamed so brilliant a red that she was certain she would be spotted. But she remained quiet. So, he *had* known! Not only that, but he had watched!

"You raped a young girl?" Ledyard asked, looking at Billy.

Billy looked over at Sheena, then quickly looked toward the floor. "Aye," he said. "I did."

Ledyard looked at Sheena, then at Billy. He laughed, longer and louder than he had at any time before.

"You are an amazing fellow, Billy Drumm. Aye, and versatile too."

"Then you intend to make him your mate?" Dog asked.

"Aye," Ledyard said.

"I claim the right of honor," Dog said.

"Dog, you got no honor," Ledyard said. "And anyhow, it won't do you no good. Even if you win, you lose. I'll not have you as my mate."

"The Articles say I have the right to fight him."

"The Articles also say there will be no fightin' among crewmen on board. Do you want to wait until we've found an island somewhere?"

"No," Dog said. "By God, I want to fight him today."

Ledyard sighed. "If the majority of the crew agrees, then you shall have your fight."

"Billy, what is this to be? A duel?" Sheena asked.

"No, just a fight," Billy said. "Assuming that the crew agrees to it."

Dog grinned, showing crooked, yellowed teeth. "Oh, they'll agree to it right enough," Dog said. "They're more'n ready for a little fun and entertainment. They are gonna' love watchin' me beat your brains out."

"You may come out on the bottom end of this ruckus," Billy warned.

Dog grinned widely. "Naw, I won't," he said. "You see, you don't know how to fight none at all, 'cept as a gentleman. 'N this here ain't gonna be no gentleman's fight."

20

By the time the sun had risen fully above the ocean, Captain Ledyard had men aloft, putting on all sail for the departure. Sheena eagerly joined them, climbing out onto the yards to handle her share of the work. So adept and skillful was she that more than one man remarked about the new first mate's good sense in choosing a faggot with seamanship.

Under press of full sail and with a brisk following wind, the *Marcus B.* started out of the harbor, headed toward the shipping lanes of the Spanish Main. She was a fast ship, so fast that she seemed to lift out of the water and skim across the surface rather than plunge through the waves. It was an exhilarating moment for Sheena. She breathed deeply, enjoying the invigorating freshness of clean salt-sea air, free of the rotting fish and heavy smoke from the fouled shore.

"Mister Drumm, you know your way around a ship at that," Ledyard commented, leaning against the rail and observing as Billy gave the orders to come about for maximum advantage of the winds.

"Thank you, Cap'n," Billy answered.

Ledyard pulled at his beard and looked at Billy through one squinting eye, for the left one, the one disfigured by the scar, remained wide open all the time, even when he was asleep. "The question is," Ledyard asked, "can you fight? Many is the ship we take which asks no quarter, 'n then it's hand to hand."

Billy looked over at Dog, who was talking to a couple of the other sailors at that moment. Dog had just made some joke, and the three of them laughed, their laughter traveling back to the quarter-deck and ringing mockingly in Billy's ears.

"I imagine we'll find that out soon enough, Captain," Billy said.

"Aye. Now Dog, he's a good'n he is. I reckon if you can take him, you can handle just about anyone. Leastwise, you'll be good enough for our purposes."

"Hey, Mad Jack, when are we gonna get to see the fight?" Hedge called.

"Yeah," another sailor said. "Unless the new first mate has asked for quarter?"

Everyone laughed. Then Dog stepped out from behind them and peeled off his shirt. He wasn't quite as tall as Billy, but he had shoulders like a bull. His chest was matted with hair the same color as his beard. Tufts of hair grew from his shoulders and on his back.

"Come on down here, you yellow-livered bastard," Dog called. "Come down here and take your medicine."

"Dog's gonna treat you proper, he is," one of Dog's friends said.

Billy smiled at the sailors, then stripped out of his own shirt. He wasn't nearly as hirsute as Dog, and he was much slimmer. But he was muscular and strong, even if he didn't have the look of bull-like power that Dog possessed.

"The fight's on!" someone yelled. Within a moment all hands were on deck, forming a ring for the combatants.

Sheena climbed the main lower shrouds until she

was well positioned to see what was going on. Hedge followed her up and took a position right beside her, then looked over at Sheena and smiled. "I aim to watch how your man can fight," he said. "If ole Dog gives him a good whippin', then like as not I'll give you a visit. I don't figure Drumm will be in too good a condition to fight for you."

"I may have something to say about that," Sheena said.

"Har," Hedge said. "You can say all you wants, but a young boy can be raped, same as a young girl. 'N if I have ter cut you up a little, why I can do that too," he added, patting the handle of the dagger that protruded from the red band he wore around his waist.

A hush fell over the sailors as they watched the two men in the ring. Billy and Dog circled about, holding their fists doubled in front of them, each trying to test the mettle of the other.

Surprisingly Sheena was able to observe the fight with an almost detached interest. She wanted to see how Billy would handle Dog. She knew it would be quickness and agility against brute strength, and she hoped to learn by watching.

Dog swung first, a clublike swing which Billy leaned away from, and Billy counterpunched with a quick jab. It was a good punch and it caught Dog flush on the jaw, but Dog just laughed it off. As the fight went on, it developed that Billy could hit Dog almost at will, but since he was bobbing and weaving, he couldn't get set for a telling blow. His scores didn't seem to phase Dog at all.

Billy hit Dog in the stomach several times, hoping to find a soft spot, but there was none there. He gave that up and started throwing punches toward Dog's face, hoping to score there, but they seemed just as ineffectual until he saw a quick opening, which allowed him to send a long left to Dog's nose. He felt the nose go under his hand, and he knew that he had broken it. The nose started bleeding profusely and the blood ran across Dog's teeth and through his beard. It was a terrible-looking sight, but Dog continued to grin, wickedly, and seemed unperturbed by his injury.

Billy kept trying to hit the nose again, but Dog started protecting it. Billy was unable to get through, though the fact that Dog was protecting it told him at least that the nose was hurting. Dog was throwing great swinging blows toward Billy, barely missing him, and Billy knew that if just one of them connected soundly, he would be finished.

After four or five such swinging blows, Billy noticed that Dog was leaving a slight opening for a good right punch, if he could just slip it in across his shoulder. He timed it. On Dog's next swing Billy threw a solid right, straight at the place where he thought Dog's nose would be. He hit the nose perfectly and had the satisfaction of hearing a bellow of pain from Dog for the first time. It was a sharp and bruising punch, but it cost Billy; he felt his knuckle snap and winced as sharp pain shot through him.

Billy gave up his right then and went back to jabbing with his left, holding his right ready for one good blow, not wanting to waste it. He was getting tired. He started moving more slowly, both with his legs and his arms. His right hand was now badly swollen and he wasn't sure he would be able to use it, even if the opportunity did present itself.

Dog realized his advantage over Billy. In fact, it had been his plan to allow Billy to tire himself out, then close in on him. He began to rush Billy, swinging both hands. It was all Billy could do to parry the blows and stay out of the way. Even his parrying had a telling effect on him, as his arms and shoulders began to hurt from the punishment he absorbed. Then Dog managed to land a straight short right. It was not one of the wild, swinging punches, just an ordinary right, and Dog wasn't even positioned well, so much of the force of the blow was dissipated. Even so, when it crashed against Billy's head, Billy dropped to the deck like a sack of flour.

Sheena heard the crowd react. She leaned forward in the shrouds to get a better view of Billy, who was now stretched out on the deck. Billy rolled over and got to his hands and knees in an attempt to rise. Dog rushed over to him and tried to kick him.

"Billy, look out!" Sheena called. In the excitement she failed to modulate her voice, so that it was a woman's shout which issued from her throat. She felt Hedge looking at her in surprise, but dared not return his gaze, certain that in so doing she would give herself away. Instead she concentrated on the fight below.

Billy reacted to Sheena's warning by rolling to one side just as Dog kicked. He managed to hop up again before Dog could recover for a second kick, and while Dog was off balance, sent a low, whistling punch straight into his groin.

Dog dropped both hands to his groin, and then Billy threw his broken right hand into Dog's Adam's apple as hard as he could. He jerked his hand back in agony but it was worth the pain. Dog choked, then grabbed his neck with both hands. He fell, gagging, to his knees. Billy wanted to hit him one more time. He drew back his hand, then he let it drop to his side. He stood there, looking down at the wheezing Dog.

"You've had your honor, Dog," he said, out of breath himself. "Let us be done with it now." Billy turned his back on Dog and started for the quarter-deck.

"He whipped you, Dog," one of the sailors shouted. "That gentleman bested you good." The others laughed; several threw mocking taunts at Dog.

Dog stood up and looked at the sailors who were now mocking him. Suddenly he grabbed a dagger from one of the men nearest him, and with a yell raised it high over his head, aiming it for Billy's back.

Sheena snatched the dagger from Hedge's waistband

and, with a quick, deft, overhand motion, threw it at Dog. It turned over, flashing once in the sun, then buried itself in Dog's chest, just as he released his knife. The impact thwarted Dog's throw, and his knife sailed somewhat wide of its mark, sticking into Billy's shoulder.

All this had happened in the wink of an eye. The sailors who had seen Dog throw his knife at Billy didn't realize that Sheena had thrown Hedge's knife at Dog a split second earlier. When Dog collapsed with a dagger sticking from his chest, they were surprised, and wondered where it came from.

"Billy," Sheena shouted. She swung out from the shrouds on a hanging rope which carried her over the heads of the gathered sailors and allowed her to drop on the deck just beside him. She pulled Dog's knife from Billy's shoulder, then grabbed the shirt he had removed earlier and used it to bandage his wound.

Dog had struggled back up to his feet. He pulled the bloody knife out of his chest and held it over his head, starting toward Billy.

"By God, you'll join me in hell!" he coughed, trying to reach Billy. He could manage only about two more steps. Then he stopped, dropped the knife, and put his hands to his wound. Blood spilled around his fingers. He looked at Sheena. Then his eyes grew wide with surprise and chilling realization. "It's you!" he said. He looked at the others, then pointed at Sheena. "Mates, we've been tricked. This be a woman." He coughed again, then fell forward on the deck, his blood spreading in a pool beneath him.

"The man went mad before he died," Sheena said nervously. "I've seen it happen before."

"Aye," one of the sailors said. " 'Tis likely to affect any man."

"Dog wasn't mad," Hedge said from his position in the shrouds. "Sean is a woman. What be your real name, girl?"

"What?" Sheena asked, laughing nervously. "What are you talking about?"

"I heard you shout a warnin' to your man," Hedge said. He climbed down from the rigging and stepped through the ring of sailors to confront Sheena. "I'm sayin' you be a woman."

"Well, now," Ledyard said. He had watched the entire affair from his position on the quarter-deck and was now speaking for the first time. "Is that right, Mister Drumm? Have you brought a woman on board in violation of the Articles?"

"He didn't know I was a woman," Sheena said quickly. "I had him fooled."

"How could you fool him, lass? Have you got men's parts?" one of the sailors asked. He laughed at his own comment.

"No, but . . ."

"I knew she was a woman," Billy said quickly, standing up and holding his hand over his wound. "I talked her into coming on board with me. She didn't know about Article Ten, mates, so don't hold that against her."

"Did you know about Article Ten?" Ledyard asked Billy.

"Aye, Captain, I knew about it," Billy answered.

"And you know what the punishment is for violating that article?"

"Aye."

"Run out the plank!" one of the sailors shouted.

"Aye, the plank, the plank," another shouted.

"Hold it!" Mad Jack said, holding his arms up to quiet the crowd. "He has a right to a trial, and I aim to see he gets it."

"Captain, I plead guilty," Billy said quickly. "I only ask that you don't punish Sheena, as she is innocent of any wrongdoing."

"I'm afraid the trial will have to decide that," Ledyard said. "Hedge, you'll have to be the new first mate, seein' as one is already dead 'n the other'n's about to be."

"Aye, Cap'n," Hedge said.

"Make ready for the trial of the prisoner. And run out the plank," he added, looking at the sun. "We've lost enough time already. I want to try him, then feed him to the fishes and get back to ship's business."

"Aye, Cap'n," Hedge said. " 'N the girl?"

"Ah, yes, the girl," Ledyard said. He looked at Sheena and smiled. "I'll think of something."

21

A captain's mast, when someone's life was at stake, was normally a very serious and solemn occasion. Traditionally, rum was passed to members of the crew to fortify them, and the accused was given a double ration.

Ledyard followed tradition and passed the rum around, but it was no solemn occasion. This could be attributed to several factors. One was that Billy Drumm was new and unknown to the crew, having just signed on this very morning. Dog, on the other hand, had, for all his faults, lived and fought with the crew for over a year and was thus one of them. Also, bringing a woman on board was in direct violation of the strongest of all pirate superstitions. Most felt that if the situation wasn't rectified, evil luck would plague them for this entire cruise.

Hedge had placed a table just aft of the mainmast, and Captain Ledyard, as presiding judge, took his seat behind it. He drained the last of his drink, then took his pistol from his waistband and banged the handle of it against the table. "Let's get started," he said. "Bring the prisoner to me."

Billy, prodded with a saber, walked across the deck

to stand before Ledyard's table. His left arm hung limply at his side and he clutched at his left shoulder with his right hand.

"Billy Drumm, the charge is that you brought a woman on board this vessel, contrary to Article Ten of the privateer's code."

"Hell, he's guilty, Cap'n," Hedge said. "Let's feed 'im to the fishes."

"Hold on there, not so fast," Ledyard said. "We gotta' have us a witness."

"A witness? What kind of a witness? Hell, Mad Jack, we all seen him come on board with her."

Mad Jack looked at Sheena. Sick at heart, she was watching the proceedings with downcast eyes. She had talked Billy into this. Now he was about to die, and she felt it was all her fault. Mad Jack smiled at her.

"Well, now, we ain't all seen that she is a woman, have we?"

"What?" Hedge asked.

"Take her clothes off," Mad Jack said. "We can't just up 'n kill a man unless we got absolute proof that he's guilty as charged."

"I'm guilty, damn your black soul to hell!" Billy shouted. "Leave my wife be!"

"His wife?" Hedge asked.

Mad Jack smiled. "I reckon you could say that," he said. "Seein' as how I married 'em." The smile left his face, and he stared at Sheena with lust-inflamed eyes. "Now, get them clothes off of her."

Hedge signaled to two of the seamen, who grabbed Sheena to prevent her from running. Sheena was so dispirited that she offered no resistance at all. Hedge walked over to her. Using his knife, he cut the buttons from her shirt, opened it, then pulled it off. Her firm young breasts popped free, and there was a collective intake of breath from the crew. Next, he opened her pants, then pulled them down, exposing her long, smooth legs. He tossed the pants aside, and Sheena stood on deck, totally nude, before the gaze of over thirty men.

"My God," someone said. "That's the most beautiful woman I've ever seen in my life." There was a moment of stunned silence as the crew looked at Sheena. Sheena, whose heart was heavy for her husband, stood mute before their pitiless gazes.

Billy walked over, picked up a piece of canvas, then carefully draped it around Sheena's shoulders. He kissed her on each cheek, stopping the silent tears in their tracks. Then he kissed her lightly on her lips, still tasting the salt of her tears on his tongue. He walked back to Mad Jack Ledyard's table and drew himself up to full height, standing at attention, holding both arms by his side with total disregard for his wound.

"You have satisfied yourself, sir, that my wife is indeed a woman," he said. "Now I stand guilty as charged, and am ready to accept any sentence as you may direct. I only ask that, as captain of this vessel, you see your responsibility toward this innocent girl."

"You're a brave man at that, Billy Drumm," Ledyard said quietly. He pulled at his beard for a moment. "I sentence you to walk the plank," he said.

Billy turned away from the captain, looked at Sheena with a small smile, then walked quickly toward the rail, where the plank had been put in place. He stepped on it, walked out to the end, and stepped off into space, without another word.

"Billy, no!" Sheena shouted, coming out of her reverie at the last instant. She started toward the rail, but the two sailors who were standing nearest her grabbed her and restrained her.

"What do you want to do with the girl, Mad Jack?" Hedge asked.

"Take her to my cabin," Ledyard said.

"Take her to your cabin? But you can't have her. You know the Articles," Hedge said.

"The Articles say no women, except prisoners, can be on board. This woman is my prisoner," Ledyard said. "Now take her to my cabin." Ledyard pointed to the ship's carpenter. "You, throw that plank overboard and let's get back to business."

"Aye, Cap'n," the carpenter said. He pulled the nails and tossed the plank overboard. Keeping the board that had been used as a plank to cast a man into the sea was nearly as strong a taboo as bringing a woman on board. For such a superstitious lot were the sailors that they believed the man's ghost would be held by the plank and would come back to haunt the ship.

Ledyard stood up and stretched. It had been an unsettling morning and now he was faced with a decision. He could either return for a new first officer, someone who could help him navigate, or he could continue on alone, being the only man left on board who knew the navigation science.

He sighed. There was really no decision to make. If he was going to intercept the H.M.S. *Goodhope* with the rich treasure he knew that she carried, he would have to continue on. That meant little rest for him on this voyage. He would have to take readings by the noonday sun and the midnight stars in order to fix their position.

He thought of the girl in his cabin, then smiled and rubbed his crotch. It might be a tiring trip, he thought, but it wouldn't be a lonely one.

22

It was approximately nine thirty in the morning when Billy stepped off the end of the plank. Sheena had been brought into the captain's cabin immediately thereafter, and was locked in. She knew the door was locked because she tried it, remembering Billy had left the door unlocked for several days without her knowing it.

At the thought of Billy, Sheena felt tears stinging her eyes. Billy had warned her about Article Ten, but Sheena had insisted that she come aboard. Now she realized how selfish that was. After all, it wasn't her life that was in danger; it was his. And she had had no right to take chances with his life.

She looked around the cabin. It was quite large for a ship's cabin. Then she realized that it had been modified, probably to accommodate Mad Jack Ledyard's large frame. She walked over to try the door one more time and found that it was still locked. She shrugged. What difference did it make anyway? Even if the door hadn't been locked, there was nowhere to go.

Sheena gazed through the stern windows and saw

the red dying sun behind them. She was somewhat surprised to discover that it was so late. She also realized at about that time that she was hungry. And no wonder, for she had eaten nothing since the stew she had cooked for Billy last night.

Sheena heard Ledyard's voice just outside the door and realized that he was about to come in. She looked around quickly, trying to find a place to hide, but knew that such an idea was foolish. So she just stood there, hearing the key scratch in the lock and watching the door swing open.

Ledyard stepped inside, then looked at Sheena and smiled broadly. "Well, now, missy," he said. "Have you had a good cry over your dearly departed husband?"

"You'll not have the satisfaction of knowing that, Mad Jack Ledyard," Sheena said.

"Satisfaction, is it? Do you think I'm a cruel man, missy, to take satisfaction in your sufferin'?" Ledyard placed his hands over his heart and assumed a look of sorrow. "I've no such intention. In fact, I feel a need to comfort you in your grief."

"I don't need comforting from the likes of you," Sheena said.

"Sure you do, missy," Ledyard said. He removed his saber and pistol, laid them on the table, then removed his belt. He looked up at Sheena with a big smile on his face and saw that she was eyeing the pistol.

"Missy," he said, wagging his finger at her. "Don't tell me you would think of shooting me with my own pistol?" He laughed and picked the weapon up, then extracted a small piece from the back of it. "There, I've removed the flint, so there's no way to fire the priming pan. It would do you no good to grab it, for it won't discharge."

The smile left Ledyard's face. "Now, missy, I'll give

you a touch o' that comfortin' I promised you." He began to undo his shirt. "I see you managed to get dressed again. That was a waste of time. Get outta' them clothes."

"No," Sheena said, backing away. "Please, Captain, allow me some time for my sorrow."

"I've been sorrowed myself," Ledyard said, still removing his clothes. "Many is the time I've lost good mates in a battle. But I've always found a good romp in bed with a pretty woman snaps me right out of it."

Sheena continued to move away from the captain, trying to keep the table between them. After a moment Ledyard realized what she was doing. He picked the table up and tossed it to one side as effortlessly as if it had been a tin cup. The pistol and saber clattered to the floor, and Sheena made a lunge for the saber. Mad Jack saw what she was going after and managed to kick it away just in the nick of time. He grabbed her.

"You got spirit, girl," he said, smiling at her from behind his thick beard. "I like that in a woman."

Sheena struggled to free herself from his grasp, but she was no match for his bulk and strength. A moment later she felt herself being laid on the oversized bed which dominated the cabin. She felt her clothes being torn away, and, soon, the sensation of air upon her naked skin.

"Lord, now," Mad Jack said, looking at her in true admiration. "Now there's a sight worth dyin' over, n' that's a fact."

Somehow, even in the midst of her struggles and fear, the genuine reverence of Mad Jack's statement got through to her, and a tiny corner of her mind took pride in the compliment.

Then Sheena felt Mad Jack's full weight upon her body. There were no preliminaries of any kind. His view of her naked body had been all the stimulation Mad Jack needed for full arousal. With powerful hands he spread her legs apart and went into her with a lunge.

He was exceptionally large, and he drove into her like a battering ram. She almost cried out in pain but held it in check, refusing to give him any response whatever for his efforts. She closed her eyes tightly, bit her lips, and turned her head to one side, trying to find the strength to endure this ordeal. She thought of Billy, and how she had led him to his death, and realized that what she was going through now was just punishment for her sin. She looked upon it as her penitence, and that helped her get through it.

Ledyard's breath started coming in shorter, sharper gasps. Then, with a groan, he finished, and she felt his semen running down her thigh. The evil thrusting halted. He lay upon her for a moment, limp and spent, and Sheena had the sudden and inexplicable thought that she had won some type of match between them. It was as if the sex had been a battle, and he had emerged spent and defeated while she was energetic and victorious! She felt a sense of triumph, and at that moment forgot all about the pain and degradation she had gone through.

Mad Jack got up from his bed and began putting his clothes back on. He looked over at Sheena, who lay stretched out on his bed. Bars of late evening light streamed in through the shutters, splashing on her in alternate lines of light and dark. She raised one arm above her head and the action brought a nipple into the light, highlighting it in the shadows. She looked at Mad Jack with lips which were slightly pouting. Her eyes were green and deep. He sighed.

"Missy, 'tis easy to see why your man could face walkin' the plank for you. You've somethin' about you that could drive a man wild."

"It's in my blood," Sheena said, for the first time taking a somewhat perverse pride in her tainted background. She sat up. "Jack, I'm hungry," she said.

Ledyard laughed. It was the same cannon-deep laugh she had heard when they first came aboard early that morning.

"I fail to see what is so funny about a person being hungry," Sheena said. "I haven't eaten all day."

"I'm sorry, girl," Ledyard said. "It's just that most of the women prisoners we get on this ship are such frightened nannies that they wouldn't think of eating on their first day. And you come right out and admit that you are hungry. 'Tis not the way of proper young ladies."

"I'm not a proper young lady," Sheena said, walking over to put her clothes back on. "And I may be your prisoner, but I came aboard of my own free will."

"Aye, that you did, lass," Ledyard admitted. "Very well, I'll get us some soup and bread."

"Jack, must I be kept locked up?" Sheena asked.

"Yes."

"Why? I can't escape. We are in the middle of the ocean."

"Because you are a prisoner," Ledyard said.

"Oh, I see," Sheena said. "In other words, you are frightened that if you don't keep me a prisoner the others will make you walk the plank, is that it?"

"No," Ledyard said. "I'm the captain of this ship. No one is going to make me walk the plank."

"You mean you aren't afraid?"

"Of course not."

"Then grant me parole to roam the ship," she said.

"You'll just get in the way."

"I'm the best sailor you have on this ship," Sheena replied hotly. "And I know the science of navigation as well as any ship's officer."

"You know navigation?" Ledyard asked, surprised by her statement.

"Yes."

"How came you by such knowledge?"

"From Billy's books."

Ledyard laughed. "Books? You think you can learn such things from books?"

"Yes."

"Impossible. It can't be done."

"Oh, but it can be done," Sheena said. "And after dinner I shall prove it to you. Provided, that is, that you allow me the use of the astrolabe and almanac. And the ship's timepiece. You do have one, don't you?"

"Aye, and a fine timepiece it is, too," Ledyard said.

Sheena dressed then, and walked over to open the *Connaissance des Temps,* an almanac published by the French government which established the known positions of all stars by hour and date. She looked through it for a few minutes, recalling the information she had read in Billy's books. She had never actually plotted a fix, but she had read how it was done so many times that she had it committed to memory and was certain that she could do it.

"I'll get us some grub," Ledyard said with a grunt. He left the cabin, leaving Sheena alone.

Sheena looked over at the floor, where the pistol and saber lay. For a brief moment she contemplated taking the saber, waiting behind the door, and killing Ledyard when he returned to the room. But the thought passed as soon as it surfaced, for she knew that such a thing would be foolish. There would be no escape after she committed the deed, and she would have accomplished nothing.

Besides, she admitted to herself, she was still infatuated with the idea of going to sea. Though she would have preferred the idyllic voyage she had planned with Billy, such was not to be, and it would be best that she accommodated herself to the facts.

Ledyard returned a moment later, carrying two bowls of steaming soup and a large piece of black bread. Sheena was sitting at the table studying the astrolabe. She had never actually seen one before, and Ledyard smiled at her. Suddenly he remembered having left both his pistol and saber in the room and looked over to where they had been in quick fear. Then, seeing that they were in the same place he had left them, he smiled even more broadly.

"Well, I see you didn't try to take my pistol and shoot me," he said. "I guess maybe that means you like ole Mad Jack just a little, huh?"

"I hate you for what you did to my husband," Sheena said.

"It wasn't me, girl, it was the privateer's code," Ledyard said. "He knew the chances he was takin'. And I mind that you did too, so don't get uppity with me. You kilt him as much as I did, girl."

Sheena felt her cheeks flame in embarrassment. She turned her head rather than look him in the eyes, because his remark had been a telling one.

"I thought so," Ledyard said. He set the soup bowls and the bread on the table. "Let's eat, girl."

The soup wasn't all that tasty, but it was hearty and filling. So filling, in fact, that Sheena was unable to eat all of hers. She sat there silently while Ledyard attacked his. Ledyard was a serious eater. He made no idle conversation while he ate, and he reminded Sheena of one of the yard dogs on her father's plantation.

That's funny, she thought. That was the first time she had thought of, or missed, her father since she had left home. And even now, sitting in the ship's cabin of a privateer captain who had just raped her, she felt no remorse for having left her family.

It grew dark outside, and Sheena could hear the sounds of the sea rushing past the ship's hull. There were groans in the wood and creaks in the rope. Occasionally one of the sails would give out a thunderclap as the canvas spilled wind.

"Do you want the rest of yours?" Ledyard asked, looking at Sheena's bowl.

"No," Sheena said quietly.

Ledyard finished her soup as well, then took the last crust of bread, sopped it across the bottom of both bowls with his fingers, and poked it through his beard into his mouth.

"Now, girl, show me your tricks."

"If I can do it," Sheena said, "you'll allow me the freedom of the ship."

"I'll think on it," Ledyard promised.

Having exacted that much of a promise from him, Sheena took the astrolabe and almanac with her and started out on deck. Ledyard followed right behind.

When Sheena reached the deck, she caught her breath at the beauty of the scene. The night air was clear and sharp in the moonlight, and the sea stretched out, rolling gently to the horizon, given texture by the whitecaps, which flickered like molten silver when a wave spilled over.

Sheena walked to the ship's rail, the better to take in the beautiful sight, and was startled by the appearance of green lights in the water. Hundreds of brilliant green streaks glowed at her, as if a city of lights were just beneath the surface.

"Them green lights is phosphor'nt fish," Ledyard said.

"Oh, I wish I were a man," Sheena said. "If I were, I would never leave the sea."

"Aye, missy," Ledyard said, sharing the moment with her with a surprising amount of feeling. "I put to sea when I was but a pup, and pray that my body will feed the fishes instead of the worms when I'm gone."

Sheena didn't want to share her intimacies with Mad Jack Ledyard. It was enough that he had her body anytime he wanted it. She would jealously guard her soul from him. She picked up the astrolabe and walked back to the quarter-deck to begin her sightings. She took the fixes of several stars, then located them in the almanac.

As Sheena was thus engaged, several of the sailors drifted back to see what was going on. The navigation instruments were strictly the domain of the officers and none of the men understood their mysteries. To see a girl with them was an amazing thing. The men stood by, so shocked by the sight that for the moment they forgot their superstitions against women.

"We'll have to return to your cabin, Jack," Sheena said. "I'll need your charts."

A few minutes later, Sheena, after working some figures, pointed to a spot on the chart. "I make us right here," she said.

"You mean you can locate us without having to wait for midnight?" Jack asked, amazed by what the girl had shown him.

"You mean you can't?"

"Of course I can," Ledyard sputtered. "It's just that—well—I didn't think you could, that's all."

"Where are we headed?" Sheena asked.

"We are going to latitude twenty-seven degrees north, longitude seventy-seven degrees west," Ledyard said. He smiled. "There's going to be a fat prize there for the taking. If we can get there in time," he added.

Sheena looked at the chart. "We're headed due south now," she said.

"Aye," Ledyard said. "That's my intention. We head due south until we come to the twenty-seventh parallel; then we head due east until we reach our spot."

"We should be going south by southeast," Sheena said. " 'Twould cut off this dog leg and save us at least two days sailing time."

"Aye," Jack said. "But 'tis easier to find our way by running down."

Sheena laughed. "I read that it was done that way in the old days. But there's no need for that with modern instruments. Jack, let me navigate for you."

"No, 'tis out of the question," Jack said.

"Why? Is it because you are too proud to admit that I can do it and you can't?"

"I can do it," Jack said.

"Jack, you'd let your pride stand in the way of a prize ripe for the picking?" Sheena teased.

"'Tis not my feelings," Jack said. "I've the crew to consider."

"But haven't you told me you are the captain? Didn't you say that you don't fear the crew?"

Jack ran his hand through his hair and looked at Sheena, finally letting out a loud sigh. "Very well, girl, you shall be my navigator," he said. "But mind, you're still my prisoner as well, and as such, you'll be expected to do my bidding when it comes to affairs of the heart."

"I'll share your bed, Jack," Sheena said easily, resignedly. "But you'll never share my heart."

23

There were four Anglo-French and Anglo-Spanish wars fought between 1689 and 1763. And though a peace treaty signed in 1713 technically ended the war known as the War of Spanish Succession, trade right disagreements in the Caribbean caused a continuous state of belligerency to exist between England and her American colonies, and France and Spain. Ships which traded in violation of these agreements were said to be smugglers and were fair game for capture by privateers flying the colors of their sponsoring nations.

The *Marcus B.* was just such a privateer. A privateer was a privately owned vessel, armed and manned at the owner's expense, for the purpose of capturing the merchant craft of belligerent nations. International law required that privateers have a commission from the government, called a letter of marque, and sail under the flag of the government which granted the letter. The owner of the vessel held one half a "share" in any booty legally captured, and the captain and crew divided up the remainder.

The most important need of a privateer was that she

be fast. Her armament need not be heavy. A privateer was not intended to fight a regular naval battle and generally avoided the enemy's naval ships and privateers, for these would only produce empty holds if captured. The privateer carried only enough cannon to influence the lightly armed merchantmen into surrendering. Should that fail, she would close with the merchantman and board her. Such encounters were nearly always decided in favor of the privateer, because she carried more crew than the merchantman, and this crew was selected for its fighting ability. Also, as each crewman of a privateer vessel had a personal stake in the prize, each had a greater incentive to fight.

Often, however, targets of opportunity didn't present themselves, and many a privateer turned pirate, just by striking the national colors it sailed under and hoisting the Jolly Roger. This served notice that it would attack merchantmen of any nation, including its own.

Because of Sheena's navigational ability, the *Marcus B.* had reached the shipping lanes in plenty of time. It was in position to move in rapidly when the sails of an approaching ship were spotted by the lookout, high in the crow's nest.

"Sail ho!" the lookout sung down.

"Where away?"

"Four points off the larboard bow!"

Sheena leaped into the rigging and climbed halfway up to look in the direction indicated. There, just over the horizon, she saw a tiny white speck.

"All hands aloft," Ledyard shouted. "Lay on all sail. Run out the spinnakers. Helmsman, we've a course close to the wind. We'll run full and by."

"Aye, aye, Cap'n," the helmsman answered.

The *Marcus B.* came alive with sailors in her rigging and in moments the wand-thin masts were bent under the press of full sail. The ship fairly leaped forward, cutting a wake across the blue-green water, flying toward the spot on the horizon that now could be seen even from the deck.

Sheena felt a keen sense of excitement building inside her. She worked alongside the sailors. Such was the cooperation that they forgot for the moment that she was a girl. They were concerned only with rigging the ship for all possible speed.

"Will this be your first fight then, Sheena?" one of the sailors asked easily.

"Aye," Sheena answered.

"Then you wouldn't mind a few words of advice?"

"No, I would appreciate it," Sheena replied, grateful that one of the men had taken the trouble to talk to her.

"You're gonna' be scared when we go aboard her. Everybody is. The only thing is, they are a lot more scared than us, so scream somethin' fierce. That scares 'em even more. Remember, they ain't nothin' but merchantmen, and we're the scourge o' the seas." He grinned broadly, and Sheena saw that three of his teeth were broken halfway down to the gum. With his grin the gap looked comical. In a hideous scream she knew it would be fearsome.

"That's right," another sailor offered. "I mind the time I was on a merchantman when we was attacked. I was that scared by the howlin' that I messed in my pants. A lot more scared than I have been since I was taken into the brethren."

"Yeah," the first said. "And he done brought up another good point. Best you go up to the head sometime 'afore we attack. Don't feel shamed by it. We all do it. Cleanin' out the bowels 'afore the battle keeps you from doin' what he done."

"And be on your guard at all times," the other sailor said again.

"Prepare for battle!" Ledyard shouted.

The sailors began scrambling around again, bringing

ropes and grappling hooks and lying them alongside
the sail. Those who had shoes removed them. Their
hair was tied back out of their way. Shot and powder
were brought into position and placed behind the
guns. Breeching ropes were checked. Sponges were laid
in to swab the barrels, and a charge of gunpowder and
a round of grapeshot were loaded in each cannon.

"Are none of the cannons loaded with balls?" Sheena
asked.

"No, for we've no wish to sink the ship. Her cargo is
of little use to us if she lies in Davy Jones's locker. A
taste of the grape, now, oftentimes that's all that's
needed to make the faint-hearted captain call for
quarter."

"Cap'n, she be flyin' the Union Jack," the lookout
called down.

"Aye, that be the *Goodhope* then."

"The Union Jack," Sheena said in surprise. "She's
English?"

"Be she in ballast?" Ledyard called up to the lookout.

"No, she's heavy-laden, for she's low in the water."

"Ah, a rich prize then," Ledyard said. "Just as I
was told."

"Jack, you can't take her!" Sheena said. "You hold
an English commission. You're flying the English
flag."

"Aye, you're right," Ledyard said. "Sheena, in my
cabin, in my desk, you'll find the Jolly Roger."

"The Jolly Roger? You're a real pirate then?"

Everyone laughed, and Sheena felt her cheeks flush-
ing bright red.

"Aye, missy, and the boldest of the sea," Jack replied. "Now, fetch the ensign, or confine yourself to
my cabin as my prisoner. It's up to you."

The others looked at Sheena to see what she would
do. Her seamanship and navigational skill over the
last week had nearly won them over. Now she was

faced with a challenge. She could either be one of them, or she could prove they were right in their superstitious feelings about women.

Sheena thought it over. What did she have to go back to? If she was recognized anywhere in the colonies, she would be returned to her father, who would send her to the convent. Billy was dead. She had only the sea for her comfort. What was it Captain Collier had said on board the *Cassandra*? He said that he had salt-water for blood. Sheena felt that same way. And where else, save on an outlaw ship, would she be likely to fulfill her dream of going to sea?

"I'll get it," she said. To her surprise her statement was greeted by a cheer from the men. When she came back with the black flag, one of the men tossed her a saber.

"Can you use that, girl?" he asked, as she caught it from him.

"Yes," Sheena said. She swung it about. "It's a mite heavier than the foil I'm used to, but I'll manage."

"Let me have it," the sailor said, holding his hand out. "We've the better part of two hours before we close with them. I'll work on the balance some; it'll make it easier for you."

"Thank you," Sheena said, surrendering her blade back to him.

Sheena walked over to the rail and looked across the narrowing gap of water toward the ship. She wondered what was going on over there. Did they realize they were about to be in a battle? Were they as frightened as she was? And how would she act? She discovered, to her surprise, that she was more frightened by how she would do than she was by the prospect of being killed or wounded. She had nearly won the men over. She didn't want to lose them now by some act of cowardice.

Sheena felt her stomach turning. Then she was conscious of a steady stream of men visiting the head. She remembered the sailor's warning and, the next time the head was free, took advantage of it.

They drew steadily closer to the other ship, and finally were close enough for Sheena to see activity on its deck. Then she heard their captain hailing them across the water, his voice being carried weakly but clearly by the megaphone.

"What ship, and whence?"

Ledyard swung the megaphone out. "Be ye the *Goodhope*?"

"Aye!" the *Goodhope* captain responded. "What ship, and whence?" he asked again.

Ledyard dropped the megaphone and looked over at Hedge, who held the black flag with the white skull and crossbones. It had already been fastened to the halyard. "Run up the Jolly Roger, Hedge," Ledyard said quietly. He swung the megaphone out. "We be the *Marcus B*. I'm Jack Ledyard, gentleman of the sea, come to make my fortune!"

At almost the precise moment the Jolly Roger reached the top of the mast and played out in the breeze, a cannonball crashed through the rail on one side of the ship, passed across the deck without hitting anything, and smashed through the rail on the other side. It splashed in the water a hundred yards beyond. It was the first time Sheena had ever seen a cannonball fired. As she had no concept of such things as the speed of sound, the fact that it had arrived and departed in silence seemed eerie. Only after the ball had passed through both rails did the sound of the cannon that fired it reach them.

"Return fire!" Ledyard bellowed, and the six cannon on board the *Marcus B*. boomed and covered the water with billowing smoke. When the smoke cleared away, Sheena saw three of the *Goodhope*'s crew facedown on the deck and two more leaning against the rail, clutching their wounds. The effect of the grape had been devastating.

"Do you ask for quarter?" Ledyard shouted.

The captain of the *Goodhope* answered by firing his pistol at the *Marcus B.*, more out of rage than in hope of actually inflicting damage.

"Helmsman, bring her alongside," Ledyard ordered. "Mates, into the shrouds. Prepare to board!"

The sailors around Sheena let out a terrifying shout and climbed into the shrouds, some holding their sabers aloft, others holding the ropes with grappling hooks, preparatory to securing the *Goodhope* to the *Marcus B*. Sheena went aloft with them and found a line she could use to swing aboard when they were alongside.

There was a crunching sound as the two ships crashed together, and Sheena was nearly knocked from her perch by the jar of the impact. The grappling hooks were tossed and the ships secured. The sailors around her gave out another terrible shout and started leaping across to the *Goodhope*. Sheena took a deep breath, then swung across before she could think better of it. Instantly she found herself on the deck of the *Goodhope*, confronting one of its sailors. Brandishing a pike, he lunged at Sheena. Sheena parried the thrust easily, then, just as she had learned in fencing, executed an immediate counterattack. The difference was that instead of touching her opponent with the blunt tip of a fencing foil, she thrust into him with the point of her saber.

It had been one thing to throw the knife at Dog when he was about to kill Billy—Dog was himself about to commit murder, and she had acted quickly and instinctively to save the man she loved—but this was something entirely different. Here was a man who was a stranger to her, an innocent seaman who had fought only to save his own life.

Sheena could have killed him by following through with her thrust. Instead she withdrew the blade quickly, cringing at the sight of its bloody tip. She watched the man fall to the deck wounded, though not fatally. He dropped his pike and Sheena kicked it away. Then, she turned away just in time to see Hedge's head lopped off in one swing by a huge man who was fighting against three other pirates, handling them all with ease. He was bigger even than Ledyard. His head was completely bald except for a single shock of hair which grew from the very top and hung, braided, down to his massive shoulders. He was barechested, and wore flaring pants of red-and-white stripes. He was laughing at the efforts of the sailors to kill him.

"Quarter!" the captain of the *Goodhope* shouted at that moment. "By all that's holy, Captain, call off your attack!"

"Hold it, mates!" Ledyard shouted, leaping up to the quarter-deck. "He's struck his colors."

"Somebody better tell this big son of a bitch!" one of the men struggling with the big sailor shouted, his voice bordering on terror.

Ledyard pulled his pistol from his waistband and pointed it at the big man. "Captain, call off your giant or I'll put a ball in his head!"

"Habib," the *Goodhope* captain yelled. "Put down your sword!"

Habib looked at the pirates. By now eight had closed around him. He laughed at them, then threw his saber into the deck in front of them. It stabbed nearly four inches into the planking, then whipped back and forth like a willow in a windstorm.

"Oh, please, terrible pirates," Habib said, holding his hands together in mock, prayerful supplication. "Please, don't hurt Habib!" He spit on the deck, then laughed again.

"Where did you get that son of a bitch?" Ledyard asked the *Goodhope* captain.

"In Istanbul," the captain said. "He can do the work of three men, but he is crazy in the head."

"Habib," Ledyard called. "How would you like to come with us?"

Habib smiled. "Habib would make better pirate than you have now."

"Good. You are one of us now. Help us to transfer the cargo. Captain, if you'll come aboard my ship, sir, I'll share a tot of rum with you."

The *Goodhope* captain ran his hand through his hair and looked at his dead and wounded. "No," he said. "I thank you for granting us quarter, and I appreciate your offer of rum. But best I stay with my ship. Will you be sinking her?"

"No," Ledyard said. "I have what I want, and you are no danger to us." Ledyard looked over and saw Sheena leaning against the rail. He smiled at her. "Missy, you did well for your first battle," he said.

"Missy?" the *Goodhope* captain said. "Glory be, you mean that is a girl?"

Sheena untied her hair and shook her head, to let it fall to her shoulders.

"Naw," Ledyard said, laughing his cannon-booming laugh. "She ain't no girl, Cap'n. She's a hellcat, she is."

24

During the brief time Billy and Sheena had been together, Billy's lovemaking had taken Sheena to the highest summits of ecstasy. At those moments she couldn't help but feel glad that she was tainted with bad blood, for she was certain that no proper young lady could enjoy sex as much as she. She had even enjoyed it the two times Billy had raped her. He was a skilled and considerate lover, and the rapes, though forceful, had not been brutal. They were fire-and-ice experiences, tender even in their savagery.

But if Billy satisfied her, Mad Jack left her totally unfulfilled. Once Sheena accepted the fact that there was little chance of escaping his demands, she believed that her own passions were strong enough to allow her to enjoy sex with anyone who was a capable and thoughtful lover.

But Mad Jack wasn't a lover. He was a brutal and inept seducer, who thought only of himself and used Sheena to fulfill his own needs.

Now, having successfully captured the prize ship and heading for Nassau to sell the goods, Mad Jack celebrated every night with rum and seldom drew a sober breath. Though he made frequent demands of

Sheena's body, liquor rendered him nearly impotent. Once he passed out on top of her and she had to struggle to get free. When she was free, she pushed him off angrily and fell into a frustrated sleep in the large bed, while Mad Jack snored drunkenly on the floor.

A knock on the cabin door awakened Sheena the next morning. She sat up in bed to see the sun's jewels dancing about in the cabin, reflections off the bright water. Mad Jack was still asleep on the floor, a line of spittle stretching from his lips to his great, hairy hands, which he was using as a pillow. Sheena pulled the sheet up to cover her breasts.

"Come in," she called.

The door swung open and Habib stepped inside. He was carrying a keg of rum.

"What is that?" Sheena asked.

"The captain asked Habib to bring more rum today," Habib said.

"The captain won't be awake for another two hours," Sheena said dryly. "But I'm sure that's the first thing he'll reach for. Put it there, on his desk."

Sheena pointed toward the desk and when she did the bedsheet fell down, exposing her breasts. She pulled the sheet back up quickly, then looked at Habib, noticing with some pleasure that the giant was staring at her.

Well, why not? she thought. She was certainly beyond the innocent virgin stage. She was little more than the captain's slave anyway, so she might as well accommodate herself to that fact and derive whatever pleasure might be salvaged from such a situation. Habib seemed strong enough and manageable enough for her purpose. Besides, none of the others in the crew interested her in the least.

Sheena looked quickly at Ledyard. He appeared to be sound asleep. She could never be sure, because his left eye, as always, was wide open. But she had grown used to that staring eye, so it didn't bother her.

"Habib," she said, smiling. "Come, sit on the bed with me."

"You are the captain's woman," Habib said.

"I am not his woman," Sheena said. "I was Billy's woman, but now my dear, sweet husband is dead, and I am no one's woman. I shall do as I wish."

Habib walked over to the bed and sat where she indicated. She smiled at him and raised one hand up to touch his bull-like neck. Again the sheet fell away, and this time she made no effort to replace it. "I have never seen a man as strong as you," she said.

Habib grinned proudly and flexed his arms to make a muscle. He took Sheena's hand and placed it on the knot of flesh, then, flexing and relaxing his arms, he made his muscles jump and quiver like something alive under Sheena's hands.

Sheena suddenly thought of the delightful irony of having the captain made a cuckold in his own bed. It served him right, for his inadequacy as a surrogate for Billy had left Sheena's nerves raw with frustration. Now she discovered that the brute animal strength of this giant was arousing her. She felt her skin begin to tingle and she labored to keep her breathing calm. She wondered if she could hold sway over him by the power of her sex. She was bound to try. She discovered that she was getting more excited by the idea of bringing such a brute to bear than she was by any actual attraction he held for her. She felt herself dampen, and a warmth spread through her body.

"You seem nervous," Sheena said to Habib. "Am I making you nervous?"

"Yes," Habib said.

"Now, why would I make you nervous?" Sheena teased. "Surely you've been with a woman before? I'll bet you've even held a woman's breast." As she spoke she moved his hand to her breast, then stared into his bulging eyes.

Habib's eyes were touched by hunger, true enough,

but there was something else in them. Something deep and sad and mysterious, and Sheena found herself wondering about it. But when Habib began to knead her breasts, she put the wonder aside and lay back to enjoy his supplication. His hands were firm, yet amazingly tender, like iron encased in velvet. It was the first time since Billy that anyone had done anything to try and respond to her needs. She sighed and pulled the sheet away from her, exposing her entire body to him.

"Oh, Habib, that feels wonderful," she purred, arching and stretching her body like a cat under the affectionate rub of its owner.

Habib beamed under her compliment. He moved one hand down her stomach, slipping gently and knowingly into all the right places.

Sheena thrust her hand deep into Habib's pants, feeling the muscles of his abdomen, the coarse bush of his hair, the large and throbbing testicles . . . and nothing else!

Sheena opened her eyes in surprise and looked into Habib's face, and saw again the sad and mysterious expression she had seen earlier. Only now it was joined by an expression of pain unlike any she'd ever seen before.

"Habib? What is it? You have no—"

Habib pulled her hand gently out of his pants, then opened them, exposing himself to her. There was nothing there except a knotty-looking piece of scar tissue.

"Four years ago Habib was prisoner of the Mongols," Habib explained. "Habib kill many before capture, and in their anger, they took this." He pointed to the emptiness. "Mongols are very smart. They know that if take everything, Habib soon not care if Habib not a man. But leave this," he hefted his testicles, "and Habib still want woman. Want, but no can have." He looked at the floor in shame.

"Oh, Habib, I'm so sorry," Sheena said, genuinely

moved by his plight. Tears welled in her eyes as she realized that her temptations had made his situation worse.

"Ha, ha, ha!" Ledyard suddenly laughed, springing up from the floor.

"Jack, I thought you were asleep!" Sheena gasped.

"This eye never sleeps," he said, pointing to the bulging socket that was always open. "So, missy, you thought to have another man in my bed, did you? Well, next time you try that, be sure you pick a man!" He laughed again.

"Habib is a man," Sheena said. "And without his parts, he would be a better lover than you, you drunken lout!"

This time it was Habib's time to laugh.

"What do you mean?" Jack sputtered. "I've bedded you every night."

"Bedded me? Why you drunken old fool, the youngest cabin boy or the oldest faggot afloat could do more for a woman in bed than you. Next time you capture a woman, capture an old hag who has had her time. She might be grateful for anything you can do. But don't come around me anymore, Mad Jack Ledyard. I'm too much woman for you."

"You're forgetting your place, missy. You're my prisoner," Ledyard said. "And you'll do anything I tell you to do."

"I'm not your prisoner any longer," Sheena said, getting out of bed and padding naked over to her clothes. "I've fought as a member of this crew and I've earned my place in it. Habib, help me move out of here. I'll find a place to throw my blanket."

"Now, you just hold on there," Jack yelled. "I'm captain of this ship, and you'll go nowhere without my say-so."

"Mad Jack, the only way you are going to stop me from going through that door is by killing me," Sheena said defiantly.

Habib moved quickly to place his six-foot-nine-inch frame between Sheena and Ledyard.

"Mad Jack kill Sheena, Habib kill Mad Jack," he said menacingly.

Ledyard looked at the two of them for a moment, then dismissed them both with a wave of his hand. "Go on," he said. "Get out of here. You deserve a man with no parts. And you," he said to Habib, "you are just what the captain of the *Goodhope* said you are. You are crazy!"

25

There were two primary reasons for men joining the brethren. First and foremost was the chance to share in the treasure captured by the ship. But another, nearly as important reason, was the lack of discipline on board pirate ships.

Merchant sailors had to be careful to show the proper respect for their officers and to respond quickly to orders; otherwise they would find themselves on the receiving end of a lashing or confined to the brig receiving only bread and water.

On board pirate vessels, the officers and crew were partners in the operation, so there was no such thing as self-abnegation. Minor punishments didn't exist. Compared with merchant mariners, pirate crews lived a life of ease.

It must be said in defense of merchantmen, however, that such strict discipline was necessary to run such a ship. Without the incentive of an illicit reward, the merchant captain had only discipline and order to rely upon. That the New World was developed into a primary market for Europe in less than a hundred years is indicative of the fact that their system of seamanship was effective.

At this precise moment the *Marcus B.,* bound for Nassau with its hold full of captured bounty, was little more than a merchant ship. True, its sailors all owned a share in the goods, but the anticipation of the hunt, the hunger of an empty hold, and the excitement of an upcoming fight were not there. Therefore, they had no incentive to make them superior sailors. And, as they had no discipline either, the *Marcus B.* was, by all means of reckoning, a sloppy ship.

Mad Jack Ledyard, whose bed had been deserted by Sheena, sought recompense from rum and scarcely ventured out of his cabin. The sailors considered their primary duty to be the capturing of a prize vessel, and as that had been accomplished and they did not have to face the wrath of a captain, they spent most of their time drunk as well. In fact, it was a wonder that the vessel was proceeding toward Nassau at all, since all necessary work was done purely on a voluntary basis.

Sheena continued the navigation. Of necessity, she was learning all the other aspects of sailing as well. She could handle the helm as well as any and better than most. She learned what sails went with what wind conditions and she could tell from the feel of the wheel if the ship was improperly rigged.

Habib became Sheena's muscles. The fact that she had not belittled him when she learned his terrible secret seemed to instill a fierce loyalty in him. He responded to her slightest command as if she were his lord and master.

It was common knowledge that Sheena had absented herself from the captain's bed, and at first the crew thought that it was in favor of Habib. But as Sheena spread her blankets on deck and slept in full view of the watch, it was soon obvious that Habib wasn't enjoying her favors any more than the captain was.

That would seem to leave the door open for anyone else to try and move in. But Sheena discouraged the few attempts which were made, and the thought of having to cross Habib discouraged any ideas that some may have had about taking her by stealth or force.

Still, the sight of Sheena was a constant reminder to the men of the pleasures of a woman. They spent many a drunken hour lusting after her and looking ahead to spending their share of the loot in the pleasure houses of Nassau.

On the last day before making Nassau all the crew seemed bound to celebrate, and, as there were signs of an approaching fog, Sheena went to Ledyard's cabin to complain of the quality of the seamanship.

"You take the ship in," Ledyard said, belching in drunkenness and staring at her with the exaggerated eye.

"Handling the ship in the open sea is one thing, Jack," Sheena said. "But bringing it in across the shallows and shoals of the islands, especially at night and during a fog, is something entirely different. I can't do it, and you know I can't do it."

"Ha," Ledyard laughed. "And so you've come to beg me to do it for you. You've need for a man after all, for all your show of needin' no one."

"If I needed a man, I wouldn't have come to you, Jack Ledyard," Sheena said hotly. "If truth were known, I don't think you are capable of taking us in either, besotted as you are."

"Methinks you're right," Ledyard said, belching again. "Give the order to furl sail and throw out a sea anchor. We'll stand dead in the water overnight and make landfall on the morrow."

"You'll have to give the order," Sheena said. "If you can find someone sober enough to go aloft, and if they will obey your order."

"Of course they'll obey my order, girl. I'm their captain," Ledyard said, hiccuping as he spoke.

Ledyard did manage to find a couple of sailors who weren't too drunk to stand, and he was able to cajole them into climbing the rigging to furl sail, though

Sheena and Habib had to do the lion's share of the work. Finally, at about nightfall, the *Marcus B.* stood dead in the water, and the sailors, content that their work had been done, drank themselves into a drunken slumber.

Shortly after nightfall the evening mist turned to fog, and it reached out with long gray fingers to cover the ship and wrap it securely in its grasp. All wind stopped. Even the movement of the sea seemed slowed by the heavy blanket.

Sheena, nervous and irritable at being on board a vessel manned by a drunken crew, wandered around the deck. She understood the men's desire for independence. It was what made a man a good pirate. But if she were captain, she would have instilled a little discipline in them.

Sheena stood near the rail on the larboard side of the quarter-deck, peering out into the fog. There was such a dreamlike quality to the scene that it was hard to distinguish fantasy from reality. There was movement on board the ship, no more than shadows gliding through the fog, moving soundlessly about. At first she didn't perceive them, and then when she did, she wasn't sure if they were real or if she was dreaming them. Initially there were only two or three, then five, then several, and then, with her hair standing on end, Sheena saw one of the figures materialize right on the quarter-deck.

"You are armed with a rapier, monsieur, use it," the figure challenged, and Sheena realized that these were no apparitions but real people, and her very life was in danger!

"Boarders!" she shouted. "All hands, we're under attack!"

Habib heard his mistress's warnings. He was on his feet at once, catching four of the invaders by surprise. They were literally pushed into the sea by him before they could react. Six others quickly took up the fight, however, and as Habib was without a weapon, managed to subdue him.

The fight put up by the drunken crew of the *Marcus B.*, if indeed it could be called a fight, was short and ineffective. Mad Jack Ledyard, in one last blaze of glory, went down fighting. He took two with him, but less than a moment after the invaders had boarded the ship, he was killed, with his head severed to be displayed on a pike. His bad eye stayed open, to stare menacingly at his murderers.

"Quarter!" the *Marcus B.* crew began to yell, and soon they were herded together under the guard of the boarders.

The short battle was over. Yet throughout the ship the ring of blade on blade continued, as two figures were engaged in combat on the quarter-deck.

Sheena was surprised by the tenacity of her adversary. Her advantage over most men lay in the fact that they tried to gain a victory by their strength, while she was content to finesse their strength against them. This swordsman, however, used skill and grace, and Sheena soon realized that she was losing ground.

"*Mon Dieu,* you have more skill than anyone I have faced in a long time," her opponent said. "But you are losing. Ask for quarter."

"No," Sheena replied. "You ask for quarter!"

Sheena thought she saw an opening and moved quickly to take advantage of it. But her thrust was parried easily, and then, in a whipping motion, the sword of her opponent clashed with hers and jerked hers free from her hand. It flew across the rail, and Sheena heard the faint splash as it hit the water.

"Now, my brave one," the swordsman said, holding the tip of the rapier against Sheena's neck, "say whatever prayers you know before you die."

"No," Habib called. "Do not kill my mistress! Kill Habib instead!"

"Mistress?" the swordsman said, looking at Sheena with a quizzical smile. "So, you are a girl?"

"Aye," Sheena said, removing her cap and shaking her hair free. "You can save your boasting, for the person you've bested is just a woman."

"Oh, no, mademoiselle, do not say *just* a woman. You do not do yourself justice, for you are a magnificent woman. I am Jean Garneau, at your service."

"Capitaine," one of Garneau's men called. "What shall we do with these English dogs?"

"Use them to transfer the booty from their hold to the *Croix de Triomphe*," Captain Garneau said. "Then cut their rudderpost and set them adrift."

"*Oui, mon capitaine*," the sailor said.

"Behold your capitaine," Garneau said to Sheena, pointing to Mad Jack's severed head. "See how his head decorates my pike? I will return it to Nassau and collect the reward."

Sheena saw Ledyard's head, then looked away quickly.

"Ah, but I am indelicate," Garneau said. "Ledyard was your lover, *non*?"

"No," Sheena said.

"Please, I am French, and therefore a . . . how do you say it? Romantic? You can tell me if he was your lover."

"He was not my lover," Sheena said.

"But he did make love to you?"

"That, sir, is none of your business," Sheena replied hotly. "You've bested me, and you've captured our ship. But I will not tell you my secrets."

"You are right," Garneau said. "Please forgive me, for I had no right to pry into a woman's secret affairs." There was a twinkle in Garneau's eyes. "For after all, we all have secrets, do we not?"

"Capitaine, the giant," one of the sailors said.

"What about the giant?"

"He refuses to work. He won't do anything until he knows what is to become of his mistress."

"She is to be taken aboard the *Croix de Triomphe*," Garneau said. "Take her to my cabin."

"I am to go aboard your ship?" Sheena asked. "Why?"

"As you say, I bested you," Garneau said. "You are at my mercy. Tell me, what is your name?"

"Sheena. Sheena Drumm," Sheena said, taking Billy's name as her own for the first time.

"Well, Sheena. Will your giant allow you to go peacefully, or must he be killed?"

"If you kill Habib, it will be expensive for you," Sheena warned. "For he will kill four of yours while dying."

"Perhaps if you spoke to him it would prevent needless bloodshed," Garneau suggested.

"Perhaps, if you let him come with me."

Garneau looked at Habib, who was glaring back. "I must say that the countenance of your giant, to say nothing of his muscles, frightens me. Are you sure you can handle him?"

"Aye," Sheena said. "And *only* I can handle him."

"Very well, you shall have your wish. He may go with you. LeClerc, take them to the ship. I shall be there shortly."

"*Oui, mon capitaine,*" LeClerc said.

Sheena was directed to the rail, then over the side and down to a waiting longboat. At a signal from her, Habib came quietly. There were two sailors manning oars in the longboat, and they began rowing through the fogbank as soon as Sheena and Habib were aboard. Sheena noticed that the oars were wrapped with cloth. As the sailors pulled them they barely cleaned the water; thus the sound, already muzzled by the fog, was made even quieter by design, and it was little wonder that their attack earlier had been such a surprise.

As if from nowhere a ship appeared in the fogbank, and moments later the longboat was alongside. The sailors, who had yet to speak a word, motioned for Sheena and Habib to climb aboard, and when a head stuck over the rail, one of the sailors yelled up in French.

"I am Monsieur LeGrande," the figure on the deck said to Sheena. "I am first officer of the *Croix de Triomphe*. Welcome aboard, mademoiselle. You are to wait in the capitaine's quarters."

"And Habib?"

"Ah, yes," LeGrande said, looking at Habib. "He can remain on deck."

"Habib go with Sheena," Habib said.

"It's all right, Habib," Sheena said. "I'll await the captain's pleasure." She looked at LeGrande. "Show me to the cabin."

"This way," LeGrande said.

Sheena followed LeGrande to the cabin, then went inside as directed. LeGrande disappeared.

Sheena had never seen anything to compare with Captain Garneau's cabin. It was large, even larger than Ledyard's, and it had a huge canopy bed. Wall hangings of white and gold silk gave it the appearance of something from a storybook. In the center sat a beautifully polished table, adorned with a silver service that rivaled her father's tea service back on the plantation. But the thing that drew her attention immediately sat in the far corner of the room. It was a large white porcelain-and-gold-trimmed bathtub.

Sheena's heart leaped in excitement. How long had it been since she had had a bath? Oh, what a delight it would be to take one now.

Even as she was thinking about it, the door opened and LeGrande and Habib came in, Habib carrying a huge bucket of hot water.

"I've had your giant fetch water for a bath, mademoiselle. Feel free to use the capitaine's tub."

"A bath, yes," Sheena said, smiling in spite of the turn of events. "Oh, what a pleasure this will be."

Habib poured the water into the tub. Billows of steam rolled away in thick clouds, subtly inviting her in.

"Oh, thank you, Habib," Sheena said. "And thank you, Monsieur LeGrande. Now if you two would leave me, I'll just have that bath."

Habib and LeGrande withdrew without another word, and Sheena hurriedly slipped out of her clothes. Soap, oil, and rosewater stood on a shelf nearby, and she treated herself to the most luxurious bath she had enjoyed in months.

As Sheena bathed, she thought of the mysterious Jean Garneau. Garneau was certainly unlike any other pirate captain she had met. Jean had a clean-cut, handsome face. Sheena had to admit that she had noticed that even as they were fighting. There was something about Jean's eyes, a sensitivity that she had seen in no one since her Billy. A sensitivity, yes, but a sense of humor, too, like her Billy. Whatever it was, Sheena found that she was attracted to him.

And the captain was obviously attracted to her, she decided, or she would not have been brought here to this cabin. Perhaps the captain intended to make love to her, as part of the spoils of war.

Sheena held her leg up and stretched it out. It was long and smooth and well-formed. She passed as a boy only because it was so unusual for a woman to dress as a boy, and the clothing itself was enough to fool most people. But there was certainly nothing boyish about her appearance. She was actually a very beautiful woman, and she knew it. Little wonder that Captain Garneau wanted her. The question was, did she want Captain Garneau?

Sheena thought about it for a moment. Not since Billy had she experienced the delights of sexual fulfillment. And if Billy were still alive, she would withhold that pleasure until once again she could share it with her own true love. But Billy was dead, and she'd been used and abused by Mad Jack Ledyard, with little in return. She owed herself what little pleasure might remain for her in this life, and she was determined to take it from whence it came. Yes, she told herself. She would respond to Captain Garneau's lovemaking. If sensitive eyes were the measure of the person, Captain Garneau would be one who could bring her to the heights of ecstasy.

Sheena stepped out of the tub, pink and squeaky clean, and picked up her clothes. They were repulsive to her. She had no idea she had been that dirty until she saw those filthy rags in contrast to her own cleanliness. She tossed them aside and opened two large doors to Captain Garneau's clothes closet, hoping to find something there that she might wear.

Sheena gasped. Inside the closet were not only the pants and shirts she hoped to find but a full array of women's clothes as well. There were dresses of all styles and colors, and one beautiful silk nightgown.

Sheena laughed. "So, my French romantic. I am not the first, am I? Then I shall be the most memorable," she said aloud.

Sheena chose the nightgown, put it on, then walked over to check herself in the mirror. The nightgown was pure white silk, and it clung to her body, accenting her curves rather than concealing them. The nipples of her breasts were very prominent beneath the soft, clinging material. She pushed at each of them, hoping to make them stay down, only to discover that such action made them protrude all the more.

"Very well," she said aloud, softly. "I won't attempt to hide them from you, Captain. I will leave them thus, for you to enjoy."

Sheena found an ampule of perfume and put just a bit on her breasts, not strong enough to be too noticeable but powerful enough to play on the passions of anyone subjected to the scent. Thus prepared, she walked over to the bed and turned the covers down, there to await her new lover.

26

Sheena lay in bed listening to the sounds of the cargo being loaded into the ship's hold. The sailors were speaking French, and though she understood nothing of what they were saying, she did sense a degree of order and efficiency. After her experience on board the *Marcus B.* such order was impressive.

Sheena was tired, the more so because the preponderance of the work had fallen into her hands during the last few days on board the *Marcus B.* Now she discovered that the sudden relaxation of responsibility was almost as soothing as was the bed itself. She drifted comfortably off to sleep.

"Oui, mon capitaine, you will not be disturbed," Monsieur LeGrande's voice was saying. The voice just outside the cabin door awakened Sheena at once. For an instant she wondered where she was, then remembered. She found herself in the captain's bed, bathed, perfumed, and seductively clothed, and she realized what she was doing.

At that instant, Sheena had second thoughts. By climbing into Jean Garneau's bed she was, in a sense, throwing herself at the captain. What if she was rejected? What if she was laughed at? She regretted what she had done and a flutter of panic rose in her stomach. She looked around the room quickly, wondering if she had time to hide somewhere before the captain came in.

Too late! The door was being pushed open, even as Sheena gave thought to those fears.

Sheena had turned the gimbal lamp down when she went to bed, but Captain Garneau turned it back up, filling the room with a golden bubble of light.

"Let me get a better look at you, Sheena," Garneau said. "Ah, you are lovely. Absolutely lovely. I see you found the bathtub, and my clothes closet. Good, good, the change becomes you very much."

"I hope you do not mind my taking the liberty, sir," Sheena said.

Garneau walked over to the bed and placed a hand on Sheena's cheek. The hand was cool, confident and, to Sheena, pleasantly stimulating. Her skin heated to its touch. "You ask if I mind, *ma chérie*? But of course I don't mind." Garneau pulled the cover away to look at Sheena. "Beautiful clothes are made to be worn by beautiful women. You do that gown justice, I must say."

"How came you by such lovely things?" Sheena asked.

Garneau smiled. "Were you not pleasantly surprised to find such beautiful clothes?"

"Aye, of course I was," Sheena said. "Though I must confess to a degree of bewilderment."

"Then the clothes have served their purpose," Garneau replied. "I am glad you have made yourself ready for me."

"What makes you think I have prepared myself for you?" Sheena asked, making one last try at saving face.

"My dear, you've bathed, put on the most alluring nightgown and, my senses tell me, adorned yourself with perfume. I'm glad you were subtle with it. Most non-Frenchwomen bathe in the stuff, when in fact it should be only a faint suggestion, just as you have done. That way it stimulates the passions without overpowering the senses."

Garneau leaned over and kissed Sheena.

Billy's kisses had been pleasurable, true enough, but they were only a prelude to what was to come. Ledyard had tried to kiss her, but Sheena had managed to avoid his kisses, and Ledyard, who wasn't really interested in kissing anyway, hadn't pressed the issue. Sheena actually had had little experience with kissing, and was therefore amazed at the sensations one could evoke.

Sheena felt as if a thousand butterfly wings had brushed against her lips. Her head began to spin. Then she felt Garneau's tongue darting about, touching her mouth lightly, tasting of mint and spreading a warmth rapidly through her body.

The sensations nearly overwhelmed her. Sheena raised both her arms, pulling Garneau down to her, losing herself in the kiss, which deepened, testing it to see how far it could take her. A moment later, with her senses reeling and her self-control slipping away, she found it necessary to pull back.

"I've . . . I've never been kissed like that before," Sheena said.

Garneau smiled. "I expect I'll introduce you to a great many things you've never done, before this night is over. Are you aware of how much pleasure a woman's breasts can feel when loved by one who has skill in such things?"

Garneau, who had rubbed Sheena's breasts through the silk, now turned the silk down to expose Sheena's creamy mounds. It seemed to Sheena that her nipples had never been so tightly drawn, or as sensitive as they were now. Garneau's fingers and hands played upon them, but so delicate was the touch, so skillful the manipulation that Sheena couldn't feel the fingers themselves, only the pulsating sensations that the fingers caused.

Garneau's hands, fingers, lips, and tongue were on Sheena's face, ears, neck, shoulders, and breasts. Then Sheena discovered that at sometime during the love-making her gown had been removed, so that she lay in bed, completely nude, totally surrendered to the skillful supplications Garneau was providing for her.

At first Sheena wanted to reciprocate, to provide for Garneau the same degree of stimulation that Garneau was providing for her, but such was her state of arousal that she was completely helpless. She lay with her arms by her side, unable to lift them, either in resistance or reciprocity.

"And now, *ma chérie*," Garneau said. "I will rid myself of these clothes and take you to heights of pleasure which few women have enjoyed."

Sheena smiled at Garneau's vanity, but she didn't question it, for already she had been lifted to states of rapture she had never experienced before. She closed her eyes and lay still, her arm loosely across her forehead, waiting for the ultimate; the joining of their bodies to keep the promise her own body was making to her. She felt the weight of Garneau slipping into bed beside her, and she turned toward the weight with an open-mouthed kiss. Their bodies pressed together, and bubbles of fire ascended from Sheena's enflamed loins . . . *but the body pressed against Sheena's was a woman's body!*

Sheena broke off the kiss and pushed away, shocked by her sudden realization. "You!" she sputtered. "You are a woman!"

"Of course I am," Garneau said easily. "Why should you be so shocked? Weren't you playing the same game?"

"No," Sheena said. "No, I made my sex known at once. You should have done the same."

"You have not enjoyed what we are doing?" Garneau asked.

"No. No, of course not."

Jean Garneau laughed a low, throaty laugh and placed her hand between Sheena's legs. Sheena could not deny the dampness, nor fight the weakness of her body as it betrayed her.

"No," she murmured, too weak to pull away. "Please don't."

Garneau paid no attention to Sheena's pitiful entreaties, but continued to make love to her, employing all the many skillful tricks at her disposal. Sheena, pushed now to the raw edge of desire, was unable to fight any longer. She made a low sound of surrender in her throat, then willingly, eagerly, gave herself over to the more experienced woman, letting Jean do as she wished. Darts of flame flashed through Sheena. Her body quivered in response. Then lightning struck her, not once but twice, three times, four times, and Sheena felt an ecstasy so intense as to be almost unbearable.

They made love again after that, and still a third time, and Sheena learned what to do to bring Jean to the same heights of ecstasy that she had enjoyed. Sheena responded to the lessons avidly, and was gratified and proud to discover that she could evoke as powerful a response from Jean as Jean could from her.

Afterward, coasting down slowly and together, Sheena still too aroused to feel guilty or have second thoughts, they drank rum, and Sheena fell asleep, sinking deeper into the arms of Morpheus than she had at anytime since coming to sea.

27

The ringing laughter sounded like breaking crystal. There was a degree of polish to it, like the elegance of delicately blown glass, but there was a harsh, brittle edge too, as if the ingredients had some imperfection, so that the end result was flawed.

The laughter had come from the lips of Liam O'Sheel, and his mirth was born of the discomfort of one of the serving girls in the tavern he was visiting. The unfortunate girl had suddenly discovered that the hem of her dress was on fire, and in order to avoid serious burns, had had to rip the dress off. Now she was standing before the crowd in her undergarments. She was trying unsuccessfully to cover her ample breasts and white thighs.

"Oh, Liam, you are absolutely priceless," one of Liam's table companions said, himself a jaded young man of the county. "One never knows what new uses one can make of a candle, does one?"

"It's all a matter of superior intellect, dear boy," Liam said, beaming under the praise of his friend. He tapped his head. "I have a brilliant mind and the keenest intellect."

An older man was sitting at a table next to Liam

and his friends. He had been shuffling cards and dealing them out, then turning each hand up to see what the cards were, before pulling them in and starting all over again. He had not spoken to anyone, had looked up only with the slightest interest when the girl, screaming, had removed her dress. Now he was once again busily engaged with his private game.

"You, sir," Liam's supportive friend said to the man with the cards. "Do you not believe my friend is the smartest man in all of Charles Town?"

The man mumbled something and continued with his game.

"What was that, sir? I didn't hear you," Liam said.

The man didn't answer Liam.

"Does this ruffian not know who I am?" Liam asked the others at his table. They laughed at Liam's comment and watched to see what he would do next. He stood up, walked over to the table, then, with a grand, sweeping motion, brushed the cards from the table. "Answer me, you buffoon!" Liam shouted.

The man stood up quickly and grabbed Liam by the scruff of the neck.

"Pick the cards up, friend, and put them where you found them," he ordered.

"Owww!" Liam shouted. "You are hurting me, sir."

"Do as I said or I will break your puny neck," the man said again, not raising his voice, but speaking in the soft, controlled tones of one who has great confidence in his abilities.

Liam started to pick the cards up.

"And tell me you are sorry," the man said.

"Surely, sir, you do not intend to make a fool of me in front of my friends?" Liam whined.

"You are already a fool, and I've had nothing to do with it," the man replied.

Those who had been laughing with Liam now laughed at him. He felt his face flaming as he replaced the cards on the table.

"And now, tell me you are sorry," the man ordered.

"I'm sorry," Liam said.

"Thank you. Now I shall return to my game, and you, sir, shall return to yours."

Liam, starting back to his table, saw the look of mirth in the faces of those who, moments ago, had been his friends. Deep inside, he knew that he was no different from them. They were wealthy, jaded young men, too old for childish entertainments but not yet the masters of their own fortunes. The result was a life dedicated to pleasure, and if they found pleasure at another's expense, then their pleasure was all the sweeter. But that their pleasure should be at his expense was more than he could bear. He tried to think of a grand and eloquent gesture which would put him back on a par with them.

Suddenly he realized what he was going to do. He stopped, halfway to his table, then turned to face the man who had just humiliated him.

"Sir, you have left my clothes in disarray," Liam said. "I shall have to arrange them."

The cardplayer looked up with little interest, then returned to his game.

Liam tucked one pant leg into his boot, then started to tuck the other one in. And that was the whole idea of this charade, for tucked into that boot was a concealed pistol. When he straightened up he had the pistol in his hand. He moved to less than three feet away from the cardplayer. As yet no one, not even the cardplayer, had an idea of what he was going to do. Liam pointed the pistol at the cardplayer's head and pulled the trigger.

"My God!" one of the young men at Liam's table shouted, when he saw the cardplayer fall across the table with a large, oozing hole just above his left ear. "What have you done, Liam?"

"I've shot the uncouth bastard," Liam said calmly.

He returned to the table and sat down. "Now we can continue our party without interruption."

"But, Liam, he's dead!"

"I should hope so," Liam said, laughing easily. "I lodged a ball in his brain for just such a purpose."

"But you've got to get out of here! You can hang for this!"

Suddenly Liam's fine joke seemed to backfire. His mind had been clouded by rage, and he hadn't thought clearly. He had wanted, somehow, to restore his position with the others, to once again be the leader. But it wasn't working out as he planned. They weren't laughing. They were frightened, and they were urging him to run away.

Run away! Yes, yes, oh, my God, what have I done? Liam thought. *This one I cannot hide.*

"I—I—I've got to go," Liam said. Now, he too was frightened, and his fear was not only of the law but of the others, even his own friends. He started backing toward the door, looking at the shocked faces of the patrons. "Don't anybody try and come for me," he warned. "Everybody stay away!"

Liam bolted out the front door and ran to his horse. A moment later he was pounding down the Charles Town Pike, headed for Bonny Isle, as fast as his horse would take him. *What will I do?* he thought. *How will I get away? Everyone in the tavern knows me. They will come for me! I will hang! Oh, God, I will hang!*

The horse labored under Liam's insistent whipping, answering his urging to go faster and faster, until its entire body was covered with lather. Still, Liam urged it on, until finally, as the animal passed through the gates of Bonny Isle, it fell dead from its labors.

Liam was thrown when the horse fell but got up without injury. With no regard for the horse, he ran into the big house and into the library, where he knew his father kept a substantial sum of money.

Liam called once for his father. When he heard no

answer he proceeded to rifle through the desk, throwing papers, books, envelopes, anything that got in his way to one side, until he saw the small sack which he knew was filled with gold coins. He hefted it, was gratified for its weight, then hurried up the stairs to pack a few belongings. He was nearly finished when the door to his room was jerked open.

Liam gasped in quick fear, then looked around to see his father standing there, looking at him.

"Oh," Liam said, breathing a sigh of relief. "It's only you. I must say, you frightened me half to death."

"Is it true?" Dr. O'Sheel asked.

"Is what true?"

"I was in Charles Town, and I heard that you murdered a man in a tavern there. Liam, could this be true?"

"It—it was self-defense," Liam said.

"No," Kevin replied. He hung his head in shame. "No, it wasn't. The story was quite specific on that. They say you murdered him in cold blood."

"Well, what if I did?" Liam exploded angrily. "The uncouth bastard had it coming to him, treating me as he did."

"But Liam, what were you doing in such a place anyway? Son, those are places of the devil!"

"Don't talk to me of the devil, you hypocrite!" Liam said. "Do you think I don't know the story of Sheena's birth? Do you think I don't know how you visited that whore that was her mother? I heard her tell the story to Sheena; then I followed her home." Liam laughed, an evil laugh. "And then I took her to bed."

"Liam!"

"Oh, why should that shock you, Father? After all, didn't you do the same thing? I could hardly be counted on to behave any differently, now, could I? I mean, we are aware of how blood will tell, aren't we?"

"But you said that she tried to entice you into her

bed," Kevin said. "That is the way it happened, isn't it?"

"No," Liam said. "I took her to bed, willingly, hoping she could make me forget the terrible lusting I have for Sheena."

"What did you say?" Kevin asked, his voice strained with disbelief. *"You have lusted after your own sister?"*

"Yes. And would have had her had I won the wager she made with me. But she tricked me, and I lost the match."

"Son, wait, you are going too fast," Kevin said. "I don't understand what you are saying."

"Oh, you understand all right, old man." Liam chuckled. "But I got even with her. She was blamed for killing Elmyra."

"You mean she didn't—it wasn't Sheena—it was—"

"Yes. It was me," Liam said. "I killed Sheena's mother, Elmyra, and tonight I killed that pig in the tavern. But too many people saw me tonight, and I have to leave." He pointed to the sack of money on the table. "I'll be taking that with me."

"No," Kevin said quietly. "You aren't going anywhere."

"Yes, I am. Don't you understand? Too many people saw me tonight. I have to get out of here, or I will hang."

"If you hang, you shall hang," Kevin said. "But will do the right thing by surrendering yourself to the sheriff."

Liam laughed, a half-choking, disbelieving laugh. "Father, you can't be serious. You mean you actually want me to surrender myself, even if it means I might hang?"

"Yes," Kevin said. "And then we shall both pray for forgiveness. You, because you have done those awful things, and I because I have been blind to your faults and to Sheena's virtues."

"Sheena's virtues?"

"I have sinned against my daughter. I shall spend the rest of my life trying to atone for those sins."

"Yes. Well, you do what you want to, old man. I'm leaving."

Liam picked up the money and started out the door, but Kevin stepped in front of him. "No," Kevin said. He grabbed the money sack and tossed it back inside. "You will wait here until the sheriff arrives."

"Get out of my way," Liam said, pushing his father away. He started for the money.

"No," Kevin said.

The two men struggled against each other, Liam trying to get away, Kevin trying to hold him. As they struggled they fell against a table, knocking a kerosene lamp onto the floor. It broke, and the spreading oil caught fire, but the men were so engrossed in their struggles that neither of them noticed.

The struggle took the men out onto the second-floor landing, where they pushed and shoved against each other, each trying to gain the advantage. Finally, with one mighty shove, Liam pushed his father over the banister. Kevin let out one short yell, then crashed, headfirst, onto the floor below. Afterward, he lay very still.

"Father!" Liam shouted, hurrying down the stairs to look at him. He knelt beside him and felt his neck. He looked into his open, vacant eyes. Kevin O'Sheel was dead.

"You shouldn't have tried to stop me, old man," Liam said quietly. He stood up, then turned to go back up the stairs to retrieve the bag of money. By that time the fire in his room had become an inferno. It burst out of the room and quickly invested the upper landing, so that the top of the stairs was a solid sheet of fire.

"No!" Liam shouted. He started up the stairs, intending to dash quickly through the fire to his room, but the heat was so intense and the flames burning so fiercely that he was forced to turn back before he could even reach the top of the stairs. The fire licked up at the ceiling. A timber weakened, then collapsed. Liam was afraid that the entire house was about to fall in on him. He let out a scream and dashed outside.

The slaves who had seen the burning building came running toward it, carrying buckets and shovels.

"We'll help, Marse Liam, we'll help," one of them shouted.

Liam looked at the flames, then laughed coldly.

"Let the son of a bitch burn," he said, walking toward his father's still-saddled horse. His laughter grew long and loud. "Let it burn, let it burn, let it burn."

"Marse Liam, where you goin'?"

"I'm going to find Sheena," he said. "I've got my own fire to put out."

He jerked the horse around, put the spurs to it, and the spirited animal, the best on Bonny Isle, leaped forward at a gallop. Above the pounding of the hooves, even above the roar of the fire, the frightened and confused slaves could hear the evil ring of his laughter.

28

Liam had already ridden one horse to death this night. He was determined to spare the next one, because he knew that after it went, there would be no more. Despite his best intentions, though, his fear drove him on, and only when he noticed his animal's labored breathing did he think of it again. Then, seeing a tavern, he decided to give the horse a breather, while having a few drinks to calm himself down.

Liam was on a road he seldom traveled, purposely avoiding anyone who might know him for fear that he was already being hunted. So when he tied up in front of the Red King, he looked at it with curiosity, wondering what it was like.

Inside, the Red King looked no different from any other tavern, except that it was dimly lit by three wheels containing candles, suspended from chains. The gloom was further increased by the cloud of tobacco smoke which hung just above the unpainted oak tables.

Liam ordered his drink and sat at a table, withdrawing into his own thoughts. His attention was finally arrested by a small man in a captain's uniform. The captain was drinking beer, and his glass was nearly empty. On sudden impulse, Liam signaled the waitress.

"Yes, sir?"

"Would you refill the captain's glass on me, please?" Liam asked.

The waitress took a beer over to the small man and handed it to him, then pointed Liam out. When the captain looked up, Liam saluted him with his own glass. As Liam hoped, the captain stood up, walked over to his table, and joined him.

"My appreciation, sir, for your charitable act," the captain said. "The name is Boyle. Garrison Boyle, at your service."

"And I am . . ." Liam hesitated. To divulge his real name might now be dangerous. "Leo Steele," he said.

"Tell me, Mister Steele. To what do I owe the honor of drinking your beer?"

"I can tell by your attire, sir, that you are a seaman."

"Aye. I'm cap'n o' the *Sea Witch*."

"Would you be interested in taking on a hand?"

Boyle eyed Liam suspiciously. "Beggin' your pardon, Mister Steele, but you've not the looks of a seaman about you."

"I've had experience as a ship's surgeon," Liam said. "It is for that berth I would apply."

"Ship's surgeon, you say?" Boyle rubbed his chin and looked at Liam. "Fact is, I don't have a surgeon at the moment, and I could use one," Boyle said. "Though I was goin' to sail without one, if need be, so don't go tryin' to hold me up on the price," he added quickly.

"I'd be willing to work at your terms, Captain," Liam said, breathing a sigh of relief. If Captain Boyle only knew that he just wanted to get away, he could probably get him for nothing, Liam thought.

"You know anythin' 'bout doctorin' niggers?"

Liam laughed. "Nigger diseases are just about my specialty. My father owned several."

"Then you've no qualms about workin' on a slaver?" Boyle inquired.

"A slaver?"

Boyle put his hand on Liam's arm. "For if you've no qualms, I'll tell you here and now they's money to be made in the trade. Aye, and a bit o' fun too, if you know what I mean."

"I see what you mean," Liam said. "I'm your man, Captain. I'll report aboard soon as you like."

"Then you'll be leavin' the tavern with me," Boyle said. "For we're anchored in a nearby lagoon, and we'll sail with the mornin' tide."

"That suits me fine, Captain," Liam said.

At the moment a large man with red hair and a bushy red beard came in. Several of the patrons knew him and greeted him. He returned their greetings. When he looked over and saw Liam and Boyle at a table, he walked toward them.

"Hello, Boyle," he said. "I hear you'll be sailin' tomorrow."

"Aye," Boyle said. "Cap'n Anders, this here is Leo Steele, my ship's surgeon."

"Do you know about doctorin' niggers?" Captain Anders asked, laughing. "For that's the only trade Boyle does."

"It pays well," Boyle said.

"Aye. And there's little chance of piracy, for who would want to steal a shipload o' niggers. The *Goodhope* was attacked on this trip, you know."

"No, I didn't know," Boyle said. "French privateers?"

The waitress brought Captain Anders a mug of beer. He drank nearly half of it before he wiped the foam from his beard with the back of his hand and answered the question.

"Naw. Hell, if it had been Frenchies, I would have tried to outrun 'em. Or at least fight back. It was Mad Jack Ledyard."

"Mad Jack?" Boyle said. "Aye. I've heard that he's gone on account."

"He ran up the Jolly Roger on me, the bloody bugger. And, get this, will you? He had a girl with him. A fightin' girl, who could handle a blade the best of anyone I've ever seen."

"A girl?" Liam asked, his interest suddenly piqued. "Could you describe her?"

"Sure can. She was a lovely broth of a lass, green eyes, flaming red hair, young, maybe eighteen or twenty. Sure'n she looked out of place where she was, I tell you, until she handled that blade!"

"Sheena!" Liam said under his breath.

"What was that you say, Surgeon?" Anders asked.

"Uh . . . nothing," Liam said. "I was just thinking aloud."

"I thought you said the name Sheena, for that is the selfsame name I heard for the girl. Sheena Drumm."

"Drumm? Not O'Sheel? But of course, William Drumm. Then something did happen as I suspected. And now I know it *must* be her!" Liam said.

"You know the girl?"

"Aye," Liam said. "I know her well. And I must find her."

"If you had been with me a while ago, lad, you wouldn't have to find her. She would've found you." Anders finished his beer, then looked around the tavern. "Now, mates, if you will both excuse me, I've been becalmed, then swept by unseasonable storms, boarded by pirates and have lost my cargo. I'm badly in need of somethin' to change my luck, if you know what I mean. I aim to find me a black wench to lie with."

"We must go too," Boyle said, standing up. "Surgeon, you'll be going with me?"

"Aye, Captain," Liam said.

The ship was within walking distance of the tavern, so Liam sold his father's horse to the tavern owner, then followed Boyle down to the beach. There, two sailors were sitting by a longboat. They jumped up when Boyle and Liam approached.

"This is Mister Steele," Boyle said. "He's the ship's surgeon, and so will be granted the respect of an officer."

"Aye, Cap'n," one of the men said.

"Did you get the girl?"

"Aye, Cap'n, them two bounty hunters had her, just like they said they would. They said she was still a virgin like you wanted, though it pained them to let her be."

"Where is she?"

"She's aboard, Cap'n. Locked in your cabin, like you said."

"Let's go."

It was only then that Liam noticed that the ship was lying at anchor about three hundred yards off shore, a long, low, black shadow on the water. Boyle was silent as they rode out, and Liam observed that, though small, he was a very intimidating man. When the men spoke to him it was always in voices laced with fear.

Once aboard, Boyle made it clear that under no circumstances was he ever to be visited in his cabin, nor was his cabin to be entered in his absence. Liam thought it a rather odd request, but he agreed readily enough. Even he was beginning to feel a bit intimidated by the diminutive captain, and he wanted no trouble with him. If the captain had a girl in the cabin, so be it. It was none of his concern. He cared about one girl, and one girl only. And now, thanks to the information from Captain Anders, he knew where she was. And he would find her, if it took him ten years.

The sky was gray and dirty when they got under-way the next day. For the first few days Liam had to fight against a recurring bout of seasickness. The ill-ness was not only uncomfortable, but he was afraid it would undermine any confidence Boyle might have in him as a ship's surgeon. It wasn't so important that he have Boyle's confidence, as much as it was that he didn't fall into disfavor with the small man. Liam knew that it wasn't beyond Boyle to demote him on the spot and force him to finish the voyage before the mast, if given cause. And that, Liam knew, would be the worst thing that could happen to him.

Liam watched the captain's comings and goings like a hawk. Whenever the little man came out of his cabin, Liam appeared to be busy, thus not to incur his wrath. When Liam felt weak from the effects of the sea, he would wait until Boyle was out of sight or back in his cabin before he would give in to it.

Liam learned that he could tell where the captain was just by looking at the padlock on his cabin door. If it was locked, then Boyle was on deck somewhere, and Liam had to be on his best behavior. If it was un-locked, Boyle was in his cabin, and Liam could afford to be more relaxed.

They were ten days out. Sailing southeast, under a hot sun, with the men working bare-skinned, when Liam saw an example of why they feared Boyle so.

The incident started innocently enough. One of the sailors teased another. In the hot, still air, the teas-ing quickly turned to torment and the victim re-taliated by shoving his tormentor. But, as so often happens in such cases, Captain Boyle saw only the victim's retaliation.

"Mason, you'll be goin' to the whipping tee for that," Captain Boyle called.

"The hell I will, Cap'n. It was all his fault," Mason responded.

Captain Boyle was shocked to hear a sailor talk back to him. "You'll be getting ten lashes instead of five for passing that remark," Boyle warned him.

"Oh, go to hell!" Mason said angrily. He had clearly been pushed to the limit, and his rage now knew no restraints. "Why don't you make it twenty, you sawed off little son of a bitch!"

The crew, which in truth had been enjoying Mason's persecution as a respite from the tedium, now gasped in surprise. It was dangerous to talk back to any captain, and especially so to talk back to Captain Boyle. And to mention his diminutive size, something the captain was extremely sensitive about, was the most dangerous thing of all.

"Mister Adams!" Captain Boyle shouted to the first mate. "Mister Steele," he called to Liam. "Prepare a ship's mast!"

The crew gasped again. The captain had the absolute authority to mete out nearly any punishment in the books. A ship's mast, requiring the captain and at least two other officers, was convened only for the most serious of punishments: hanging, which could be done only if the continued life of the prisoner endangered the ship; dismembering, cutting off a finger or fingers, or in some cases even a hand, for stealing; and keelhauling.

"Cap'n Boyle, the table is set up, sir," Liam said, reporting to Boyle after making the arrangements.

"All right," Boyle said. He looked over at two men, who now held Mason between them. Mason had his arms tied behind his back, though, in truth, he was no longer belligerent. The mention of a ship's mast had frightened even him into submission.

"Cap'n Boyle, sir, I'm awful sorry 'bout what I said 'n done 'n all," the prisoner said nervously. "There's no need to bother with a ship's mast. Why, I'd be glad to take whatever punishment you feel is fittin'."

"Bring the prisoner before the mast," Boyle ordered coldly.

The two sailors dragged the hapless man before the table. Liam examined him more closely now, since the man was standing not three feet in front of him. The prisoner was tall and thin. His eyes shone with his fright. He was shaking as violently as a man in the most advanced chill.

"Prisoner, how speak ye?" Boyle demanded.

Mason barely opened his mouth. As he mumbled, a fleck of spittle ran down his chin.

"We can't hear you," Boyle said. "Speak up, damn you!"

"Please, Cap'n, sir," Mason said, a little louder now. "I plead guilty 'n I throw myself on the mercy of the mast. I'm but a poor miserable sailor, not worth the time or effort of such fine gentlemen as yourselves, and I beg of you to have pity on me. I'm heartily sorry for what I done."

Captain Boyle looked at the other members of the board. "Is there any question in any mind o'er the guilt o' the prisoner?"

"He's guilty," Adams said.

"Guilty," Liam agreed.

"Prisoner, prepare to hear your sentence," Boyle said, looking at him with cold, expressionless eyes.

The frightened man fell to his knees and bowed his head in the position of prayer.

"Please, Cap'n, sir. Please, you other gentlemen. Talk to the cap'n for me. Beg him to have mercy on me."

Showing no indication that he had even heard the pitiful pleas, Boyle began to pronounce the sentence. "It is the sentence o' this mast, legally convened o' ship's officers, that you be keelhauled no fewer than ten times."

"No! My God, sir! No!" the man screamed.

"Prepare for a keelhauling," Boyle ordered.

The prisoner was dragged, crying and pleading, amidships, where a harness was fixed to him. An outrigger was hung from side to side of the ship. A rope was threaded through a tackle on the starboard rig, then taken down through the water and passed up on the other side.

"Captain Boyle, sir, I must confess to ignorance on this," Liam said. "But I am curious. What, exactly, is keelhauling?"

"It's a simple, but most effective punishment," Boyle said. "They tie the prisoner into that harness, then drag him beneath the ship and up the other side. It's rigged so he'll drag against the barnacles and such on the ship's bottom, you see."

"Oh, yes, I do see," Liam said. He smiled. "I must congratulate you, Captain, on this marvelous diversion."

"And in this blessed heat, it'll be a welcome diversion for the men too," Boyle said. "I think it'll perk 'em up a bit."

"They'll like you for it, I'm sure."

Boyle chuckled. "I don't need them to like me, Mister Steele. Just fear me."

Mason was stripped naked and then swung out over the side of the ship, mumbling and whimpering. His eyes were tightly shut. Liam felt a strange, almost erotic thrill at watching this take place.

"Haul him through!" Boyle directed.

The sailors on deck pulled the rope and Mason lowered to the water. He took a deep breath of air, a sobbing, bubbling sound, just as he went under.

The sailors pulled on the rope for what seemed like a minute or more. Then someone shouted, "He's a'comin' up on this side!"

Liam looked to the port side and saw the man appear feet first. He was dragged across the deck, leaving a wet trail of seawater and blood, his body having been savagely cut upon contact with the ship's barnacle-encrusted bottom.

Liam crossed the deck with him, then looked into the man's terrified face as he went over the side and down for the second time. The man opened his eyes just as he went over, looking into Liam's face with a terrifying, insane look. It was a silent, useless plea for help.

Liam couldn't explain the thrill he was feeling over witnessing this. It was sensual and erotic. He suddenly thought of Sheena, and knew at that moment that the supreme thrill of all would be to take Sheena to bed, use her brutally, and then keelhaul her, naked and bleeding, in front of the crew. The thought made him come close to an orgasm, and he held on to the rail tightly to prevent it.

There was dead silence during all this time. Nothing could be heard except the squeaking of the block-and-tackle rig, and the splashing of water.

The man appeared on the opposite side and was dragged across the deck again. This time he trailed almost as much blood as he did seawater, and his eyes were tightly shut as he passed over and into the water a third time.

The next time he appeared on deck his eyes were open, but they appeared to be unseeing. His mouth was open too. It was a gaping, bloody hole, and his face was blue.

The block-and-tackle detail paused a moment. One of the men bent over the bloody, wet mess, which until a few moments past had been a living, whole man.

"He's dead, Cap'n," the man said.

At the man's words one of the detail men began to loosen the harness holding the prisoner.

"What are you doin'?" Boyle asked harshly.

"The man's dead, sir."

"I heard that he was dead, but why are you cuttin' him loose?"

"He's dead, sir!" the man said again, as if frustrated that he couldn't be understood.

"That makes no difference," Boyle said patiently. "The punishment is to be hauled ten times, and he will finish his sentence, dead or alive. Unless, of course, you wish to finish it for him!"

"Aye, sir, the punishment will continue," the sailor replied meekly. He began to haul on the tackle, once more pulling the prisoner across the sloppy deck.

The keelhauling went on. It was an eerie tableau. The crew stood by, watching. Not a word passed from the lips of anyone, and the silence was interrupted only by the macabre symphony of sound made by the creaking windlass, the splash of water, and the scraping of the body as it was dragged, lifeless, across the deck.

After the tenth revolution the man stopped. The body lay still, dripping water, blood, and bodily fluids onto the deck.

"Surgeon," Captain Boyle spoke. "Examine the prisoner."

Liam looked at Boyle as if he hadn't heard him correctly. "Sir, the prisoner is dead."

"Examine him, please," Boyle commanded, paying no heed to Liam's answer.

Liam moved toward the mass of flesh. He stood over the unmoving form for a second, then knelt beside it. He gingerly rolled the body over and looked into what had been Mason's face. It was purple, bloated, and forged into a look of sheer terror. The unseeing eyes were bulging nearly out of their sockets. The entire length of Mason's body, from the top of his head to the bottom of his feet, was scraped raw, and his flesh was hanging in strips. His stomach was open and part of his intestines protruded from the opening.

Liam looked into the man's eyes, stuck his finger in

his mouth, and felt for a pulse. There was no sign of life from the grotesque remains.

"He is dead, sir," Liam said quietly.

Captain Boyle looked at his clerk. "Clerk, make an entry to the fact that the prisoner was pronounced dead by the ship's surgeon after concludin' punishment duly authorized by a ship's mast."

"Aye, Cap'n," the clerk, a red-faced man wearing spectacles, answered.

"Sailmaker, prepare a shroud. The prisoner will be buried at sea, with Christian services. The rest of you, return to your duties. Surgeon, come with me. I have another task I wish you to perform."

"Aye, sir," Liam replied, following Boyle toward the captain's cabin. It would be the first time he had been in the captain's cabin during the entire voyage. He knew there was a girl in there, from the conversation he heard when first reporting on board, but he had not yet seen her. Now, at last, he would see why she was so special that she had to be kept locked up.

"You said you knew nigger doctorin'," Boyle said, as he unlocked the padlock to his cabin.

"Yes, sir. It is an art I know well."

"Can you tell if a girl is a virgin?"

Liam laughed. "Sure. That's one of the first things I learned to do."

Boyle looked at him with a stern expression which told Liam that he was in no mood for jokes.

"I'm sorry, Cap'n," Liam said. "But to answer your question, yes, I can tell."

"We're goin' to see a man tomorrow in Nassau," Boyle said. "He's the one who'll be givin' us the money for the niggers we'll be pickin' up in Africa, 'n I got a little gift for him. But first, I gotta be sure this nigger girl's a virgin. Virgins are the kind he likes best."

Boyle opened the lock and swung the door open. Liam stepped in behind him.

"That's why I been keepin' the door locked," Boyle explained. "If anyone got in here and pestered her, she'd be worthless to me."

"Where is she?"

"She's around," Boyle said. "You, girl, are you hidin' in the closet? Come out here. I want the surgeon to look you over."

There was no answer to Boyle's call, so he walked over to the closet and jerked the canvas curtain to one side.

"Oh, there you are," he said. "Come on out here, girl, where the surgeon can get a thorough look at you. He's gonna check out to see if you are a virgin, like you said."

The girl stepped out of the closet and into a patch of light, which spilled in a golden square through the stern windows. Liam saw her close then, for the first time, and he gasped.

"Tricia!"

Boyle looked at Liam sharply. "See here, do you know this girl?"

"Aye," Liam said. "I know her."

"I'll be damned. Have you pestered her?"

"No, Captain," Liam said. "But I wanted to."

"I don't care what you wanted. She's got to be a virgin, do you understand that? She's got to be."

"Well, Tricia, you ran away from home and got your mama killed protecting your virginity. Is it still intact?" Liam asked.

"If I could take it all back, Master Liam, I would," Tricia said, tears flowing down her cheeks.

"Wouldn't we all, Tricia, wouldn't we all?" Liam replied. "Now, get up on the bed, girl. I'm going to examine you."

Boyle paced back and forth nervously as Liam spread the girl's legs and checked her out. After a moment, Liam raised up and smiled at the small captain.

"Well?" Boyle asked anxiously.

"She's a virgin."

"Good. That will please Don Bustamante greatly."

29

"Non, non, non, monsieur. You will have the opportunity to buy at the auction. The same opportunity that everyone else shall have."

"But Captain, that doesn't seem fair. After all, by your own admission this is the same cargo I had consigned to the *Goodhope."*

"Oui, monsieur, but I did not take it from the *Goodhope.* I took it from the *Marcus B."*

The arguing voices were right outside the cabin door, and Sheena groggily sat up in bed, wondering what was going on. She walked over to the door to listen, and as she did, she saw her nude image in the mirror. At that instant Sheena recalled what had happened the night before in vivid detail, and her cheeks flamed red with embarrassment.

The cabin door opened and Jean swept in, dressed once again in the men's clothes she wore as captain of the *Croix de Triomphe.*

"Get dressed, *chérie,"* she said breezily. "We are in Nassau, and we shall visit the city before we return to auction our prize."

"What—what's going on? Whose are all the voices?" Sheena asked.

"Bidders," Jean said. She laughed. "Leland Stand-hope is on deck, pleading that he should have first rights to these goods, as they were his by consignment on the *Goodhope*. But he is the biggest thief in the islands, and it is time he paid a good price for a change."

Sheena took a pair of pants and a shirt from the closet.

"Non, ma chérie. You will wear women's clothes," Jean said.

"I wish to wear these," Sheena said.

"You may wear such at sea," Jean said. "But in Nassau you will wear women's clothes."

Sheena started to protest again, but for some reason that she couldn't understand, she acquiesced to Jean's demands and returned the men's clothes to the closet.

"Ah, that's good," Jean said. "Now, I must go to the customhouse to declare my prize. You will meet me there in one hour, and I shall show you the city."

"You, a pirate, can register your prize?" Sheena asked.

Jean laughed. "No," she said. "Ledyard was a pirate. I am a privateer, commissioned by the govern-ment of France."

"But this is an English island."

"Ah, but this prize was taken from a pirate ship," Jean said. "Had it not been, I would have had to go to one of the French islands. But I must go quickly to register. What do you wish to do about your giant?"

"Habib?"

"He waits on deck to serve you. Why is he so loyal to you?"

"Because I can keep a secret," Sheena said. "Jean, I— I have no money to give him. I was to have a share of our prize."

Jean laughed and took a couple of coins from the

small money purse which hung from her belt. "Here," she said, tossing the coins to Sheena. "This should be enough to keep even a giant of his size in food and drink for a while."

"You have my thanks," Sheena said.

"Remember, the customhouse in one hour," Jean said, stepping outside the cabin.

Sheena put on a robe, then stuck her head out the door to call for Habib.

"Habib, here," she said, handing him the money. "Go downtown and have a good time."

Habib looked at the money, then, quizzically, at Sheena.

"I'm all right," Sheena said. "I'm getting dressed to go downtown too. Don't worry, Habib, I'm in no danger."

"Habib can come back to Mistress?" Habib asked.

Sheena smiled. "Aye, Habib. I'll be right here. You have a good time, but don't get into any trouble."

"Habib be good boy," Habib said, grinning broadly and putting the money in his pocket.

Sheena watched Habib leave the ship, happily anticipating his time ashore. She thought of the terrible tragedy which had deprived Habib of his parts, and she couldn't help but wonder just how he did spend his time ashore. But the thought was a depressing one. She put it aside quickly, then returned to select something to wear to the customhouse. If she was going to be a woman, she was going to be a beautiful one.

"If it is true, as you say, Captain, that you have the head of the pirate Ledyard impaled upon a pike, then I am authorized to pay you two hundred and fifty pounds as reward money," a fat, sweating customs official said. "But I shall have to see the head with my own eyes."

"Do you know him?" Garneau asked.

"Aye, I know him. An ugly and sinful man, with a hint of sulphur about him, and an eye that never closes."

"Then view his head quickly and dispose of it," Garneau said. "I find little satisfaction from such a decoration on my ship."

"'Twill take a short time. Then we will bury his head in the pauper's graveyard, as prescribed."

"No!" Sheena said from the doorway of the customhouse.

Jean and the official turned to look at her. She had just arrived, and stood in the doorway wearing a golden-colored silk gown. It had a very low-cut bosom, was pinched in at the waist, then flared out into many tiers. Her crimson hair was fashioned into one long braid which fell softly across her left shoulder. Her skin glowed, and her eyes sparkled. She licked her lips, her tongue darting out through perfectly spaced, brilliant white teeth, and a flash of light sparkled from the dancing earbobs she had found to wear.

"Who is this beautiful creature?" the customs official asked.

Jean Garneau beamed proudly. "Monsieur Whitehall, may I introduce Mademoiselle Sheena Drumm? She was, until yesterday, held prisoner by Mad Jack Ledyard. She was rescued by my brave crew."

"How fortunate for you, madam," Whitehall said. "Though what an ordeal you must have gone through."

"Why did you say no to the suggestion of burying Ledyard's remains in the pauper's cemetery?" Jean asked.

"I—I just remembered something Jack, uh, Mr. Ledyard said," Sheena replied. "I'm certain he would have preferred to be buried at sea."

"But surely, madam, you harbor no sentiment for

240

the evil brute?" Whitehall sputtered. "After all, you were his prisoner."

"Aye," Sheena said. "But the man's dead now, and there's only his soul to reckon with. For the sake of his soul, I would ask that he be buried at sea."

"I can understand that," Jean said. "He was a sailing man, same as myself, and I would prefer the sea as my final resting place."

"This is highly irregular," Whitehall said. "If I pay the reward, then I must claim the remains. That is the rule."

"Then don't pay the reward," Jean said. "We will bury the capitaine when we return to the sea."

"But—but I must see him at least," Whitehall said.

"No," Sheena said. "If you won't pay Captain Garneau, you have no right to view the remains."

"But see here, young lady, I must make a report to the governor that Mad Jack Ledyard is dead! And I cannot make that report if I don't see him!"

"Perhaps he isn't dead," Sheena said. "Perhaps he is still roaming the seas, waiting to plunder the king's ships."

"No, that will never do," Whitehall said. "For don't you see? As long as there is a suspicion that Mad Jack is alive, most anyone would have license for piracy. They could blame it on Mad Jack."

"Unless you pay the reward, there will always be that suspicion," Sheena said.

Whitehall sighed and looked at Garneau. "You say you rescued this creature. Are you certain she is not working for you?"

"She speaks only the truth," Jean said.

"Very well, I will pay the reward," Whitehall said. "But only if I can see the remains."

"That you can do," Jean replied. "Be on board the *Croix de Triomphe* at three o'clock this afternoon. That is when I shall hold the auction."

"The auction, yes," Whitehall said. He folded a

piece of paper and handed it to Jean. "Here is your authorization."

"*Merci*, Monsieur Whitehall," Jean said. "You are most kind."

"And you are most clever, Captain, to bring English goods into an English port on board a French privateer, and sell them to English businessmen."

"It makes life interesting, *non?*" Jean said. "Good day to you, sir."

Jean offered her arm to Sheena, as would a man, and Sheena took it as they left the customhouse.

"He thought you were a man," Sheena said.

"*Oui*, as does everyone else with whom I do business," Jean answered. "I trust you will not give my secret away?"

"No, of course not," Sheena said. "What about your crew? Do they know you are a woman?"

"Only one knows," Jean said. "Monsieur LeGrande. The others are unaware, and I prefer to keep it that way."

"I tried to hide my sex," Sheena said. "But I couldn't."

"That is because you still think as a woman," Jean replied. "I no longer think as a woman, and it is easy for me."

"Is that why you—" Sheena started to ask if that was why Jean chose to make love with her the night before, but she felt too shamed to put it into words. She didn't finish the sentence, because Jean understood.

"*Oui*," she said. "I have strong passions, but I cannot give in to them with a man, for then my sex would be known. Also, I might become great with child, and then I would be beached until the child was born, and perhaps afterward as well. So, I choose to satisfy myself with women. It is a satisfying way of sex, *non?*"

"No," Sheena said.

"Non?" Garneau's eyes sparkled, and she looked at Sheena with an expression of disbelief. *"Ma chérie,* you cannot lie to yourself. Admit that you enjoyed what we did."

"Yes," Sheena said. "I enjoyed it, but it wasn't natural."

"Oh? And the sailors who turn to their own kind to ease the pain of long voyages—is that natural?"

"That's different," Sheena said. "The others accept it, and speak no ill of it."

"There is no difference between women and men when it comes to being denied the opportunity to make love," Garneau said. "Women will turn to their own kind, just as a man will. And as you discovered, the comfort is great."

The two women were walking down a busy cobblestoned street. When a drunk accosted them Sheena held on to Jean's arm for protection as naturally as she would the arm of a man.

"Be off," Jean said to the drunk.

"Sure mate, but would ye be willin' ter share the looksome wench on yer arm there?"

Jean's sword was out in an instant, and the tip of it touched the drunk's neck. "Mind your tongue, monsieur, or I shall cut it from your mouth!"

"Ayiiee, no, don't do that, Cap'n, sure'n I beg of ye. I 'pologize to yer lady fren'."

"Then be off while I'm in a charitable mood," Jean said.

The drunk took a few steps backward, then turned and ran. Both Jean and Sheena laughed. Sheena realized that at this moment she actually thought of Jean as a man, though, except for the role she was playing, Jean certainly wasn't masculine. Last night, Sheena realized with delight, Jean had been a very beautiful woman.

Sheena didn't know exactly why she was feeling as she did right now, but for some reason she was perfectly content to abandon her own role-playing and be just as she appeared to be, a lovely girl on the arm of a handsome escort.

"In here," Jean said, pointing to a brick building. "I came earlier to make reservations for us."

"This is a restaurant?" Sheena asked. "It looks just like a house."

"It's a private club," Jean said. "None but the very wealthy come here. They have excellent food, and, as the patronage is refined, we won't be disturbed by any nasty incidents as are likely to occur downtown."

A uniformed and bewigged black man met them just inside the door. "May I have your name, please?" he asked

"I am Capitaine Jean Garneau. I have a reservation."

"Yes, Captain. If you would check your sword with me, please, I'll show you to your table."

Jean hesitated for just an instant, then shrugged and removed the sword. The doorman hung the sword from a wall hook, then led them into the dining room.

The dining room was beautiful. Two large crystal chandeliers hung from the ceiling, and the highly polished tables were set with sparkling china, glistening crystal goblets, and shining silver utensils. The men and women who were there were elegantly dressed. Sheena was surprised to see that many of the women were black, or mixtures. There were even a few black men, all of whom seemed to fit in with the group.

"There is no prejudice on the island then?" Sheena asked.

"*Oui*, there is prejudice here," Jean said. "For prejudice is in men's hearts. But, there is perhaps less prejudice here than in other places."

Sheena and Jean were seated at their table, where

they dined sumptuously on roast pork, fresh vegetables, fruit, and cheese. Sheena had long been restricted to sea fare, and she ate with a ravenous appetite.

"Don Bustamante, you must come," one of the men at a nearby table was saying. "Ask anyone on the island; they will all tell you that I give the most magnificent parties."

"Oh, yes, Señor Bustamante, last week he had two girls; nubile, nude nymphs, as it were, fighting in a vat of mud," another said. He laughed. "Fighting, mind you. It was hilarious."

"And I'm told you are a man of discriminating tastes," the party-giver said. "I'm sure your presence at my party would make it a tremendous success."

"I'm sure it would, señor," a tall, black-eyed swarthy gentleman answered. "As my appearance at any party makes it a success." He was dressed in the most elaborate finery Sheena had ever seen on a man: a lace shirt with many frills, a green and gold brocade jacket with large, puffy sleeves, and mustard-colored breeches. He was obviously a man of much substance, and the others hovered around him like bees around a flower.

"That is Don Pedro Ricardo Bustamante, supreme emissary and Spanish grandee in the Caribbean," Jean explained. "Some say he is the wealthiest man in the New World."

"Sure'n he dresses the part," Sheena whispered. "He looks like a peacock."

Both women laughed at Sheena's comment.

"I'll be comin' for sure 'n certain," another man spoke up. He was a small, evil-looking man, dressed in a captain's uniform and looking ill-at-ease among the others.

"Captain . . . Boyle, I believe, isn't it?" the party-giver spoke.

"Aye, Boyle it is, cap'n o' the *Sea Witch*."

"Captain Boyle, I believe someone told me you were a slaver."

"Aye, headed tomorrow for Coramantine to pick up a load." He laughed. "I'll turn a fair profit too, I don't mind tellin' you."

"You will forgive me, sir, but I've no wish to see you at any party I give."

"Then you'll have no wish to see me either, señor," Don Bustamante said. "I would rather have enjoyed the captain's stories. I'm sure you have many, do you not?"

"Aye," Boyle said, grinning broadly at this intervention on his behalf. "I've brought nearly two thousand niggers to the New World."

"How many of them lived, sir?" the party-giver asked.

"Them's the ones that lived," Boyle said easily. "I started out with better'n twice that number."

"You mustn't be harsh with people like the good capitán," Don Bustamante said. "After all, if it weren't for people like him, we wouldn't enjoy creatures like this, now, would we?" As he spoke he chucked the chin of a beautiful chocolate-colored girl who sat near him. "I daresay a shipload of these lovelies would be a delightful experience for its crew."

"Aye, we've a fine time with the nigger wenches, that's for sure 'n certain," Boyle said.

"Yes," the party-giver said, now won over by his desire to please Don Bustamante. "Yes, I can see the possibilities. Captain, forgive my outburst. You are more than welcome at my party."

"I'll be there," Boyle said.

Don Bustamante took an apple from the bowl and began peeling it with a golden-handled dagger. "I'll be there as well," he said. He looked toward the party-giver. "That is, on promise of something amusing."

"You'll be amused, Don Bustamante, I promise you that."

"Good, good, I have a very low threshold of boredom," Bustamante replied. He signaled for a waiter, gave him the pared apple and dagger and whispered instructions in his ear. The waiter placed the apple and dagger on a silver tray and carried it over and laid it before Sheena.

"What is this?" Sheena asked.

"Excuse me, ma'am," the waiter said. "It comes from the grandee."

Sheena looked over at the grandee, then nodded her head in thanks, though she would have preferred to be ignored by the man. For all his wealth, he had a brutish air about him which Sheena found unappealing.

"It is customary to say thank you for such gifts," Bustamante said.

"I'm sorry, sir," Sheena replied. "I meant the nod of my head to be taken as thank-you, since I had no wish to interrupt your conversation."

"I don't consider that a thank-you at all," Bustamante said.

"Then allow me to express my thanks," Sheena said, growing more uncomfortable.

"Your behavior is as poor as your table manners," Bustamante said. "You were eating like a pig. I thought perhaps you would want to stuff the apple in your mouth." He squealed like a pig, then laughed, and the others at his table, anxious to please him, laughed with him.

The anger flared so quickly that Sheena acted before she thought. She picked the knife up, then whipped it across the room, pinning Bustamante's voluminous sleeve to the wall.

Bustamante's face registered first terror, then anger, before he brought himself under control. Everyone

else was quiet, waiting to take their cue from Bustamante.

"I've grown rusty, señor," Sheena said. "I meant
to pin your ears to the wall."

Bustamante stared at Sheena for another few seconds, then broke into a smile. It was a controlled
smile, which didn't reach his eyes. Nevertheless, it
broke the tension in the room and allowed the others
to laugh at the incident.

"Then I can only say a prayer of thankfulness that
your aim was off," he said. "Forgive me, señorita, I
was merely seeking a means to lessen the boredom of
the moment."

"Good day to you, sir," Sheena said.

"Waiter, the charges please," Jean called.

"No, please, señor, you must allow me to pay for
the meal," Bustamante said. "By way of apology."

"We—" Sheena started angrily.

"Accept," Jean finished. "Let's go, Sheena," she whispered under her breath.

Sheena wanted to say something else, but at Jean's
urging she left. "Oh," she said, once they were outside.
"How I wish he had a sword in his hand."

"He would never meet you on a field of honor,"
Jean said. "But we can take a little from his purse."

"You mean the meal? If he is as rich as you say, he
will never feel it."

"*Non,* not the meal. The Capitaine Boyle. He leaves
tomorrow for Coramantine, did you not hear him say?"

"Yes, but what does that have to do with Don
Bustamante?"

"Boyle will have money. A great deal of money. And
though Bustamante would keep it secret, I know that
the money is his."

"And we are going to take it from him?" Sheena
asked.

"*Oui.* If you wish to sail with me."

"Yes!" Sheena said, squealing in delight. She hugged Jean around the neck in her happiness.

"Here, now," Jean said. "There will be plenty of time for that later."

"Aye," Sheena said, accepting the remark without question.

30

The *Croix de Triomphe* was tied up at the foot of Nassau's King's Wharf. Its masts stabbed into the sky and its rigging hung from the crossarms, now free of the billowing canvas which propelled it across the seas. It rocked gently back and forth as the heavy barrels of its cargo, tobacco, spices, and rum, were rolled across the deck and down the gangplank to be auctioned.

A carriage moved along the cobblestoned street, with its iron-rimmed wheels humming against the pavement, accompanied by the hollow clumps of the horse's hooves. Two young girls, laughing and whispering to each other, waited for the carriage to pass, then hurried across the street to stand in the crowd and watch the auction.

The auctioning of a privateer's goods always brought large crowds, for there were bargains to be had in helping the buccaneer rid himself of his booty. The going rate was from half to three quarters less than prevailing market prices on the same goods. Often, businessmen found that they had to repurchase the same goods they had consigned barely a month earlier. Still, it was cheaper than replacing their consignment at market price, so though they complained bitterly and cried about being robbed, they were among the most spirited of the bidders.

"And now the rum," Garneau said. "If I get a good price, I'll sell it by the lot. If not, I shall sell it a barrel at a time."

"Seventy-five pounds for the lot," one bidder called, knowing that the price was far too low.

"Eighty," another countered, and the bidding was on.

Behind the bidding businessmen there sat an enclosed coach, pulled by four matching horses and flanked by uniformed liverymen. The carriage was red and white, trimmed with gold, and bore the royal crest of the Spanish grandee.

The grandee himself, Señor Don Pedro Ricardo Bustamante, sat in the shaded interior of the coach, watching the proceedings. He was holding a black cane with a gold, jewel-encrusted head. The fingers which clutched the cane were themselves adorned with rings. There were two beautiful girls in the coach with him, provided for him by the local consul and highly recommended for their inventiveness and skill in bed.

"Señor Bustamante," one of them purred. "How could an auction be more interesting to you than what we have to offer?"

"Yes," the other said. "There is little to do here. Take us to the consulate building, and we can show you a good time."

"Be patient, my pets," Bustamante said, continuing to stare out the window at the auction. Or at least the girls with him thought he was staring at the auction. In fact, he was staring at the beautiful young girl who had thrown the knife at him in the club.

The girl fascinated Bustamante. Never in his life had he been so insulted by so lovely a creature. It was an exquisite situation, a beautiful, desirable woman needing to be punished. And punishing women was an area in which the grandee excelled.

"*Merci beaucoup, monsieurs,* for the spirited way in which you bid for my prize. You have made the voyage of the *Croix de Triomphe* a successful one."

"Señor, surely the bidding has not ended?" Bustamante called. He signaled for one of the liverymen, and the footman opened the coach door to allow him to step outside.

"*Oui,* it is ended, monsieur. I have nothing else to sell."

"That isn't true."

Jean's eyes flashed angrily. "Are you calling me a liar, monsieur?"

"No, no, of course not," Bustamante said quickly, laughing somewhat to defuse Jean's wrath. "But I am told that you have the head of the pirate Mad Jack Ledyard."

"*Oui.*"

"I will pay a handsome price for it," Bustamante said.

"But why would you want such a thing?" Jean asked.

"It amuses me," Bustamante said. "I enjoy amusement."

"*Pardon, monsieur,* but it is not for sale."

Bustamante smiled and removed a paper from his pocket. "I have a signed order by the governor general. It directs you to sell the pirate's head to me."

"How come you by such an order?" Jean asked.

Bustamante chuckled. "I represent the Spanish government in the Caribbean. The English wish to maintain good relations with me. This was a small concession."

"You can't have it," Sheena shouted, stepping up to the rail with flashing, angry eyes.

Bustamante smiled. So, the customs officer was right. The beautiful young girl does have some sentimental attachment to the pirate's head. It was for this very reason that Bustamante wanted to buy it. Through such a purchase, he hoped to have some leverage over Sheena Drumm.

Bustamante looked at one of his liverymen and wagged a jeweled finger at him. The liveryman took off on the run.

"As you can see, I've just sent one of my coachmen to secure an armed detachment from the governor. When he returns they shall board your ship and take the head by force," Bustamante said.

An anxious murmur ran through the crowd, and they turned to look toward the ship to see how Captain Garneau would respond.

"What makes you think they can take it by force?" Jean asked.

Bustamante chuckled again. "My dear capitán. Look at your vessel. You have only yourself, that somewhat dimwitted-looking giant there, and the young lady. Your men are all ashore, besotted, or bedded down with whores. And skillful though your lady friend may be at throwing a knife, I scarcely think she will be of much aid in repelling a determined armed force."

"Habib," Sheena called. Habib walked over to hear Sheena's whispered instructions, then hurried away.

"What did you tell your giant friend?" Bustamante asked. He laughed. "Whatever it was, it must have frightened him, for see how he runs about."

Bustamante was having great sport with Jean and Sheena, and the crowd was beginning to appreciate his sense of humor. They laughed at his jokes, and at the small crew of the *Croix de Triomphe*.

"Oh, dear me, the governor's troops are on their way now. Decide quickly, Señor Captain, and I shall pay you handsomely for the brute's head. Delay, and I shall have it for free."

A detachment of twelve armed men arrived, bearing muskets across their shoulders. The commander of the detachment halted the men, then reported to Bustamante, bringing his hand up in a sharp salute.

"Excellency, I am Lieutenant Thompson at your service, sir. I have been ordered by my government to take possession of the pirate's head for you. Do you know what this is about?"

Bustamante pointed at the ship with his cane. "Yes, señor. As a concession between governments, your governor has decreed that the head of the pirate Mad Jack Ledyard, now on board this vessel, is to be turned over to me. Capitán Garneau, who is French and feels no compulsion to obey your governor, has refused to comply with the request."

"I shall retrieve the head for you, Excellency."

"*Gracias*, Señor."

Thompson ordered his men into a single file, then faced them toward the ship.

"Captain Garneau, by order of the Governor of Nassau, you are commanded to surrender the pirate's head at once," Thompson said.

"Monsieur, I have no intention of heeding those orders."

"I remind you, Captain, that you are in an English port and subject to those orders."

"Then I shall weigh anchor and depart at once," Jean said.

"I'm sorry, Captain, but you will not depart without surrendering the head."

"If we must fight, then we will fight," Jean said.

Thompson looked at Garneau and Sheena. There was no one else visible on board the ship. He turned to look at Bustamante. "Is there only the captain then?" he asked.

"And one frightened giant," Bustamante said. "He has gone below, no doubt to cower in some corner of the ship's hold."

Again the crowd laughed. They drew closer, tin-

gling with excitement at the prospect of being witness
to a battle.

"Detail, raise your weapons," Thompson said.

As one, the line of muskets came up to the shoulders
of the soldiers and were pointed at Jean and Sheena.

"Ready," Thompson yelled.

"What do you say, Sheena? Do we give them the
bastard's head, or do we stand here and get shot?"
Jean asked.

"Wait," Sheena said.

"Wait? *Mon Dieu, chérie,* wait for what?"

Suddenly the crowd was startled by the loud boom of
a cannon being fired from the gundeck. A puff of
smoke billowed from the mouth of the cannon on the
bay side of the ship, and a round black object sailed
through it, then dropped as a small dot, far into the
sea.

"My God!" Thompson shouted. "What was that?"

"That was the pirate's head," Sheena said. "Mad
Jack has just been buried at sea."

Jean had been as shocked as the others to hear the
cannon's report. Now, recovering and realizing what
Sheena had done, she began to laugh. She laughed so
hard that she had to lean against the mast for support,
and the sudden release of tension affected the crowd
so that they, too, joined in the laughter.

"Señor Thompson, I demand that you shoot that
rebellious capitán at once!" Bustamante shouted,
pointing at Jean.

"I'm sorry, sir," Thompson said, having trouble
holding a straight face himself. By now even his soldiers were laughing. "I have no orders save to recover
the head. That now seems to be impossible."

Habib came back on deck and looked out toward
the crowd, smiling broadly.

"Well done, giant," one of the crowd shouted, and
all cheered, so that Habib flexed his muscles and
basked in the glory that was his for the moment.

Bustamante whirled about angrily and climbed back into the coach. He banged on the side of the coach and shouted something in angry Spanish at the driver. The coach jumped ahead, chased by the laughter of those on the dock.

"Sheena, that was a very brave thing you did," Jean said, wiping away the tears of her laughter. "But it was also very foolish, for you've made an enemy of a man who has influence throughout the Spanish Main."

The man who had influence throughout the Caribbean was still seething in anger as his coach clattered over the cobblestoned streets, bound for the consulate offices and the bedroom apartment there. The focus of his anger was Sheena Drumm. He would have no rest until he had punished her.

"I'm glad we left that old auction," one of the girls with him said.

"Me too," the other agreed. "Now the fun is about to start."

Bustamante looked at them, and for the moment at least was able to lay his anger aside. He didn't have Sheena Drumm to punish, but he did have these two lovely creatures. He thought of the ropes, masks, chains, and whips he had brought to Nassau with him, now waiting for him in the bedroom. The palms of his hands grew sweaty, and his breath came in shorter gasps.

"*Si, mi bonitas,*" Bustamante said, thinking of the exquisite agony they would soon feel when his whip cut into their flesh. "The fun is about to start."

Liam was visiting all the grogshops, trying to find out about the *Marcus B.* He knew that Sheena was on board, and when he heard that the *Marcus B.* had been spoken, rudder-damaged but only one day's sailing from Nassau, he decided that he would leave the *Sea Witch* and wait for her arrival.

Liam could have jumped ship, but such was his fear

of Boyle that he chose to go and see the little man and request his permission to stay ashore. He finally found him at a party.

"Surgeon," Boyle said, looking up when Liam was directed to him. Boyle had a naked young girl on each arm and was himself nude. In this state he presented such an unimposing figure that Liam wondered why he was so frightened of him. But he had only to recall the keelhauling incident to understand the reason. "What are you doing here?"

"Captain, I've heard that the *Marcus B.* will be arriving on the morrow. I should like to meet it."

"That's impossible," Boyle said. "We'll be leaving with the mornin' tide."

"But I must meet it," Liam said.

"I told you, that's impossible."

A door opened from a nearby room, and a tall, black-eyed man stepped out. His skin was bathed in a sheen of perspiration, and he patted at his lips with a perfumed handkerchief.

"Oh, there you are, Capitán Boyle. Allow me to express my thanks once again for your gift. She was exquisite."

"I trust she was a virgin as I promised?" Boyle said. "This man is my surgeon and he verified the fact, so if you have any complaints, you may take them up with him."

"Oh, I have no complaints at all, Capitán," the man said. "Indeed, she was such a lovely creature that had she not been a virgin, I could have still enjoyed it. As it is, I have taken exquisite delight in satisfying my own pleasures while leaving her virginity unspoiled."

"What? I don't understand," Liam said. "How could you have your pleasures while the girl is yet a virgin?"

The man laughed, a shrill, almost feminine laugh. "My dear, dear boy. You've a great deal to learn, and yet, from the looks of you, I've no doubt but that you would be an excellent student."

"I must confess, sir, that I do enjoy the pursuit of pleasure and would appreciate learning of new experiences."

The man laughed again. "What is your surgeon's name, Capitán? I like him."

"Leo—"

"Liam O'Sheel," Liam said, interrupting Boyle with his right name.

Bustamante laughed again. He wagged a finger at Liam. "Ah, and you found it necessary to give the good capitán a fictitious name, eh? No doubt, escaping some devilment in the Carolinas."

"Yes, sir," Liam admitted.

"Well, my name is Don Bustamante. I insist that you remain as my guest for a while."

"Captain?" Liam asked, looking at Boyle.

"If Don Bustamante wants you to stay, you shall stay," Boyle said.

"Oh, and to compensate you for your loss, Capitán," Bustamante said, "I shall send the young girl back with you. I imagine she will fetch a fine price at the auction in Coramantine. And you shall be able to enjoy the pleasure of her company on the long trip over. I imagine you have been wanting to sample her delights, have you not?"

"Aye," Boyle said. "I must confess to that. Though realizing the value you placed on her virginity, I abstained."

"Well, you need abstain no longer, my dear fellow. She is now yours to enjoy. To you, Capitán, I wish a pleasant trip. And you, Liam, I bid come with me. I have more entertainment lined up. Your first lesson shall begin tonight."

"Good-bye, Captain," Liam said to Boyle. "I hope you enjoy Tricia. I never had the pleasure."

"I shall enjoy her, Surgeon. I shall indeed," Boyle said, looking toward the room with a gleam of anticipation in his eye.

31

Sheena was home again. At least that was the way she regarded it, for never had she found a place more to her liking than the open sea. As she stood on the quarter-deck of the *Croix de Triomphe* and watched New Providence Island sink into the sea behind them, she was at peace with herself.

Gone was the woman's finery she had worn in Nassau. Once again she was dressed in pants and a shirt. This time the shirt was much smaller and less cumbersome, thus allowing her more freedom of movement. It also clung to her body, advertising her breasts, but as it was no longer necessary to conceal her true gender, it didn't really matter.

Jean had been walking the deck, checking the rigging, and she came back to climb the three short steps up to the quarter-deck. "It is good to be at sea again," she said. "I do not like the land."

"Not even France?"

Jean laughed. "In truth, *chérie*?"

"In truth."

"I've never been to France. My father was a French naval officer during the wars with England. He sneaked my mother on board. She died giving birth to me while we were at sea. When the French government discovered this, my father was cashiered from the navy, so he acquired a ship and became a privateer. He kept me with him, disguised always as a boy, to protect me from the sailors. I learned navigation, seamanship, and the art of fighting, first by watching as a curious child, then later, by participating myself. I've known no home but a ship for my entire life."

"I've known many," Sheena said. "But I've no wish to know any other. This is what I want to do for the rest of my life."

"Ah, *ma chérie*, and therein is the rub," Jean said. "As a pirate, or even a privateer, you have to be prepared for the fact that you may not have a very long life."

"I don't care," Sheena said. "Sure'n to my way of thinking one year at sea is worth four ashore."

"*Oui*," Jean said. "But I have devised a plan which will perhaps lengthen your life."

"Oh? How so?"

"When we close with the *Sea Witch*, you will maintain the helm. You will not board her with the rest of us."

"No!" Sheena said. "I *will* board her."

"Your share of the prize will be the same, Sheena, but in this way you will have less risk."

"Jean, have you forgotten that I nearly bested you in swordsmanship? You yourself said that I was the most skilled you had faced."

"*Oui*, but I did best you."

"Aye, but you can best everyone, so that is no measure. Besides, I boarded the *Goodhope* when Ledyard took her and I handled myself quite well on that occasion."

Jean put her hand on Sheena's cheek. "*Ma chérie*, it is because I care for you that I ask this."

"Jean, I have shared your bed, and I will continue

to share it, but I will not be treated as something you possess. I will board the *Sea Witch*."

"Very well, Sheena. If you insist upon this, I shall not try to stop you."

Sheena smiled. "Thank you. Besides, I'll have Habib with me. Who would dare hurt me with Habib by my side?"

"That is right. Who would risk coming near your giant?" Jean agreed.

As they spoke his name they looked forward to see Habib, the muscles in his six-foot-nine-inch body bulging as he hoisted canvas, doing alone the job which normally required three men.

The *Croix de Triomphe* held fair winds and calm seas for the next month. During those days Sheena increased her knowledge of seamanship, and even began studying the psychology of command, observing how Jean was able to maintain discipline and morale in her crew.

Sheena learned things at night as well. She explored the extreme limits of her sexual sensitivity and rid herself of any lingering sense of doubt or guilt she may have felt. Thoughts that she might be doing "evil," or "wrong," no longer came to her mind. There was only a sense of sharing, and the awareness that sex was a great gift to be enjoyed.

But there was something else. Something that Sheena couldn't quite put into thought, let alone words. Sex with Jean had been gratifying . . . but not satisfying. It was promising, but not fulfilling. After the initial flush of new sensations, Sheena discovered that there was still more to be had. Though she would take no overt action to terminate her relationship with Jean, Sheena knew that for her this could only be a temporary thing. She could never abandon herself to it entirely, as had Jean. And now more than ever, she realized what she had lost when Billy stepped off the end of the plank.

Habib made a special sword for Sheena. He took a regular sword and reshaped it, working it very carefully to adjust the balance just perfectly. On several occasions over the next few days he would place Sheena's hand in the handle, take measurements, then pull the sword back and work on it more. Finally he handed the weapon to her, smiling broadly at her reaction.

"Habib, it is amazing!" Sheena said, whipping the sword through the air in a series of movements. "Why, it feels as light as my fencing foil, yet it has the strength of a cutlass. You have done a magnificent job, and I thank you for it."

"Do you think you can use that sword, Sheena?" Jean asked, peering through the spyglass toward the open sea.

"Aye, truly, Jean, it is a work of art."

"That is good," Jean said. "For you will soon have the opportunity to put it to use."

"Why do you say that?"

Jean handed the spyglass to Sheena. "Look, there, one point off the starboard bow."

As Sheena put the glass to her eye and circled in the distance, she saw a tiny flash of sail. "It's the *Sea Witch*!" she said excitedly.

"*Oui*, and making good speed." Jean took the spyglass back and snapped it shut. "Helm, south-south-west. I'm glad we have the proper angle. I don't know that we could outrun her, as fast as the *Croix de Triomph* is."

Sheena watched the distance close between the ships. Just as she'd observed when on board the *Marcus B.*, she was aware of the almost steady parade to the head by the sailors who were preparing the ship for combat. Then she noticed that the cannoneers were loading ball into the cannon.

"Jean, your men are loading ball," she said.

"*Oui*. It has the greater range and can strike a mortal blow to the ship."

"But shouldn't you use grape?"

"*Chérie*, grape is a nasty business," Jean said. "It has one use, and that is to kill or maim men. Ball can only damage the ship."

"But if the ship sinks, won't we lose our prize?"

"You forget, Captain Boyle carries gold for payment to this slave-seller. It can be transferred quickly, even as the ship sinks."

"And the crew of the *Sea Witch*?"

"They will be put over in the captain's launch. They are but five days' sailing time from the nearest inhabited island," Jean explained.

As they drew closer to the *Sea Witch*, her lines became more clear. She was long and lean, a rakish ship, far more beautiful than anything Sheena had ever seen before. The thought of sinking her was breaking Sheena's heart.

"Isn't she beautiful?" Sheena asked.

"*Oui*. She is built for speed. The faster she can return, the fewer of the poor devils who must die in her holds."

"Wouldn't such a ship make a magnificent privateer?" Sheena asked.

"*Oui*, but even if one could find a shipbuilder who would do business with a privateer, one could not afford to pay the price for such a vessel."

"Jean, let's capture her and make the ship our prize," Sheena suggested.

"Do you mean take her in tow?"

"No," Sheena said. "We would put a crew on board her. Jean, we could have two privateers, and share the profits!"

Jean looked at Sheena and laughed. "Have you any idea who might command such a vessel?"

"Aye," Sheena said. "I would command her."

"I thought as much," Jean said, laughing again at the suggestion.

"Do you think that I could not?" Sheena asked hotly.

"*Non, non, non, chérie.* I think that perhaps you could. But what crew would follow a woman commander?"

"Your crew follows you."

"They do not know I am a woman."

"Monsieur LeGrande knows, yet his loyalty is just as great."

"*Oui,* you are right about LeGrande." Jean rubbed her chin. As they drew closer she looked at the *Sea Witch,* waiting patiently for the impending battle. "I'll tell you what, *chérie.* If you can get ten of my crew to volunteer to go with you, and ten of the crew of the *Sea Witch* to agree to stay, then I'll say we will do it."

"Very well, muster all hands and I shall put it to them," Sheena said.

Jean stepped forward on the quarter-deck and asked LeGrande to assemble all hands. A moment later the entire crew was assembled aft of the mainmast, waiting to hear what their captain had to say.

"Messieurs," Jean began. "It has been proposed that we take the *Sea Witch* as a prize ship."

"But, Captain, where could we sell her? She is not in violation of French maritime law, and to take her would be outside our authority as a privateer," Le-Grande pointed out.

"*Oui,*" Jean replied. "But if we did not sell her, but put a crew aboard her instead, we would have two privateers, and double the prize money to split between the crews."

"*Oui, mon capitaine,*" a few of the men shouted. "That is a marvelous idea."

"Who will command her?" LeGrande asked.

"I will," Sheena said, stepping up to stand beside Jean.

"You?" many sailors asked as one. "But you are a woman."

"Aye. And a navigator, and a seaman, and a fighter. I need ten brave lads who will come with me, and we'll make history!" she shouted.

" 'Tis bad luck to sail with a woman aboard," another said.

"I am aboard now," Sheena said. "Do you feel bad luck?"

There was a general grumbling of discontent among the men, and Sheena felt that she was losing them until she received help from a surprising source. LeGrande held up his arms to call for quiet.

"Messieurs, hear me," he spoke. "I think the mademoiselle would make a fine capitaine, and you would do well to sail with her."

"You, Monsieur LeGrande? But by rights you should command the new ship," one of the men said.

"I have no ambition to do so," LeGrande said. "I served proudly with Capitaine Garneau's father, and I serve just as proudly with Capitaine Garneau. I do not wish a command of my own. But Mademoiselle Sheena has shown not only seamanship, but courage. You have been told of the trick with Mad Jack Ledyard's head. Who among you would have had the courage to do as she did?"

LeGrande had chosen the correct example to cite, for the story of Ledyard's head being fired out to sea from a cannon had kept the crew entertained from the time they quit New Providence Island.

"I'll serve with mademoiselle," LeClerc said. He looked at the others. "You may remember what a fight she put up when we captured the *Marcus B*. She impressed me then, and I didn't even know she was a woman."

"I'll serve as well," another said, moving over to stand with LeClerc. Within a moment there were ten men standing nearby, volunteering their services to man the new ship. With Habib that made eleven, and Sheena turned to Jean with a smile.

"I didn't think they would do it," Jean said. "But I will honor my word, *chérie*. We will capture the *Sea Witch*. What will you name her?"

"She is the *Sea Witch* now, and so she shall remain," Sheena said. "In view of her commander I think the name is appropriate, do you not?"

"*Oui*, very appropriate," Jean said. "So, my little one, you have realized your dream to become a capitaine. And I . . . I have lost your sweet company. *Mon Dieu*, what have I done?"

"You have become an admiral," Sheena said.

Jean smiled. "*Oui*. An admiral. Not even my father had such an honor. The title will be cold company to an empty bed, but I shall somehow content myself with it."

"Capitaine, the *Sea Witch* is showing signals," Le-Grande said.

The *Croix de Triomphe* was close enough to the *Sea Witch* now for Sheena to see easily the sailor who was running up the flags. She also saw Boyle, staring back at them through his spyglass. She gave him a big smile and waved coquettishly at him, then laughed when she saw him lower the spyglass and close it in anger.

"What . . . is . . . your . . . intention?" LeGrande said, reading the flags.

"Monsieur LeClerc," Jean called suddenly.

"*Oui, mon capitaine.*"

"Fire a shot across the bow of the *Sea Witch*. Then fire two more shots, to show that we have her bracketed."

"*Oui, mon capitaine.*"

"Monsieur LeGrande, show signals: come dead in the water or be sunk."

"*Oui*, Capitaine Garneau."

LeGrande affixed the flags to the halyard and ran them up to flutter in the breeze.

"Monsieur LeClerc, you may fire."

The three guns flashed and roared, and a white feather of water shot up in front of the *Sea Witch*, then two more, one on each side of the ship. The gun crews immediately began swabbing the barrels and preparing to reload.

"She's spilling air, Capitaine, she's backing down," LeGrande said. Even as he spoke Sheena saw the great billowing sails flatten as sailors pulled on the spilling lines to kill the wind's thrust.

"Prepare to board," Jean said, and, as on board the *Marcus B.*, sailors went into the braces carrying their weapons, preparatory to swinging aboard the *Sea Witch*. Moments later the two ships were alongside, and twenty pirates, including Jean, Sheena, and Habib, leaped onto the deck of the *Sea Witch*.

"Quarter, quarter!" Captain Boyle called, holding his arms up as Sheena and the others boarded his vessel. "Why have you boarded me? Could you not tell that I was in ballast? I have nothing for you."

"That's not quite true, monsieur," Jean said. "You have the gold you are to pay out for the slaves."

"What? How did you find that out?" Boyle asked, genuinely surprised that Jean knew.

Sheena took a dagger from her belt, and in a quick, whipping motion snapped it toward Boyle, pinning his sleeve to the bulkhead behind him.

"You! I know you! You are the girl in the club!" Boyle said, suddenly realizing.

Sheena, Jean, and their men, who had by now heard the story, all laughed.

"Now you know how we know about the gold," Jean said. "So bring it on deck, Capitaine."

"It's in my cabin. I'll get it," Boyle said.

"I'll get it," Sheena put in quickly. "Habib, come with me."

Sheena stepped into Boyle's cabin. It was nothing like Jean's cabin, nor even as large as Ledyard's cabin had been. It was much more spartan, like Captain Collier's cabin on board the *Cassandra*.

"There, under the bed," Sheena said. "That must be it."

Sheena heard a movement behind her. She whirled quickly, bringing the point of her sword to bear. There was a cloth hanging over what appeared to be a clothes closet, and she could see the cloth moving.

"Come out of there," she said quietly.

There was no response.

"Come out of there," she said again. "Come out of there, or I'll run you through."

A young girl stepped out, covering her face in fear. She had skin the color of golden honey, and long, luxurious, blue-black hair. There was something hauntingly familiar about her.

"My God," Sheena said. "Tricia, is that you?"

The girl dropped her hands and looked at Sheena. Her face lit up in recognition, then thankfulness, and she leaped at Sheena with a shout of joy, throwing her arms around her in an embrace.

"It is you," Sheena said. She put her arms around the girl, comforting her. Tricia's body quivered, like a frightened bird. Sheena could understand the fear Tricia felt. "Don't be frightened, little one," she said. "You are safe now."

32

There was much work to do to convert the *Sea Witch*
to a privateer. The *Sea Witch* had only four cannons,
plus two swivel guns, so two more cannons were transferred from the *Croix de Triomphe*. There was little
useful hold to the *Sea Witch,* as shelves had been built
to allow the human cargo to lie in chains. Those
shelves had to be removed.

As Sheena was the new captain of the *Sea Witch,*
she naturally stayed aboard to supervise the new fit-
tings. Jean and the ones who would remain with her
returned to the *Croix de Triomphe,* which stayed
alongside during the work.

Though more of Boyle's crew were willing to stay,
Sheena selected only six of them, not being satisfied
with the quality of the others. They set Boyle and his
crew adrift in the captain's launch, a seaworthy vessel
which was more than adequate to make the journey
to a nearby island. Boyle left, cursing them soundly
and promising that they would pay for their crime.
Sheena's crew laughed and threw insults at Boyle.
Sheena noticed with some surprise that those men of
Boyle's crew who had stayed with her were just as

vociferous as her own men in heaping insults upon the little man.

The work continued until after sunset. By the light of a very bright moon and several lanterns, the carpenters went on. Sheena was standing on the quarter-deck—her quarter-deck, she thought with a smile—when Jean and some of her men returned to the *Sea Witch*.

"Will you be ready to get underway by tomorrow?" Jean asked.

"Aye. Repairs are proceeding rapidly."

Jean handed a package to Sheena. "Here," she said. "I'll bet you haven't eaten."

"Sure 'n I have not," Sheena said. "I've been that excited that I forgot entirely."

"I thought as much. That's why I brought dinner to you."

"How is Tricia?" Sheena asked, biting into the bread.

"She's had a bad time, Sheena. She was terribly abused. There are scars all over her body. She is such a beautiful creature, with skin so lovely. To think of her being disfigured is awful."

Sheena looked up in surprise. "How came she by such punishment?"

"The poor girl sobbed the story out to me as I put soothing balm on her wounds," Jean said. "It seems she had a run-in with your admirer, the grandee."

"Tricia and the grandee? How could that be?"

"Tricia was captured by bounty hunters."

"Yes, that would be. My brother and father authorized bounty hunters. But it was to return her to Bonny Isle that they were hired."

"Bounty hunters sell to the highest bidder. In this case it was Boyle."

"And that bastard raped her?"

"*Non*. At least not then," Jean said. "Boyle knew a good thing, and he knew that a beautiful, very young

virgin girl would put him in good with the grandee.
So he took her to Bustamante. Bustamante took his
pleasures with her, then gave her back to Boyle to de-
prive her of her virginity."

"But—I don't understand. What pleasures did Bustamante take?"

Jean laughed softly. *"Chérie,* for one who has known
so much adventure, you still know so little. There are
men who get their pleasure by inflicting pain and torture on women. Don Bustamante is such a man. He
whipped our little Tricia, then held a hot iron to her
skin, and inflicted tiny cuts with his knife."

"Oh, how awful," Sheena said, shuddering involun-
tarily as she thought of the torture Tricia had gone
through. "How did Tricia escape?"

"She didn't have to. As I said, when Bustamante
finished with her he gave her back to Boyle in exchange for—*mon Dieu."* Jean put her hand to her
mouth. "I nearly forgot. *Chérie,* I have some bad news
for you."

"What news?"

"Your papa, Sheena. I'm afraid he is dead."

"Dead? But—but how? I don't understand."

"Your brother, Liam. Tricia told me the news.
There was an awful fight. Liam killed your papa."

"My poor father," Sheena said with a sigh. "He
was so blind to Liam that the blindness finally killed
him." She was amazed that she had no tears to shed.
Though, in truth, she did feel a sadness, and was com-
forted to know that she had some human decency left.
"I wonder where Liam is?"

"He is in Nassau," Jean said.

"He is?"

"Tricia said that he was on this same ship, but
stayed in Nassau as a guest of Don Bustamante."

"Aye," Sheena said. "I can believe that, for Liam
and Don Bustamante are cut from the same bolt of
cloth."

"That is how Tricia was returned to Boyle," Jean said. "Don Bustamante gave her back to him, in return for taking Liam off his ship. Liam was serving as his surgeon."

"It is lucky for the crew of the *Sea Witch* that none became ill," Sheena said derisively. "Perhaps I should take Tricia with me. After all, she was my father's slave girl, and I do feel responsible for her."

"*Non, ma chérie*," Jean said. "I will take her. As admiral I claim that right."

"You are talking of her as if she is a prize."

"She is a prize. After all, didn't I claim you as my prize when first we met?"

"No, Jean, you were never cruel, but still—"

"Still, you were my prize. And now Tricia is. I will be most gentle with her, I can promise you that. I feel that she will welcome a woman's touch after all she has been through. Besides, you have deserted my bed, *chérie*. I need some recompense."

"Promise me you won't force her to do anything," Sheena said.

Jean laughed. "*Chérie*, I do not force women . . . I persuade. Do not fear for your little one. She is in good hands."

Sheena gave a throaty laugh and took Jean's hands in hers. "Aye, 'n I can vouch for that," she said in a sultry voice.

Jean enjoyed the private joke with her, then turned to look toward the *Croix de Triomphe*. The stern windows glowed golden, while red and green lanterns shone on deck. It was quite a beautiful sight. "I'll be returning to my ship now, Sheena," she said easily. "Tomorrow, we will split up, the better to patrol the shipping lanes. Let us agree to meet in two months in Martinique."

"Aye," Sheena said. "Martinique it is."

Jean started to leave, then stopped and turned toward Sheena. "One thing you should know," she said. "My commission authorizes me to stop only those foreign ships which are trading in violation of French maritime law. Smugglers they are, officially. I've violated that now. I have crossed the line. I'll hang when caught. It's not too late for you, but the first ship you stop will make you a true pirate, Sheena. You could suffer my fate."

"Aye," Sheena said quietly. "I know that, Jean. But I was a pirate the moment I set foot on the deck of the *Goodhope*, the king's own ship."

"As long as you know," Jean said.

"I'll be going after only Spanish ships now," Sheena said. "I've a score to settle with the grandee."

Jean laughed. "I thought as much. It is just as well I've violated my commission, for Spain is an ally to France." She shrugged. "It doesn't matter. We are true pirates now and any ship fat for the taking will be fair prize."

"Aye," Sheena said with a smile. "And I hope the prizes are fair for the picking."

"Good-bye, and good luck, Sheena."

Sheena watched as Jean and those who came with her rowed the short distance back to the *Croix de Triomphe*.

"Capitaine, the repairs are concluded," LeClerc said, coming aft to the quarter-deck. "The new cannons are mounted and the hold is cleared away. Shall I set the watch now?"

"Aye," Sheena said, still glowing from the term, "captain." It was the first time she had been so addressed and it was a thrilling moment for her.

"I'll toll out the men, then."

"Mr. LeClerc, be prepared to get underway at sunup."

"*Oui, mon capitaine*," LeClerc said. "Oh, and Capitaine, if I may say something?"

"Yes, of course, LeClerc."

"Do not attempt to hide the fact that you are a

woman. The men will serve you with great pride, mademoiselle. You have no need for subterfuge."

"Thank you, LeClerc," Sheena said. "I am proud that you hold such an opinion of me."

"It is the opinion of your entire crew, Capitaine. Good night."

"Good night," Sheena said. She left the quarter-deck and went into the captain's cabin to spend her first night in command of her own ship.

33

The eastern sky began to grow lighter. First a gray in the blackness, then a pale silver, and finally a soft pink as dawn broke. Sheena, too excited to sleep, had come on deck long before dawn and now stood at the rail watching the sky brighten in brilliant bars of color.

"Signals from the *Croix de Triomphe,*" LeClerc called to her.

"What do they say?"

"Martinique . . . two . . . months . . . bon . . . voyage," LeClerc read. "Do you wish to reply, Capitaine?"

"Yes," Sheena said. "Say, treat prize gently."

"*Pardon, Capitaine?*" LeClerc asked, clearly puzzled by the strange message.

"Treat prize gently. Captain Garneau will understand."

"*Oui, Capitaine,*" LeClerc said, hoisting the signals.

A moment later the flags were changed on the *Croix de Triomphe,* which was now beating off on a bearing of north by northeast. LeClerc read them to Sheena.

"Prize . . . agrees . . . in . . . good . . . hands," LeClerc read. "Do you understand that, Capitaine?"

"Yes," Sheena said, laughing. "And thank you, Mister LeClerc. We'll be getting underway now."

The canvas boomed and stiffened in the wind, and the *Sea Witch* heeled over to answer the breeze. She ran as smooth as she looked. Sheena paced around the wheel and compass, looking aloft, looking amidships, sometimes walking over to the rail and leaning over to gaze along the side of the sleek hull. She had never known such pride, or felt a more thrilling moment than when walking the quarter-deck of her own ship while underway.

Sheena had the good fortune to inherit a well-drilled and disciplined crew. During the next week she and her crew learned the ways of the new ship. They practiced stripping her down for battle, also backing down, coming about, tacking, and all other such maneuvers as they might need in the plying of their avocation.

During that week they spotted five ships. The first two appeared to be running in ballast. The third one, riding low in the water and obviously fat with cargo, was also English, and the crew was certain it would attack. Sheena declined, saying they weren't quite ready. In truth, even though she was already classified as a pirate, Sheena had no desire to attack an English ship as yet, and the crew surmised as much, so they didn't complain over their lack of action. The other two ships sighted that week were French, and one of them was a war frigate.

On the eighth day the lookout sung down a new sighting.

"Where away?" Sheena called.

"Dead starboard," the lookout replied. Sheena ran to the right side of the ship and opened her spyglass to search the wide blue horizon. She found it, a puff of white against the blue, and stared at it for a long moment. She was aware of someone by her side and turned to see LeClerc, then handed the glass to him.

"What might she be?" Sheena asked.

LeClerc stared for a moment, then smiled and snapped the glass closed. "From her rigging and freeboard I'd say she is a Spanish flute," he said. "She is likely to be lightly armed."

"Spanish?" Sheena said. She hit her fist into the palm of her hand and gave a little whoop of joy. "Now, Mister LeClerc, we attack," she said.

As a type of ship, the flute originated with the Dutch, but its design afforded a tremendous carrying capacity and thus was soon picked up by many other countries as well. It was round-sterned, high and slab-sided, stubby-beaked, and ship-rigged. It offered great stability in heavy seas but very little in the way of speed. The *Sea Witch*, which was a topsail-rigged schooner, was more than twice as fast as the Spanish flute, and she closed rapidly on the target.

The Spanish ship fired one badly aimed broadside at the *Sea Witch* as the *Sea Witch* closed, and Sheena ordered one volley of return fire. The cannonball from one of the guns raked the poop of the Spanish ship, killing the helmsman and carrying away the steering gear. With the flute out of control the *Sea Witch* came alongside easily. Sheena led her men across the way, onto the deck, and amidst the jumbled pieces of gear of the Spanish ship. Shots rang out as soon as they boarded, and she heard the railing beside her splinter with a heavy ball.

Habib was by her side. He took two men down within the first few seconds. One of her men screamed, and from the corner of her eye she saw him tumble over the rail with a pike through his chest. A bearded face loomed before her. She parried his thrust easily as steel clanged against steel, one clash sending sparks flying.

There were curses in Spanish and French, and wild shouts of hate and fear, but Sheena's band of men soon prevailed and the flute captain asked for quarter. The Spanish sailors, hearing their captain surrender, dropped their weapons and threw up their arms. The level of sound diminished immediately. When the last, lingering echo of ringing steel died, there were only the quiet moans and cries of the wounded and dying.

"What is your cargo, Captain?" Sheena asked.

"*Dios,* you are a woman!" the Spanish captain said.

"Captain Sheena Drumm at your service," Sheena said easily. "Now, what is your cargo?"

"Pigs," the captain said.

"You have admirable courage, Captain, to call us pigs while at our mercy. You also have poor manners."

"No, Captain, I do not call you pigs," the Spanish captain said quickly. "My cargo is pigs."

One of Sheena's crew opened a hatch cover, then pulled away, making a face at the smell. *"Mon Dieu,* he is right!" the sailor said, turning around and holding his nose. "What a smell!"

The others laughed at the sailor, but Sheena felt disappointed. She wanted her first prize to be one which could be easily converted into money for her crew.

"Do not worry, Capitaine," LeClerc said easily when he read the disappointment on Sheena's face. "There will be other prizes. And for now, we shall confiscate two of the animals and prepare a feast of roast pork."

"God's beard, Captain," Sheena swore. "Why did you put up such a battle? Men were killed and wounded for nothing. You knew we would not want your cargo."

"I—I couldn't be sure," the captain answered. He licked his lips apprehensively and looked at his crew.

The squeals of pigs interrupted them as a few of Sheena's men carried two of the squirming animals over to the *Sea Witch,* which was bouncing on the seas hard alongside the Spanish ship.

"Are you ready to quit this ship, Capitaine?" LeClerc asked.

"Aye," Sheena said disgustedly. " 'Tis but a puzzle

to me why men would fight so for no reason." She started toward the railing, then stopped and looked back toward the Spanish captain. It might have been her imagination, but she thought she saw just the slightest trace of smugness on his face, as if he had won a major victory.

But he hadn't won a victory, Sheena thought. He had lost a battle, and had had some of his crew killed for nothing. So what reason would he have for smugness? Unless . . . "Mister LeClerc, wait a minute!" Sheena called out.

LeClerc looked at her with a puzzled expression on his face.

"Check the good captain's cabin," Sheena said.

"No, señor, you can't go in there!" the Spanish captain said, moving toward the door.

Sheena smiled. "Perhaps there is something else in this pigsty, yes?"

LeClerc ordered two men into the captain's cabin. Sheena and the others waited for them on deck. No one talked or moved for several seconds, and there was only the hum of the wind in the rigging and the rustle of the furled sails to accompany the lapping of the sea. After several seconds there was a shout of elation from the captain's cabin, and the two men came running out on deck, carrying a chest. It was filled to overflowing with jewelry: diamond rings, emerald necklaces, ruby pins, gold and silver goblets, loose precious stones, and gold coins.

"That is the personal property of the supreme emissary, His Excellency, Don Pedro Ricardo Bustamante, Spanish Grandee of the Caribbean," the Spanish captain said.

"No, Captain," Sheena said easily. "That is the prize of the crew of the *Sea Witch*!"

Sheena's men, cheering and laughing at their good luck, carried the treasure chest with them to their own ship. This time when Sheena started across the railing she looked into the face of the Spanish captain and saw not the smug look of victory but the crestfallen look of defeat.

It was an exuberant crew on board the *Sea Witch* that night. The rich smell of roast pork hung in the air. There was music and dancing and much celebration. But through it all a watch was maintained, for Sheena applied well the lesson she had learned on board the *Marcus B.*

34

Don Bustamante and Liam O'Sheel now shared a common goal. Each of them wanted to capture Sheena, each for his own reason. The fact was, however, that Bustamante had no idea that Liam wanted her for himself. Had he known of Liam's need to quench the terrible inferno Sheena had ignited in him, he would have recognized at once the incompatibility of purpose, and sought Sheena on his own.

As it was, Liam convinced Bustamante that he could find Sheena and would deliver her to him, if only Bustamante would furnish and outfit a ship. And so Bustamante entered into an unholy alliance with Liam, for the express purpose of finding Sheena.

Liam found a ship, bought it, outfitted it, and manned it all at Bustamante's expense. He manned it with American and English sailors, ostensibly to avoid a language problem. In fact, he manned it in such a way as to ensure that the crew would be loyal to him, and not to Bustamante. Had Bustamante realized that Liam had no intention of returning Sheena to him, Liam would have been unable to hire English-speaking sailors. In fact, Liam would have hired no sailors, for Liam would have been dead.

Liam had a brilliant plan. He disguised his ship to look like a fat merchantman, riding low in the water, as if heavily laden with rich prize. It would sail slowly through the Spanish Main. When spotted by the *Croix de Triomphe* it would strike its colors and beg for mercy. Then, when Captain Garneau and the others boarded, Liam would spring upon them with concealed men, kill or capture them all, and save Sheena for his own personal entertainment.

And Liam knew just what the entertainment would be. First he would use her, spending his passion on her until he was completely satiated. And when he wanted her no more he would strip her naked and have her keelhauled before his crew.

Already Liam could feel a tingling in his groin as he thought of the pleasure that lay before him.

"Cap'n, sails!"

"Where away?"

"One point off the larboard stern."

Liam looked through the telescope but could see only a dot on the horizon. As yet, it was too far away to tell.

"Reduce sail," he ordered. "I want that ship to catch us before dark."

"Aye, Cap'n. Do you think that be it?"

"I don't know," Liam said. He looked through the telescope again, though he knew such a gesture was useless.

The day wore on. Noon came and passed. Liam ate hardtack and salt meat at his post, watching the ship advancing under full press of sail. It had been definitely identified now as the *Croix de Triomphe* by several of the men who had seen the ship in Nassau.

"She'll be showin' signals soon, Cap'n," Liam's mate said.

"When she shows signals press on all sail. Make a show as if we're running," Liam said. "Then, when she fires a warning shot, we'll strike colors."

"Aye, Cap'n. Shall I arm the men now?"

"Yes, but for god's sake keep them out of sight. If the men are seen before the pirates board us, they'll rake our stern with shot, then pull away, and we'll lose them. The men must stay out of sight. Do you have that? They must stay out of sight!"

"Aye, Cap'n. Not to worry. They're good men, the lot of 'em."

"They are wharf rats and sea bums," Liam said. "The man who gives us away will be keelhauled for his stupidity."

"Aye, Cap'n."

"Cap'n, she's showin' signals," the lookout shouted down. "Heave to for boarding."

"We've got them!" Liam shouted excitedly. "Put on more sail. Let's make a show of running for it."

"Aye, Cap'n," the mate said, hurrying to carry out Liam's order.

Liam watched the reaction of the *Croix de Triomphe* to the addition of more sail. Then, just as he predicted it would, the *Croix de Triomphe* fired a round from its bow chaser. Liam saw the bright flash, then the puff of white smoke. A cannonball arced toward them, passed through one of the sails with a ripping sound, then splashed into the water beyond. The dull thudding boom of the cannon reached his ears a moment later.

"Signals changing, sir. Heave to or she will sink you."

"Very well, we shall heave to," Liam said. "All right, men, into your positions! Clerk, strike our colors and run up a white flag!"

"Aye, sir," a bandy-legged little man answered. The colors, a Spanish ensign, were struck, and a white flag was raised.

The *Croix de Triomphe* glided majestically toward them, then maneuvered into a broadside position. Grappling hooks were thrown across the way, and the ships were pulled together. Seconds after, a dozen pirates leaped on board, led by their rather smallish captain.

"Quarter, quarter!" Liam shouted, holding his hands up. "Are you Captain Garneau?"

"Oui," the small captain answered. Captain Garneau looked around, puzzled by what she saw. "Capitaine, are your men all gutless? You've made no fight at all."

"Why should we fight?" Liam said. "We have no—"

"It's him!" a young girl's voice shouted. Liam looked toward the *Croix de Triomphe,* riding at anchor next to them, and was surprised to see Tricia standing on the deck and pointing at him with a look of terror on her face.

"Watch for a trick, Jean!"

Jean was suddenly placed on guard by Tricia's warning, and Liam had no choice but to order his men into action.

"Now," Liam shouted. Three dozen well-armed men leaped from their places of hiding and, having the advantage of both surprise and numbers, quickly overpowered Jean Garneau's brave band. The fight was short and bloody, as not one of Garneau's men asked for quarter.

As soon as the fighting began Liam, with the men he had designated for the purpose, jumped across to the *Croix de Triomphe.* Liam hoped to find his sister there, but he found only a lone helmsman, whom he killed with a shot from his pistol, and Tricia. Tricia ran screaming into the captain's cabin, but Liam ran her down. Grabbing her by her hair, he dragged her back out onto the deck.

"Where is she?" he demanded.

Tricia continued screaming.

Liam, who had one barrel of his pistol still charged, stuck it in her face and cocked the hammer. "You mean nothing to me, you black bitch!" he said. "Now, you tell me where my sister is or I will shoot you where you are."

"She's not here," Tricia said. "She's got her own ship now."

Liam looked back toward Jean Garneau and saw the small captain surrounded by the bodies of six of Liam's men and fighting off four more.

"Hold it!" Liam shouted. "Let the captain live!"

"Let *me* live?" Garneau shouted defiantly. "You had better ask me to let your miserable worms live." Even as Garneau spoke, another of Liam's men staggered back, clutching his hand to his chest, looking in surprise at the blood which spilled over his fingers from a wound so quickly and cleanly inflicted that the victim didn't even feel the blade sinking in.

Liam held Tricia's head in front of his pistol. "You have only this girl left alive," he shouted. "I will kill her now."

"*Non,*" Garneau shouted. "*Non,* don't kill her. She is but a child."

Liam smiled. He had figured when the girl ran into the captain's cabin that she might mean something to Garneau. He was right. "Throw down your sword," he ordered.

Jean did as Liam commanded. Then the men of Liam's ship, realizing that total victory was theirs, let out a rousing cheer.

"Men, you may divide what booty Captain Garneau has," Liam said, and the men, with another loud cheer, rushed over to the *Croix de Triomphe* to plunder its hold.

Liam climbed back across the railing, pulling Tricia with him. "This girl says my sister has gone. Is that true?"

Jean laughed. "So, you are Liam."

"Then you do know my sister."

"*Oui.*"

"Where is she?"

"That I will not tell you."

"Captain, don't you realize that you are going to hang? I'm taking you to Port of Spain, where your body will feed the crows."

"Then, to what advantage would it be to betray my friend?" Jean asked.

"Maybe we can strike a bargain."

"Why would I want to bargain with you?"

"Because it is within my power to save your life," Liam said.

Jean spat in his face. "I will not give you the satisfaction of exercising that power, monsieur."

Liam brought the barrel of the pistol across Jean's face in a wicked backhand motion, and Jean fell to the deck, unconscious.

"You," Liam said to one of the sailors who was returning with a set of jeweled earrings. "Lock this prisoner in the brig."

The sailor grabbed Jean by the legs and started dragging the small body across the deck. Tricia, who had been released by Liam when he struck the captain, started after the sailor.

"Where are you going?" Liam asked.

"I'm going with my captain."

"No," Liam said. He got a deep, lustful gleam in his eyes. "Once before I asked you to help me put out a fire and you wouldn't do it. This time, I'm not going to ask you."

"If I please you, Master Liam, will you spare the captain?"

"The captain?" Liam asked, with a wicked smile. "But of course I will, Tricia. The captain is going to be hanged in Port of Spain, just as I said. It's you you should be worrying about."

"I'm not a virgin anymore," Tricia said. "I'm not worried."

"Oh, but you don't understand," Liam said. "You

see, I had something special planned for my sister. Something very special. She isn't here, so you'll just have to take her place."

Erotic images of what was to come played across Liam's mind. It wouldn't satisfy him, he knew. But it would help ease the craving, just a bit. And the men would no doubt enjoy watching Tricia as she was keelhauled. That wasn't a sight one saw every day.

35

Sheena came to Martinique as agreed, but there was no *Croix de Triomphe*. She waited for one week; then, because she had an uneasy feeling about the situation, she put back out to sea. The men, who felt the same sense of uneasiness, left willingly, but not before the cargo had been auctioned and each of them had been rewarded with a healthy purse.

"Why do you suppose Capitaine Garneau did not keep the rendezvous?" LeClerc asked.

"I don't know," Sheena admitted. "I'm a little worried."

"Do you wish to return to Martinique and wait?"

"No," Sheena said. "I'd rather be sailing. We might run across them. At least it's better than sitting around doing nothing."

"*Oui, Capitaine*. On that I agree."

"In the meantime we shall look for more ships to plunder," Sheena said. "It will keep our mind off any possible danger to Captain Garneau. And when we do see them, we shall have a rich prize to share."

"Shall we head for the shipping lanes then?"

"Aye," Sheena said. "For if Captain Garneau has

not fallen into danger, that's where the *Croix de Triomphe* shall be."

LeClerc agreed. He carried the news to the others that they were returning to the shipping lanes. The crew was happy and enthusiastic, and proud of their woman commander. They vowed to sweep the sea clean of Bustamante's traders.

Two more ships had already fallen victim to the *Sea Witch* when the lookout spotted a third one, fat for the taking. It offered no resistance, striking its colors as soon as it was challenged. The Spanish captain even maneuvered his ship so that the *Sea Witch* could easily come alongside.

"I don't like this," Sheena said, as the ships maneuvered to close together. "It may be a trap."

"The cannons are loaded and laid in, Capitaine Sheena," LeClerc said. "I've gunners standing by with slow-burning matches. We can fire immediately if we have to."

Sheena had been looking at the Spanish ship through the spyglass. She closed it and brought it down. "I don't understand," she said. "They've made no effort to clear their decks for action. Their guns aren't run out, and the men are mustered in plain view."

"They are running up flags now, Capitaine," LeClerc said.

"What do they say?"

"Request . . . parley," LeClerc read.

"Reply, will board your vessel in force," Sheena said, and LeClerc ordered the appropriate flags sent up.

Moments later the two vessels were side by side, and grapnels were swung across. Sheena and her pirates jumped over the rails, holding their cutlasses at the ready, cautiously looking over the deck of the Spanish ship.

There was a table in the center of the deck, and on the table a bottle of wine and two golden wine goblets. The Spanish captain was standing by the table, wearing his finest uniform and smiling a welcome to Sheena and her men.

"Ah, Captain Sheena Drumm," the Spanish captain said. "I bid you welcome."

"You know who I am?" Sheena asked in surprise.

"But of course. Everyone knows the famous Sheena Drumm. Your name is whispered in every port from Boston to Barbados."

"Did you hear that?" one of Sheena's men asked the others, proudly. "Our capitaine is famous."

The others gave a loud cheer, but Sheena, with a troubled look on her face, held her hand out for silence. "How come I to such fame?" she asked.

The Spanish captain laughed. "Captain, any pirate achieves some fame. But a very beautiful señorita, who is also a pirate, ah, that is a story worth telling."

"Oh, but this is terrible," Sheena said. "Mister LeClerc, if this is true then we have no place to go, save those festering holes which are controlled by pirates."

"*Oui, Capitaine,*" LeClerc said.

"*Por favor, Capitana,*" the Spanish captain said, holding his arm out toward the table and the wine. "Won't you enjoy some wine with me as we discuss business?"

"We have no business to discuss," Sheena replied shortly. "Save the business of relieving you of your burden."

"But I have no cargo," the Spanish captain said. "You may see for yourself if you wish. I came to sea hoping to encounter you, so we could discuss business."

"LeClerc, send two men into the hold," Sheena ordered. "Send two more to search the captain's cabin."

"Be my guests," the Spanish captain said. "And

when you've finished your search, you men may drink
rum with my men in friendship."

"My men will not drink your rum," Sheena said.

"Of course," the Spanish captain replied. "A matter
of discipline, to be sure." He poured a stream of dark
red wine into the golden goblet and handed it to
Sheena. "But you will join me?"

"No, thank you," Sheena said, setting the wine down.
"What business would you discuss with me, Captain,
if you have no booty aboard?"

"Just this," the Spaniard said, removing a letter
from his pocket and handing it to Sheena.

Sheena opened it and glanced at it, then closed it
quickly. "It's in Spanish," she said.

"*Sí.* It is a letter of marque from the Spanish grandee
himself, authorizing you to serve as a privateer in his
service and granting you a pardon for all past crimes."

"Why would he do that?" Sheena asked.

"Quite simple really. The Spanish grandee would
rather have you in his service than fighting against
him. You have taken a terrible toll of our shipping,"
the Spanish captain said. "In return for his pardon he
asks only that you attack his enemies instead, and that
you share your prizes with him."

"That's impossible," Sheena said. "I already have
a partner."

"You are talking about Capitán Garneau, I suppose?"

"Yes," Sheena replied.

The Spanish captain began to laugh, and his men
laughed with him.

"What is so funny?" Sheena asked.

"You, Capitana," the Spaniard said. He wiped the
tears the laughter had produced from his eyes. "You
have been sailing around, attacking ships, building up
a treasure to share with Capitana Garneau."

"And?"

"Capitán Garneau is dead," the Spaniard said. "Excuse me for laughing at a matter as serious as death, but we discovered an amazing thing with the death of the capitán. It seems that the capitán, like you, was a woman."

"My God, then she *is* dead!" Sheena said.

"Capitaine Sheena," LeClerc said in disbelief. "Does this Spanish dog speak the truth? Is Capitaine Garneau a woman?"

"Aye," Sheena said. She shook her head sadly. "And there is no way he could have known, unless Jean really is dead."

LeClerc crossed himself, as did several other of Sheena's men.

"So, you see, Capitana," the Spaniard went on, "you now have no ally. Not one ally in the entire world. Your only hope is to accept the generous offer of the grandee."

"You say Jean—Captain Garneau—was hanged," Sheena said. "Who had it done?"

"The grandee himself," the Spanish captain said. "And this shall interest you. She was captured by none other than your brother."

"Liam?" Sheena asked in surprise.

"*Sí*. So, you see, even your brother joins the grandee in asking that you join with us."

"I see," Sheena said.

"Capitana, what can I tell your brother?" the Spaniard said. "And the grandee? What will your answer be?"

"You can tell them both that when we meet again, I hope it is in hell," Sheena said defiantly. She tore the paper into pieces and scattered it on the wind.

"But you are left without allies," the Spanish captain said.

"I have all the allies I need with my crew," Sheena replied defiantly.

Sheena's crew let out a mighty roar of approval at their captain's remark.

"Capitana, I fear you are making a great mistake," the Spaniard said. "The grandee makes a fearsome enemy."

"I had thought only that he made a rich purse, fat for the picking," Sheena said, and her men laughed with her at the taunting remark.

The four men who had searched the ship returned then with assurances that the ship was, indeed, empty.

"Return to the *Sea Witch*," Sheena ordered. She looked at the Spanish captain. "When was Jean hanged?"

"Ten days ago."

"And what happened to her body?"

"It yet hangs from a gallows in Trinidad," the captain said. "Her body will feed the crows as a warning to others."

Sheena felt a shudder of revulsion pass over her, then a terrible pall of sadness. But she had been through too much to cry.

36

The grisly remains of Jean Garneau swung in the afternoon breeze, so ghastly now as to frighten away the idly curious. Those who approached the scene did so because they were driven by a power far beyond idle curiosity. One such man, a tall, dark-headed seaman, stood looking at the sight for a few moments, then read the sign which had been posted by the governor of Trinidad. It was written in Spanish and English to accommodate the unique social structure of this island, a Spanish colony, the majority of whose inhabitants were English.

> The bones of Jean Garneau
> Are hanging here.
> Gaze upon them, dear friend,
> But have no fear.
> A pirate she was
> And a pirate she died.
> Let this be a warning, Sheena Drumm,
> You've no place to hide.

The man turned and walked back to the carriage he'd hired earlier.

"Ugly sight, ain't it, Cap'n?" the carriage driver asked, spitting a stream of tobacco juice over the wheel.

"Aye," the man answered. He twisted around for one last look as they were driving away. "I had to satisfy myself that it wasn't Sheena Drumm," he said.

"Have you ever seen Sheena Drumm?"

"Aye."

"And now you are lookin' for her, is that it?"

"Aye. I'm looking for her. And I'm going to find her, you can count on that."

"There's many more besides you lookin' for her. The reward on that she-devil pirate is higher'n any reward ever offered. Even higher'n the amount paid for Mad Jack Ledyard."

"There is no comparison between the two," the seaman said. "Sheena is twice the sailor that Mad Jack Ledyard was. And a better leader too. That will make it much harder to find her." The man rubbed his shoulder and looked up at the sky. "There must be a rain coming," he said. "Healing wounds make you feel such things."

The driver snapped the reins and the horse broke into a trot. "Not to worry, Cap'n. I'll have you in your favorite tavern 'afore you feels a drop."

The carriage rolled quickly through the streets of Port of Spain, Trinidad. True to his word the driver reached the Sea Turtle Inn a moment before the early afternoon squall began.

Once inside, the captain took his ale to his table, where he drank quietly, reflectively, and watched the heavy drops fall. When he turned his eyes back inside the tavern he saw the girl.

She was lithe of form and moved with an easy grace. She had long auburn colored hair . . . perhaps a bit too dark, but close enough to cause the sailor to look a second time. Once the girl glanced up to catch him looking at her. She smiled and blushed, and returned to her task of clearing away the empty tables. There was no doubt that the smile was meant for him, as he was the only customer in the place at this early hour.

He signaled for the bartender.

"You've drink before you already," the bartender said, approaching his table. "And the hour is early for food. So what would you be wantin'?"

The man pointed to the girl who was wiping tables. "That girl," he said. "She's a very pretty thing. Who is she?"

"She's my daughter," the bartender answered easily.

"How old is she?"

"Nineteen."

"Nineteen you say?" the sailor replied. He took another drink of his ale and regarded her coolly over the rim of his cup. "She's just the right age. Unless of course, her being your daughter, you've no wish for me to continue this conversation."

"Who are you, sir?"

"I'm Captain Smith of the schooner *Scorpion*, arrived today."

"Oh, yes, you're the pirate-chaser. You call yourself Smith, do you?"

"That's the name I'm using," the man said. "In my business it is not always wise to give your true name."

The bartender rubbed his hand on his chin and looked at the captain, taking measure of him. There were those who took a commission from the government to plunder the shipping of competing nations, and there were those who took letters to stop the privateers. The bartender felt little affection for either breed of man. Both were generally ruffians of the lowest order, though this person before him certainly looked like a respectable enough gentleman.

"I must constantly be on guard for her, as I'm sure you can appreciate," the bartender said. "The men who come in here aren't always men of means or manners, and I couldn't allow my own daughter to bed with just anybody."

"But you do allow her to bed occasionally?"

"Aye," the bartender said. "If the man is well mannered and is generous with his purse."

"Have you a room for such purposes?"

"Aye. You'll find it at the head of the stairs," the bartender answered, pointing to it.

Captain Smith took a handful of coins from his pocket and stacked them on the table in front of him. "Have her bring a bottle of wine," he said as he stood.

"She'll be right up," the bartender said with a smile, scooping the money off the table into the pocket he made with his apron.

The captain watched the bartender weave his way through the empty tables and speak to the girl. The girl set the empty ale tankards on a table and wiped her hands with the cloth as she listened to her father. Then, when her father pointed to the captain, she looked over toward him. She smiled shyly again, and Smith nodded his head ever so slightly, then walked up the stairs and pushed open the door.

The shutters to the window were open, and here the sound of the rain was quite loud. Smith could hear it drumming against the roof and trailing off the eaves. He removed his shirt and rubbed the wound scar on his aching shoulder.

The door behind him opened and the captain turned to see a woman carrying a pitcher, bowl, and towel. She placed the objects on a chest and poured water into the bowl from the pitcher.

"Millie will be up shortly," she said, backing out of the room with a small bow.

The captain crossed over to the bed and removed his boots. The girl was about the right height and build, and the exact age. But was he right to seek comfort in this way? Did it ease his pain, or make it worse?

There was a quiet, almost hesitant knock on the door.

"Come in."

Millie stepped through the door, then closed it behind her. She stood in front of it and smiled self-consciously at the captain.

"Did your father tell you why you are up here, girl?" the captain asked.

"Yes, sir," the girl said.

The captain reached for the wine, but when he saw no glasses he pulled the cork and drank right from the bottle, never taking his eyes off the girl, trying to make her over in his mind. Perhaps senses dulled by drink would help.

Millie undid the ribbon which held her hair and shook her head to let it tumble down. It was the right color, but not the right shade, the captain decided, though suggestive enough to serve his purpose.

The captain wiped his mouth with the back of his hand, and when he raised his arm the girl could see the terrible scar.

"Oh, sir, how came you by that?" she asked.

"I had a small wound," the captain answered. "But the blood attracted sharks, and they left me with a greater wound."

"Sharks?" the girl asked, shivering in fright. "How awful!"

" 'Twas my good fortune that the sharks took but one bite and let me be," the captain said. "For I had no way to fight them, or to escape them."

The girl touched the scar gently, with cool, soft hands. The captain put his hand on the girl's and held it for just an instant. His need for her grew strong and he moved his hand from hers up to the top of her dress, where he could feel her warm, heavy breast through the material.

"I'll get undressed now, sir," the girl said.

She looked at him through smoke-gray eyes and began removing her clothes, pulling the dress off her shoulders and pushing it down her body. The captain was treated to the sight of the girl's breasts, firm, well-rounded, and tipped by red nipples drawn suddenly tight by their exposure to the air. They were a bit smaller than he thought, but certainly adequate for his purpose.

The captain slipped out of his trousers quickly and stood there naked as he watched Millie continue to remove her clothes. She folded them carefully and placed them on the chest near the water basin, then turned to face him once more. Her body was subtly lighted by the rain-dimmed light. The area at the junction of her legs was darkened by the shadows and by a tangle of dark red hair which curled invitingly at her thighs.

The captain grew impatient now. He pulled Millie to him, kissing her open mouth with his own, feeling her tongue darting against his. He moved her toward the bed, then climbed in after her and crawled on top of her.

Millie warmed as quickly as the captain had and received him happily, wrapping her legs around him, meeting his lunges by pushing against him. She lost herself in the pleasure of the moment, until a few minutes later she could feel him jerking and thrusting in savage fury, spraying his seed into her and finally collapsing across her, calling a name.

But it wasn't Millie's name he called. It was another.

A short time later they lay side by side in the shadows of the room, without touching and without speaking. The shutters were still open and it was still raining, and the rain made music.

Finally Millie spoke.

"Who did you call?" she asked.

"Another."

"Do you love her?"

"Yes."

"I'm sorry."

"You're sorry that I love her?"

"No. I'm sorry that I could not be her for you."

The captain slid his hand across the bed and took Millie's. "You tried, and for a moment it was almost as if you were."

Millie squeezed his hand tightly. She thought of what true love must be like. She had never known it. A tear slid from her eye and ran down her cheek into her hair as she thought of what she must be missing.

"It hurts," she said.

"I know," the captain answered, not knowing of Millie's pain, but feeling his own.

37

"It is a dangerous risk, Capitaine," LeClerc said.

"We are in danger every day we sail," Sheena replied. "Danger is not new to us. Besides, we must either sell our booty or cast it overboard. We've no room for more, and the added weight has slowed us down."

"It is a fine plan, I will say that," LeClerc agreed. He put his hand on his chin and looked at a piece of paper Sheena had handed him. It was a drawing of the *Sea Witch*, but a few lines had been changed here and there and the name changed to *Fidelity*, so that it appeared to be an entirely new ship.

"It is a perfect plan," Sheena said. "Our carpenter can easily disguise the *Sea Witch*, we can change her name, and I will once again affect the disguise of a man. We will slip into port, take care of our business, and slip out again."

"What port could we visit, Capitaine? We are too well known in Martinique and Nassau. Even with the ship in disguise I fear someone will recognize her."

"My thought exactly," Sheena said. "It is for that

reason that I feel we should visit a new port. One we have not seen yet."

"What port?" LeClerc asked.

"Port of Spain, Trinidad," Sheena answered resolutely.

"*Mon Dieu, Capitaine!*" LeClerc said. "That is Spanish territory. You would sail into the grandee's own home!"

"Aye," Sheena replied. "But, think on it, LeClerc. Though Trinidad is Spanish, 'tis mostly English who live there. And there are many French as well. We would not stand out there as we would in other places. Besides, the grandee would never expect us to come there."

"*Oui*, he would never expect anything so foolish," LeClerc said. He sighed. "I am against it, Capitaine, but we can put it to a vote and I will support the majority wish."

"There is one more thing I want to tell you before we put it to the vote," Sheena said.

"What?"

"If it is still there, I am going to remove Jean's body from the gallows and bury her at sea."

"*Oui*," LeClerc said. "I thought as much."

"According to the Spanish captain, everyone on board the *Croix de Triomphe* was killed. But only Jean's body was not buried."

"*Oui*," Le Clerc said. "It is time now for the vote."

The crew was mustered and the plans were explained. They were cautioned about the dangers involved but told also that, for men of courage and daring, nothing was impossible.

"I will cast the first vote," LeClerc said, after Sheena finished her presentation.

Sheena looked at him, waiting to hear arguments against her proposal. She was surprised when he said simply, "I vote *oui*."

Sheena's plan received a yes vote from every member of the crew. Not one spoke against it, and afterward they fell to the task of altering the appearance of the ship with all the enthusiasm and eagerness of those embarked upon a new adventure.

Sheena, gratified by the reception of her plan, went into her cabin to study the charts and plot their course for Trinidad. She had been working for ten minutes or so when there was a light knock on the door.

"Come," she invited.

LeClerc stepped in. *"Pardon, Capitaine,* for my earlier words of disagreement. Please do not think me disloyal."

"Don't be silly, LeClerc. As my first officer you are supposed to express your opinion. That is your duty."

"It will be dangerous."

"I know."

"After we are successful where do you plan to go next?" LeClerc asked.

"I shall go to Boston," Sheena said, giving utterance for the first time to a plan she had long considered in her mind.

"Boston?"

"Aye. Boston is a fine seaport city. I could take my share of the prize to Boston and buy a ship of my own. I could become an honest sea captain."

"If you have such a wish, why not put the *Sea Witch* into such service? I am certain that the crew would back you."

"No, LeClerc, the *Sea Witch* is a pirate ship, stolen on the high seas. I could not go into the honest seafaring business with a stolen ship."

"And you have no love for the life of the freebooter?"

"My love is for the sea," Sheena replied. "It is my only love now, though once I had another." Sheena got a faraway look in her eyes.

"How is it that we found you a pirate on Mad Jack Ledyard's ship, then?" LeClerc asked.

" 'Twas the only way my husband and I could go to sea."

"Husband? You are married then?"

"Aye, I was, to William Drumm. But when my presence was discovered on board the *Marcus B.* my sweet Billy was made to walk the plank for violation of Article Ten of the Pirate's Code."

"I know of the Pirate's Code," LeClerc said. "Until you became our capitaine, I thought Article Ten a wise law. But now I know differently. You have proven that a woman can be on a pirate's ship and do well."

"As did Jean," Sheena said.

"*Oui.* Though it is hard for me to realize that Capitaine Garneau was a woman. How long before Trinidad?" he asked, changing the subject.

Sheena picked up a pair of dividers and walked them across the chart she had been examining. "I make it three days till we reach Trinidad," she said. "Tell the helmsman to come to course south by southwest."

"*Oui, Capitaine,*" LeClerc said, once again the loyal first officer.

The run to Trinidad was, as Shena expected, three days in duration. Night had fallen by the time they reached the mouth of the bay, but the moon was bright and the sea spread out like an ocean of molten silver before them. They could easily see their way in. Moreover, Sheena felt that under cover of darkness there would be less chance for the *Sea Witch* to be recognized. For, though the carpenters had given her a high poop and slab sides, she still sailed like a sleek schooner, and if one could see her closely he would be surprised to see a scow moving so gracefully.

"Set the watch, Mister LeClerc," Sheena said when anchor was dropped. She had donned men's clothes.

Even though LeClerc knew she was a woman the transformation was amazing.

"Habib ready now," Habib said, coming on deck at that moment.

"Good," Sheena said. "Mister LeClerc, you have command until my return."

"Where are you going?"

"Habib and I are going to take care of a little business," Sheena said.

"But surely you won't do that tonight?"

"Yes. Why put it off?" Sheena asked.

Before LeClerc could answer, Sheena was climbing over the rail and going down the rope to the small skiff Habib had just launched. Habib was right behind her.

Moments later the boat scraped against a dank wooden pier. Its two occupants scrambled ashore. Then Habib picked the boat up and carried it over to a growth of bushes where he hid it.

"Let's go," Sheena whispered, and the two of them hurried off into the night.

It was very late, in fact past midnight, and the streets were completely deserted. The doors and windows of the houses they passed were boarded shut for the night. There was no light to be seen anywhere. Sheena was thankful for the full of the moon, for though it could reveal their presence, it also lighted the way for them.

Somewhere a dog barked. The sudden intrusion of noise startled Sheena, and she could feel her skin jump. She took a deep breath to control her nerves and continued on.

"There, in the distance," she said. "I see the gallows."

A few steps further and the gallows was clearly visible, a stark, black, inverted el, silhouetted against the large silver disc of the moon. Hanging from the arm of the gallows was a body.

Sheena and Habib closed the remaining distance to the gallows, then stood there for a moment in front of the sign. Sheena read it, noticed the reference to herself, then steeled herself to look at Jean.

There was little flesh remaining on the body, and it bore no resemblance whatever to Jean Garneau. Somehow Sheena was able to take some comfort from that, for if this poor creature had still been easily identifiable, Sheena didn't think she would have been able to do what had to be done.

"Cut her down," Sheena ordered.

Habib had brought a piece of sail canvas with him. He spread it out below the body, then climbed onto a rock and cut through the rope. The body dropped onto the canvas with as soft a sound as a falling clod of dirt.

Habib folded the canvas over it, then slung it across his shoulder and carried it easily back to the boat.

When they returned to where the boat was hidden, Habib weighted the canvas with a few large rocks, then put the package in the boat. They paused halfway back to the ship and, as Sheena recited a prayer, Habib slipped the canvas over the side.

They watched the package sink, then rowed back to the ship, scraping lightly against its side. Sheena called out quietly, and the ropes were dropped over the rail. Habib and Sheena grabbed them and started climbing back up to the deck.

Sheena should have realized something was amiss when she didn't see LeClerc's head over the side. But her heart was still full of grief for her friend, and she wasn't paying as much attention as she should.

"*Buenas noches, Capitana,*" Bustamante greeted when Sheena stepped over the rail. Two men grabbed her roughly.

Sheena saw that a cannon was aimed right for the rail. A grinning Spanish sailor stood by the breech, holding a slow-burning match just over the touchhole.

"Habib, go back!" Sheena screamed in warning.

But Habib's personality was such that he went toward danger rather than away from it, especially if his mistress was in trouble, and he continued to climb the rope, determined to save her.

When Habib reached the rail he saw that two men held Sheena captive, and he saw the hated Don Bustamante. He did not see the cannon pointed right at him, because he was blinded by anger and duty.

Habib let out a roar and took two steps across the deck, bound to rescue Sheena, but his anger was blasted away by the crash of the cannon and the smash of the ball into his body.

Sheena's ears rang from the closeness of the explosion. She stared dazedly at the pulped remains of Habib. The ball had cut him completely in half, leaving his lower torso still on deck while sending his upper parts out into the bay.

She retched at the sight, as the Spaniards around her laughed.

"Señor Liam," Bustamante called. "Is this puking woman your sister?"

Liam stepped out of the shadows and looked at Sheena. His search was now over. She stood before him. But how would he satisfy himself with her? She was clearly the property of Don Bustamante, who obviously had his own plans for her.

"Yes," Liam said. "That is Sheena."

"Good, good. I am a generous man, am I not, Señor Liam?"

"Yes, Don Bustamante. Yes, you are."

"I have done many things for you."

"Yes," Liam said.

"And, as your last act, I have let you see your sister again."

"Yes," Liam said. Suddenly he realized the ominous implications of Bustamante's remark. "Don Bustamante, did you say 'as my last act'?"

"Before I have you killed," Bustamante said easily.

"But—but why?" Liam asked. "Why would you want to kill me?"

"Oh, there are many reasons," Bustamante said. "One could say it is because I have grown tired of your company. Or one could say it is because I know you intended to cross me and kill your sister as you did the black girl, Tricia, thus denying me my pleasure with her."

"Don Bustamante, but I intended no such thing," Liam said, now realizing that his life was in danger.

"Do not lie to me, señor. Your first mate told me this just before I had him killed. Do you think I did not wonder why you chose the crew you chose? It was to usurp their loyalty."

"No," Liam said. "Don Bustamante, you don't understand," he pleaded.

Bustamante smiled a slow smile, then waved his finger, as if dismissing him.

Liam felt a jarring blow at his neck . . . then a stinging sensation, like a cut while shaving. That was followed by a blast of cold air and the sensation of falling. Suddenly Liam realized that he was lying on the deck of the ship, looking up at a laughing Bustamante and at a grinning sailor with a bloodstained sword, and . . . *oh . . . my God! A headless body! My body!* He realized that even as his mind began to dim into eternal blackness.

38

Don Pedro Ricardo Bustamante stood just inside the door and looked into the windowless room. The room was bathed in a flickering gold light produced by two oil lamps, and the atmosphere was permeated by a sickly sweet smell from the incense in the oils.

In the center of the room on a small bed, lay Sheena Drumm. Sheena was completely naked, secured to the bed by ropes which held her arms and legs outstretched. As Bustamante looked at her he felt a growing pressure in front of his pants, and a shortening of breath. Oh, it was going to be good. It was going to be so good. Better even than when he had killed the beautiful young black girl who had been with Captain Garneau, and that had been exquisite. He would have enjoyed the captain too, had he known she was a woman. But that discovery wasn't made until after she had already been hanged. Don Bustamante felt cheated because of that. All the more reason that he would enjoy Sheena. She owed him this pleasure, not only for what she had done to him, but to compensate him for what he was denied by not realizing Jean Garneau's true sex in time.

Sheena would compensate him, he thought as he

rubbed himself. She would compensate him adequately.

It hadn't been just luck which delivered Sheena to him. Bustamante knew that she would come for the body of Jean Garneau. All he had to do was have everything in readiness for her when she did show up. When a strange ship was reported slipping into the bay under cover of darkness, he had mustered his men to board her.

They nearly let the ship get away because it was so cleverly disguised. In fact, Bustamante had already given the order to recall his men, when he saw the giant on the deck of the strange ship. The giant, he knew, had to be Sheena's giant.

When Sheena and the giant left to take the bait of the dead pirate captain, Bustamante had his marines slip out to the *Sea Witch* and board her. So surprised was the crew that they scarcely had time to defend themselves, and they were all killed without one shot being fired. All Bustamante had to do then was wait for Sheena and the giant to return. The rest was easy.

Now there was only Sheena left. And she was his prisoner, hopelessly spread-eagled before him. Oh, it was going to be so good.

Sheena couldn't see Bustamante standing in the doorway. For one thing, tied as she was, she couldn't move her head far enough to get a good view of him, and for another, she was in the light and he was in the shadows, making it even more difficult. She strained against her bonds, but to no avail. Thus far nothing had happened to her, but she knew that she would soon fall victim to Bustamante's lust.

Sheena heard footsteps, and she turned her head toward the noise. She gasped, for there, standing in the edge of the light, was a man, completely nude, save for a black mask of the type worn by executioners.

"Who are you?" Sheena asked.

The man neither spoke nor moved for a long time.

He just stood there looking down at her, and though the mask hid the expression on his face from her, Sheena could easily measure his lust by the enlarging of his manhood.

The man stepped back into the shadows for a moment. When he returned he held a leather whip in his hand, caressing it lovingly.

"Bustamante," Sheena said. "So it is you. Is this how you scarred poor Tricia?"

The man didn't answer. Instead he took two steps toward her, raised the whip over his head, then brought it down sharply across her breasts.

The lash seared into her flesh like a burning brand, and Sheena screamed out in pain and fear. She looked down and saw that already her body bore marks. A tiny line of blood oozed from the whip-inflicted wound.

Sheena screamed again, but the man took no heed of her pitiful entreaties. He continued to strike her, again and again, flailing at her breasts, stomach, legs, and thighs with the whip, until Sheena's entire body burned with the pain. She no longer saw separate lash marks. She was one solid mass of pain, from her shoulders to her knees.

Finally the beating came to a halt. Then the man in the mask did a strange thing. He brought a glass flask of amber-colored liquid and placed it beside her. It glowed in the golden light, as if it had captured liquid fire. She had no idea what it was.

The man, who had yet to speak a word, began silently applying the oil. It had a soothing effect. Within moments the painful fire which had been ignited by the whipping, changed to a warm, almost pleasurable sensation.

The man rubbed the oil over her arms, shoulders, stomach, and legs. Then he came up to her firm, up-tilted breasts. Despite herself, she felt the nipples harden to the sensual touch of the oil. When his hand spread the soothing oil inside her thighs and up to the junction of her legs, she even let out an involuntary moan of pleasure.

The oil rubdown stopped, and the man removed the flask and walked off into the shadows, leaving Sheena alone.

She was alone for several seconds, and during that time she wondered where he was, what he was doing, and what would happen to her next. It had been a strange and bewildering sensation to feel the fires of pain change to the warmth of pleasure, but the overriding sensation was still one of fear. What was going to happen to her?

When the man returned a moment later he was carrying two golden clamps. These he fitted over each of her breasts. The clamps were affixed with a screw device whereby he could increase the pressure to varying degrees by tightening the screws.

"No, please," Sheena said, watching him as he slipped the devices into place.

Despite her plea the man continued with his work. Then, as she feared, he started tightening each of them. They were not designed to bring pressure directly to the nipple itself but rather just behind the nipple, which would force blood out into them, causing them to distend and protrude as if they were two fingers thrusting upward.

The sensations passed from pressure to pain, and from pain to agony, eliciting yet another scream from Sheena, before the clamps were released. By then, even though the clamps were no longer in place, the nipples remained congested with blood. They strained upward, rose red atop her bruised breasts.

Again Sheena was anointed with the soothing oil, and again she passed from pain to pleasure as the warming fluid was spread on her. But after that he returned with the whip, setting her afire with its sting once more.

And this time, while still in pain, she had the added humiliation of feeling him penetrate her, driving into her brutally, grunting out his lust on her. As he abused her, he squeezed the tender nipples so hard that the pain of it was enough to make her faint.

When she awoke some time later he was gone. She felt not only pain but humiliation and shame from the ordeal. She lay there, expecting him to return at any moment. She knew that she was his prisoner, with no hope of rescue, for Habib and her entire crew had been killed.

Sheena wished that she too had been killed. As she lay there she prayed for God to strike her dead where she was, rather than allow her to be subjected to another encounter with Bustamante.

At that moment Bustamante returned, this time without the mask, and wearing clothes. But, she noticed with dread, he was still carrying the whip, caressing it lovingly. When he reached her, he flipped it out to allow the lash to trail between her thighs, not painfully, just as a reminder that he was her master and had it in his power to inflict pain any time he wished. He smiled at her and spoke for the first time.

"What do you say, my pretty one? Are you ready for some more fun?"

He released the fastenings on his trousers.

39

For three days Sheena had to suffer the indignities of Bustamante's perversion. Her humiliation was continued even to the way she was made to eat. Bustamante placed a golden collar about her neck, tied her hands behind her, then held her by a leash as if she were an animal. Sheena was forced to eat from a plate put on the floor, using only her mouth, as would a dog.

At first Sheena refused to submit to this final degradation. She disdained her food. But by the third day she determined that if escape were ever to be possible she would need her strength, so she closed her mind to the shame of it and ate ravenously.

"Yes, my pet," Bustamante cooed, watching her eat. "That's a nice pet. Eat all of your nice food now."

Bustamante reached down to pat Sheena on the head, and Sheena, jerking away from him, upset her bowl, spilling some of the food on his boots.

"Oh, you are a naughty, naughty pet, you are," Bustamante said, his oily voice sliding out in a tone which grated Sheena almost as much as his actions. He stuck his boot out in front of her face. "Now I'm afraid you will have to lick my boot clean."

Sheena turned her face away.

Bustamante moved one hand down on the leash to grab her by the collar. With the other hand he grabbed a handful of hair and began pulling, until the pain on Sheena's scalp was excruciating.

"I said clean my boots!" Bustamante repeated, this time shouting the order.

"No," Sheena said.

Bustamante released her hair and grabbed the ever-present whip. He brought it down sharply across Sheena's bare backside, and a quick fire erupted in her. There was no part of her body which had been immune to the whip in the last three days, and the slightest touch of the lash anywhere on her body would bring on instant agony.

"Clean my boots!" Bustamante ordered again.

"No, Bustamante, you clean them," a man's voice suddenly interrupted.

"What the— Who are you?" Bustamante demanded, startled by the intruder.

The visitor stepped into the room, holding his sword before him, challenging Bustamante to do battle. "Tell him who I am, Sheena, lass."

But Sheena was unable to answer. She had been more than startled. She had been shocked. So shocked that she fainted.

"How did you get by my guards?" Bustamante asked.

"I killed a few. The rest have been taken prisoner by my men. Now there are just the two of us."

"I am unarmed," Bustamante said. "Would you kill an unarmed man?"

"After what you have done to Sheena I could kill you, and gladly," the man said. "But I think I will get even more pleasure from seeing you squirm while fighting for your life." The man saw a sword in a rack on the wall. "Here is a sword," he said, reaching for it. "Use it."

But as the visitor reached for the sword, he gave Bustamante the opening he was looking for. Quick as a striking snake, his whip snapped out, pulling the sword from the hand of Sheena's rescuer.

"I much prefer to have you unarmed," Bustamante said.

The would-be rescuer reached for his sword, but Bustamante snapped his whip against it, knocking it out of reach. Another slash, and the man went down.

"Now, my unwelcome friend," Bustamante said, grinning evilly. "I've always thought that a person could be killed by a whip, if the one using the whip was sufficiently skilled."

Bustamante swung his whip over his head, the lash making a whistling noise. Then he brought it out with full force, slashing into the man's face, leaving a bloodied streak.

"And again," Bustamante said, whipping it around to cross the streak with another, laughing at the efforts of his victim to escape.

Now his laughter ceased. Bustamante held the whip poised over his head for a moment, feeling the power of being in complete control of the situation. "I've grown tired of my game," he said. "I shall demonstrate the ease with which a man's neck can be broken."

Bustamante flipped the whip toward his victim, but at the last minute the beleaguered man managed to roll to one side. In the same motion he caught the end of the lash and jerked. The movement was so sudden that it caught Bustamante unaware, and he was pulled off his feet.

The man made no attempt to play games with Bustamante, but went straight to work wrapping the leather lash around Bustamante's neck. He tightened his hold. Bustamante's face turned blue, and he let out a gasping death rattle. The man drew the leather lash tighter, squeezing until Bustamante's eyes bugged out and all signs of life were gone.

He stood up then and looked for just a moment at the lifeless body on the floor. Then he turned quickly and ran to untie Sheena. He sat on the floor and cradled Sheena's head in his lap, gently giving her water, until she regained consciousness.

Sheena's eyes fluttered open. She looked into the face of her rescuer and gasped again.

"Wait," the man said, smiling, holding out his hand. "Don't faint on me again, Sheena, lass."

"Billy! Then it is you? But how? I mean . . ."

Billy laughed. "Did you think I'd gone to Davy Jones's locker?"

"I *saw* you," Sheena said. "Mad Jack Ledyard made you walk the plank. You couldn't swim all the way to shore!"

"It would have been a far swim at that," Billy said. "But you'll remember also that the plank I was made to walk was tossed into the sea after me."

"Aye."

" 'Twas that selfsame plank which saved my life, girl. It made a fine raft. Well, not a real raft, mind you. But I discovered that I could cling to it and keep my head above water. I floated for two days, and was discovered by a sloop heading back for Charles Town."

"Sure'n God was with you," Sheena said. "And with me, as witness my rescue. But how came you here?"

Billy smiled broadly. "I've a surprise to show you. Come, let's dress quickly and quit this foul place. The grandee was an important man, for all his evil ways. I've no wish to linger around when his allies discover what has become of him."

The surprise Billy had for Sheena was the sloop *Scorpion.* "She's all mine, Sheena," Billy said proudly, pointing to it as they rowed across the bay. "Paid for with honest prize money made as bounty on pirates gone bad."

"Billy, I've no wish for you to do that type of work anymore," Sheena said.

"Would you want to go back into piracy again?" Billy asked, surprised.

"No. But I'll not earn money on the blood of adventurous men either. I made many friends—now all dead—and I couldn't do this and live with myself."

"Then we won't do it," Billy said. "We'll go into the honest trade, as you wanted before. Would that be more to your liking?"

"Aye," Sheena said.

It was dusk by the time the *Scorpion* cleared the harbor. Sheena stood at the rail in Billy's arms, watching as the last color faded from the western sky. She was startled by what appeared to be fire on the ends of the yardarms, stays, mastheads, and other protrusions.

"Billy, we are afire!" she gasped, pointing to the apparition.

Billy looked up, then laughed.

"No, lass, 'tis nothing to worry about. Do you mean to say that in all your adventuring you've yet to see Saint Elmo's fire?"

"Saint Elmo's fire? What is that?"

"No one knows," Billy said. "But it comes on occasions. It's considered good luck to see it. I take it as a good omen that we are seeing it now."

Sheena closed her eyes and laughed softly.

"What is it, my love?"

"I know how I can see it anytime I want."

"How so?"

"Like this," she said, putting her arms around his neck and drawing his lips down to hers for a kiss. The kiss grew deeper, and they clung to each other passionately. Finally Sheena removed her lips from his. "Did you see it?" she asked softly.

"I saw it," Billy replied, returning her smile. "Now I'm going to feel it."

Billy picked Sheena up and, with their lips once more locked in a kiss, carried her to the cabin they would share, and to his bed. There, in a release of passion which dimmed the fireballs of Saint Elmo and rivaled the sunset, they made love. Afterward they lay in each other's arms, enjoying the closeness, sharing their moment. Outside the cabin the sounds of normal ship activity continued: the subdued rush of wind in the canvas, the creaking of ropes, the groaning of wood.

"Atop!" the deck officer on watch called. "What lies ahead?"

"Calm waters ahead, sir!" the lookout called down.

Dell Bestsellers